GENOCIDE
by
GMO

Jim West

ISBN
Hardcover: 978-1-964289-35-9
Paperback: 978-1-964289-20-5

Other Books by Jim West

DNAlien
DNAlien II
DNAlien III

Page Blank Intentionally

ACKNOWLEDGMENTS

First, I would like to thank the people who keep reading my books. Without them, I would have given up long ago. Without readers, a writer is useless.

Then there are the people who help you tell the story in a sensible and coherent manner. That would be my good friend John Fleenor and my cousin Kay Pratka. Tirelessly reading each chapter, they both kept telling me, "Try again!"

But the idea behind the story came from a gentleman named Chris Hawk. I owe him the biggest thanks. Discussing GMOs over beers one evening, he told me about one he had worked on that caused sterility in the test animals and was quickly abandoned. That discussion led to the 'what if' topic of genocide.

You just never know from whom or where good story ideas come from. Pay attention to the people around you! There's always something interesting out there. Keep your ears open and your mouth shut. Just remember, you've never said anything you didn't already know.

Thank you!

Page Blank Intentionally

Chapter 1

It was very early in the morning when Jim Jackson rolled over and snuggled against Maria Pompillio's warm back. The sunlight was just beginning to peek through the dusty Venetian blinds that covered the windows of his one-bedroom apartment in College Station, Texas. Dust motes slowly floated in the light as he opened his eyes and looked at the flowing tresses that were more than slightly mussed after their night together. Knowing that he really liked what he saw, he put his arm across her waist, pulled his legs against hers, and felt her push back slightly.

Kissing the back of her neck, Jim whispered, "Are you just going to lay there all day, or do you plan on waking up?"

Maria smiled softly and answered, "Not sure. Do you have something in mind that might make me want to wake up?"

As she rolled onto her back, Jim answered, "There's lots I'd like to do, but there are even more things that I've got to do today."

"More important than this?" Maria smiled as she put her arms around his neck.

1

"Certainly not more important," Jim said as he kissed her, "but more pressing,"

"You're no fun," she pouted as she crossed her arms over the T-shirt she'd borrowed from Jim's chest of drawers. "I was hoping for a whole day without any interruptions."

Jim cocked his head and said, "I told you yesterday that I had to finish some research at the library today. And you're a little behind in your research, too."

"You seemed awful fond of my 'little behind' last night," she teased.

"The 'little behind' I'm speaking of now has nothing to do with last night," Jim joked as he slipped his hand under the T-shirt.

Maria shoved his hand out and told him, "Oh, now you're interested in something besides research?"

"Always," Jim answered as he rolled away from her. "But if I don't get this project completed by the end of the month, I won't graduate this year. And I can't afford another semester in school."

Jim swung his legs over the side of the bed and stretched his arms over his head as he cracked his neck from side to side. Reaching down, he picked up the *tighty-whiteys* he'd pulled off as he got into bed last night.

Standing while he pulled them up, he remarked, "I seem to remember you telling me your Dad was about through sponsoring you and your education. I think we better make sure we finish this year, or we both may have to take jobs at Wal-Mart."

Maria sat up in bed and asked, "What are you working on today?"

"Still tracing a patent that was issued back around 1981," Jim answered as he padded over to the chest of drawers.

Selecting a clean T-shirt from the neatly arranged drawer and pulling it over his head, he continued, "The project seemed to be a success, and then it just disappeared as far as I can tell."

Maria slipped from the bed and stepped behind Jim, asking, "Tell me again about what this gene thing was supposed to do."

Jim turned in her arms and said, "Make better seeds. Grow better crops. Feed more people."

"Is that all?" she asked as she slipped from him and moved to the chair where her clothes from yesterday had been hastily thrown.

"Pretty much," Jim told her as he pulled on his jeans. "Sounds simple, but the science behind it is truly amazing. That's what I'm interested in. I want to know how to make totally new plants. Or animals. Either."

"What are you looking for today?" Maria asked as she stepped into her jeans.

"Well," Jim answered as he put his socks and boots on, "the patent covers a specific type of barley that was combined with the DNA of a mouse."

"You gotta be shitting me!" Maria laughed. "Just how do you get a mouse to breed a barley plant?"

"Not much breeding," Jim replied. "Just rather mundane mouse gene insertion into the barley DNA."

"Why would anyone want to do that?" she asked.

Dressed, Jim headed for the tiny kitchen, pulled a carton of orange juice from the almost empty refrigerator, and answered, "To make a better barley plant. Juice?"

Following Jim into the kitchen, Maria took one of the two chairs at the table and said, "Yes, please. How does that make a better plant?"

Jim took two plastic glasses, one from Taco Bell and the other from What-a-Burger, out of the sparse cupboard, poured them half full, and sat opposite Maria. Handing her a glass, he continued, "Sometimes you're trying to improve the protein content, maybe make it drought resistant, or insect resistant, or possibly just make the plant produce more or bigger seeds."

"Tell me again exactly what field you're trying to get your doctorate in?" she asked as she sipped her juice.

"Molecular biology," Jim answered. "You can relate it to your master's program in Archaeogenetics, tracing the DNA trail back in history. We just try to transfer some specific trait from one plant or animal to another through their DNA."

"Even cross-species?" she asked. "Isn't that a little unethical?"

"Nope," Jim answered as he rose to put his glass in the sink. "This sort of thing has been going on for centuries."

"DNA splicing?" Maria responded, taking her glass to the sink. "I doubt that."

"Not the DNA part, just trying to cross-breed or cross-pollinate," Jim told her. "This goes back to when man first domesticated animals in 12 thousand BC. Or crops 2,000 years later."

"What exactly do you call the current work? Cross DNA-ing?" she asked.

"No, the correct term would be Genetically Modified Organisms or just GMO," he answered as he reached for his hat. "Where do you need to go?"

Chapter 2

Jim took a quick look around the apartment as he held the door open for Maria. Satisfied that all of the lights were off, no water running, and the stove off, he followed her down to his used-to-be gray elderly Volkswagen. Now, it was still sort of gray but with several brownish rust spots and numerous visible dings and dents.

He'd been driving the car for the last seven years, trying to save as much money as he could for such mundane necessities as his apartment, utilities, food, and the occasional night out.

Coming from a rather lower-middle-income family, the small assistance he got from his folks for tuition was all he could expect. They'd paid for his Bachelor's degree, but since then, they'd only been able to help a little with the tuition.

The rest of the expenses had been paid for with part-time jobs or summer jobs. The bulk of it was from student loans, and they were accumulating at an astronomical rate.

At least the car always started and was reliable even in the worst weather. As soon as he and Maria were seated, he turned the ignition and waited for the little four-cylinder car to break into the familiar purr that came from the rear-mounted engine.

"Have you figured out where you need to go?" Jim asked as the exhaust began emitting a slightly gray haze, reminding him that the poor little engine needed some attention.

"I guess I need to go back to the dorm," Maria said, smiling at Jim. "I need to shower and get some fresh clothes before I start my day."

"Not a problem," Jim answered, pulling smoothly into the slight traffic. "What do you plan to do after that?"

"I do need to study," Maria told him. "And you're right about that research. I'm just not sure I've picked the right subject, and I hate to waste time on something that I don't enjoy."

As Jim threaded his way back to Maria's dorm, he asked, "Want to meet at the library later? Then maybe lunch."

"That sounds fine," she answered. "How long will you be at the library?"

Pulling in front of Maria's dorm, he answered, "Probably all day, but I'll take a break around noon, and I'd love to have lunch with you."

Maria leaned over and kissed Jim, saying, "Great, I'll see you at the library in about an hour."

Opening the door and sliding out, she joked, "Just don't be thinking about cross-pollinating without me!"

"Not a chance," Jim retorted as she shut the door. "I've never met a barley that I was attracted to. Maybe a cabbage since they share almost 50% of our DNA anyway."

Maria flipped Jim the finger as she turned and headed up the sidewalk to her dorm. Watching her for a few seconds,

Jim smiled and wondered how lucky he was to have met her at a local pub just a few weeks ago.

Slipping the car into gear, Jim drove slowly across the campus to the library. As he watched the numerous buildings slide by, he thought back to the years he'd spent here. First, there'd been four years of floundering, trying to figure out exactly what he wanted. Then, almost two more after his initial degree in biology, he got his Master's Degree in Molecular Biology.

Now almost complete with his Ph.D. His interest in the field sprang mainly from his time on the farm watching how a variety of plants were spaced with different ones interspersed to cross pollinate. The haphazard results were meager compared to today's science.

Even the cross-breeding of the cattle took generations, therefore years, to determine if the result was what had been desired. When he first started reading about GMOs, it was as if he saw his future for the first time.

The particular strain of barley he was researching had actually been an accidental discovery. He'd been looking for a project that had as complex a history as possible but also a dramatic positive result. What Jim really wanted to do was follow the GMO from its beginnings and see what benefits had been derived.

It was rather disappointing to find that this strain of barley had all but disappeared after it had been patented. He wasn't exactly sure when the research had begun, but since the US Supreme Court didn't rule until 1980 that genetically altered life forms could be patented, it must have been an ongoing project before that.

The one thing Jim had learned about GMOs was that it was expensive, and the results were more than likely to fail. The success rate had gone up as more and more information was available to assist the research, but it was still a gamble every time a new project was started.

Pulling into the library parking lot, Jim found a slot relatively close to the main entrance. Reaching into the back seat, he grabbed the well-worn briefcase that held his previous research notes. Even this late in the process, he was considering finding another program to follow. He intended to present a success story that dramatically proved the value of GMOs and maybe quiet some of the adverse publicity that surrounded them.

Chapter 3

Climbing out and shutting the car door, Jim watched as dozens of students wandered up and down the sidewalks, coming and going to classes. Now almost 25 years old, Jim recalled his early days and what it was like to be far from home for the first time and how life differed from his youth.

The kids he saw were generally six to eight years younger than he was now and seemed more interested in the social life than the academic one. Pretty much the same as he'd been back then; 19 or 20-year-olds continued to act like 19 or 20-year-olds.

Reaching the library, he entered and walked straight to the computer section. Glancing around, he found two computers side by side that were currently vacant. Hoping to hold one for Maria, he sat his briefcase in one of the chairs and sat down next to it.

Booting up his computer, he started where he'd left off during his last search. Finding the program he needed was relatively easy once he'd learned about the company that had developed the barley. Tracing it forward to the patent had been a piece of cake. Working backward, he gleaned the basics from the data, but the specifics were still hidden.

Probably to prevent any other person or company from benefiting from the protected research.

Knowing that he wouldn't be able to show the exact sequence of genes or the DNA, he was left with trying to follow the patented name of the GMO. Listed as 'Barley MBM-106729, Jim began a new search for that specific name.

Again, the only data found was the patent and the company that had filed for the patent. Jim sat back and started thinking about another approach to the problem. There had to be some way to find out what had happened.

Going into the US Government's Patent Office site, Jim started looking for the barley patent. Using the 'Barley MBM 106729' name to start, he again found the patent number and the company that had filed for it. Nothing new.

A couple of hours later, as he was sitting back in the chair staring at the screen, Maria walked up and said, "Doesn't look like work to me. Daydreaming about last night?"

"Hey, Maria," Jim replied as he took his briefcase from the chair and placed it on the table.

Maria put a notebook on the table and clicked on the computer, asking, "Any progress?"

Jim turned back to the screen in front of him and answered, "Nothing. I know the company, I know the patent number, I know the product's name. I just can't seem to find out anything more."

"Have you researched the company?" Maria asked as she rapidly typed her information into the school's security system to access different areas.

"Yes, I've looked them up, and they're a large Agri-Chemical company," Jim answered. "They've got thousands of patents, including this one."

"Have you looked at each of their patents," Maria questioned, busy with her keyboard.

"Nope, that'd take too long," Jim answered. "Like I said, they have thousands."

"What if they sold the patent?" Maria suggested. "Maybe some other company owns it now, and it's being marketed under a different name."

"It's still listed under the original company," Jim told her. "If they'd sold it, the patent should be listed under another name."

"Maybe," Maria retorted, "but maybe the patent office only lists the original company that was granted the patent. I would think that if a patent was sold several times, they would only keep the name of the company that applied and was granted the patent."

"That's possible," Jim said, nodding his head. "Now, how do you think I can track that? As I've said, I've looked at every site I can think of with the patent number or the brand name. I can't think of any other way to find it."

"Where's the company located?" Maria asked, using her mouse to highlight areas of her screen.

Jim typed a new search into the computer and followed the prompts until the company's website was on the screen. "Holy shit," he said. "I knew they were huge, but they're bigger than huge; they are gia-enormous!"

"They have offices all over the world!" Jim continued as he clicked on the next link. "Damn near every state in the US, too."

Maria leaned over to look at his screen, pointed to where it listed the offices in Texas, and said, "Looks like there's an office here in town."

Jim continued to scroll through the lists, looking for a central contact number, but found none. Opening a new screen, he typed in 'College Station, Texas, phone book' and waited for the information to pop onto the screen.

Once in view, he searched for the number using the company name, and almost immediately, the phone number and address appeared on his screen. "Got you," Jim said, writing the information onto the top sheet of his notebook.

"What now?" Maria asked as her fingers flew over the keyboard and the information she was seeking came into view.

"I'll give them a call," Jim said, scooting his chair back. "I'll be back in a few minutes."

Chapter 4

Jim walked quickly to the head Librarian's office and knocked on the open door's frame. "Good morning, Dr. Lindsay," he said. "Any chance I can borrow your phone?"

"Hey, Jim," Kay said, looking up from the neat stacks of paper on her desk. "Sure, come on in."

"Thanks," Jim told her, "I just need to make a quick call to the company that holds the patent on my pet project."

Over the years Jim had spent countless hours at the library and had come to know Dr. Kay Lindsay very well. "How's it going?" Kay asked as Jim dialed the number he'd written down.

"Could be better," he answered, waiting for the phone to be answered.

After several rings, a voice answered, "Monogenic's."

"Good morning," Jim replied. "I was wondering if there was a chance that I could stop by this morning and talk to someone regarding a patent Monogenic holds on a certain strain of barley?"

"What's the purpose of your interest?" the voice asked.

"I'm a Molecular Biology Ph.D. candidate here at Texas A&M," Jim told him. "And I'm working on my thesis that involves the benefits of GMOs. The specific program I've been researching was patented by Monogenic, and I'd like to follow the program to its conclusion. The problem is that I can't seem to find what happened to the product after the patent was issued."

"I'll have to get permission from the Branch President," the voice told him. "Is there a number where I can reach you?"

"Sure," Jim told him. "You can reach me at 979-369-1083."

"Got it," the voice replied. "I'll try to give you a call in the next couple of hours."

"Sounds great," Jim told him. "Any chance that I could stop by around noon? I won't be back home until later tonight, and maybe I can get your answer when I stop by."

"That'd be fine," the voice said. "Just tell the receptionist who you are and that you've talked to Jerry. I may not be here when you come by, but my replacement will have the answer."

"Thanks," Jim said, "I'll be there in a couple of hours."

"By the way," the voice said, "What patent are you looking for?"

"Patent number 5676976," Jim answered. "I believe it's known as Barley MBM 106729."

"Okay," the voice said. "I'll pass that along."

Hanging up the phone, Jim told Kay, "Now, maybe I can find out if I've selected the right program to follow."

"A lot of dead ends in research," Kay replied. "What are you hoping for when you get an interview?"

"I'm hoping that they can tell me what happened to the barley seed they patented," Jim answered. "So far, I can't find out if it ever went into production or was abandoned."

"Do you have the patent number?" Kay asked, interested in Jim's dilemma as she was in every student at A&M.

"Sure," Jim said. "But I can't get anything about it after it was patented."

"Give me the number," Kay said. "I may have a friend in the Patent Office that might be able to shed some light on it."

"That'd be great," Jim told her. "At least if I knew what had happened to the program, I could determine if I need to follow this specific program or switch to another one that has a suitable outcome."

"What do you consider suitable?" Kay asked.

"I'm hoping to find a complex GMO that has made significant advances in the field," Jim answered. "I'm hoping that I can show how GMOs have contributed to solving the food problem. Specifically in third world countries where famine is most prone."

"What do you consider a complex GMO?" Kay asked as she thumbed through her ancient address book.

"I'd prefer something that combines animal and plant," Jim answered. "But I'd settle for a bacteria, plant, or animal splicing. The main thing, as I said, is to find one that flourishes in what could be termed 'inhospitable' conditions. At least will survive and reproduce in arid climates."

"Is that what drew you to this project?" Kay asked as she looked at her watch before picking up the phone.

"More or less," Jim answered, watching her dial.

Standing quietly while Kay waited for the connection, he glanced around her office. The walls were covered with pictures of more or less well-recognized former students of A&M. There was, of course, the occasional 'Aggie' joke that every student knew would be inflicted on them for the rest of their lives.

"Hello Gary," Kay said into the phone. "It's Kay Lindsay."

Waiting for the response, she then said, "I'm fine. I just need to ask you for a favor."

Listening for a moment, she continued, "If possible, could you determine what was the disposition of a patented barley seed?"

"That'd really help," Kay said a few seconds later.

Holding her hand over the phone, she asked Jim, "Do you have the patent number with you?"

Jim laid the notebook on her desk and pointed to the number he had written in it several weeks ago.

"It's 5676977," Kay said into the phone. "I believe it's listed as Barley MBM-106729, if that helps you."

Listening for a few seconds, Kay said, "Thanks, Gary. I appreciate your help, and I'll be waiting for your call. Have a good day!"

She replaced the phone and told Jim, "It'll take a couple of hours at least. Stop back by this afternoon before we close."

"Thanks, Dr. Lindsay," Jim said, picking up his notebook. "You've been a big help, as always."

Kay stood and walked around her desk, saying, "Not a problem, Jim. I'm here to help. If there's anything else I can do for you, just let me know."

Jim took her outstretched hand and replied, "I'll certainly do that. And I really do appreciate your help. Again, as always."

Kay shook his hand and started back to behind her desk, saying, "When you're ready to finish your report, stop by and let me have a look. Sounds interesting."

"I'll do that," Jim said, turning for the door. "I'll be sure to be back before you close today."

Jim hurried back to the computer room and sat beside Maria, saying, "I may have some help from the US Patent Office."

"How'd you manage that?" Maria asked keeping her eyes on the computer screen as she kept highlighting places to deepen her search.

"Dr. Lindsay," Jim answered as he logged off his computer. "She has some friend in Washington DC that works in the office."

"Good," Maria replied as she made a few notes and logged off. "Ready for lunch?"

Chapter 5

Jim gathered all of the notes, loose pages, and miscellaneous articles from around his computer and placed them in his briefcase. Pushing his chair back under the desk, he waited while Maria neatly placed all of her material together.

"Ready?" Jim asked as she pushed her chair against the desk.

Smiling at him, Maria answered, "Sure. Got any idea where you want to go?"

"How about Dickey's BBQ?" Jim suggested as they walked toward the exit.

"Sounds good to me," Maria replied. "Can we stop by the dorm?"

"What do you need at the dorm?" Jim asked as they reached the car, and he opened the passenger door for her.

"I thought I'd put my notes away and freshen up a little," Maria said as he closed her door.

Jim walked around the front of the VW and opened his door. Tossing his briefcase into the rear seat, he asked, "Are you through studying for the day?"

"No," she answered, "but I'm thinking of doing something else for my thesis."

"Such as what?" Jim asked, starting the engine.

"Not really sure," she told him. "Maybe something that is closer to my Sociology minor."

Jim checked out the side window and mirror before backing out of the parking slot. "How do you plan to do that?" he asked as he headed for the street.

"Maybe find an early population and show how the DNA from that society moved across an area or where it ended up today," Maria answered.

"That sounds more like a Doctoral thesis than for a Master's program," Jim said.

"That's kind of my thinking," Maria said as she looked at Jim, wishing they could skip lunch and go back to his apartment.

"By the way," she continued, still thinking about an hour or two alone. "Any chance of getting the BBQ to go?"

"Go where?" Jim asked as he headed for Dickey's.

"Back to your place," she smiled.

Jim took a quick look at her smiling face and said, "What about your 'freshening up' thing?"

"I thought I could do that while you're talking to that company," she answered.

"You mean Monogenic's," Jim told her as he slowed for the upcoming stop light.

"I guess," she told him. "I wasn't paying much attention when you were talking about them. Sorry."

Sitting at the red light, Jim leaned over and kissed her briefly, joking, "You need to start paying attention to everything I say. You may miss something very important one of these days.

As soon as the car in front of them pulled away, Jim eased the clutch out and accelerated behind it.

"When do you plan on saying something important?" Maria asked, watching Jim shift through the four gears.

"By definition, everything I say is important," Jim said as he watched for the turnoff from University Drive onto Earl Ruddy Freeway South.

"Oh really?" Maria asked mockingly.

"Of course," Jim said as he merged onto the access road. "Just think of it this way, you're working on your Master's degree. Most of your professors have a PhD or are working on one."

Spotting Dickey's ahead on the right, Jim continued, "So, since I'm the same as one of your professors, and everything they tell you could be on an exam, and you must pay attention, then everything I say must be considered the same. Don't you think?"

"Number one," Maria retorted, "you aren't one of my professors. Number two, not everything they say is important. For example, one of them strayed from the course material the other day about some member of his family."

"Now," she continued as Jim found a spot in the almost full parking lot, "I certainly don't think I'll see that on the exam."

"But you remembered it," Jim quipped as he parked. "Proves my point. Even if you don't think it's important, you should still remember what I say as you did your professor."

"I'll tell you what I *will* remember," Maria said as Jim opened her door.

Stepping out and looking him directly in the eye, she said, "I'll definitely remember every time you say something completely stupid."

"When have I ever said something stupid?" Jim smiled as he shut her door.

"Besides just now?" she replied.

"Yes," Jim said. "That is, if you think what I just said was stupid, name one, just one other time."

"We don't have time," Maria said as she headed for the restaurant. "Maybe if you have a week or so with nothing else to do, then we'll start early, and I'll review the last few weeks for you."

Following Maria through the parking lot, Jim smiled to himself as the odor of mesquite smoked meat wafted across the area. Knowing that he would never possibly win any argument with Maria, he wisely decided to just keep his mouth shut.

Once inside, Maria followed Jim to the 'Order' area and waited in line to select what they each wanted. The line moved quickly as two or three individuals told the women behind the counter what they wanted.

"Figured out what you want?" Jim asked, looking at the posted menu.

"Sliced sandwich and a couple of ribs," Maria answered as she put her hand on the small of Jim's back.

"Half a pound of sliced brisket and four ribs to go," Jim told the lady across from him.

"Help yourself to the beans and fixin's," she told him as she passed the written order down to the server. "Next."

As Jim started moving down the line, Maria whispered, "Do you still think I want to spend time alone in your apartment? After what you just said?"

Jim turned slightly and quietly said, "Up to you. If you'd rather, I'll divide the food and drop you off at your dorm."

Before she could answer, Jim told the cashier that they also needed two glasses of tea and handed her a 20-dollar bill.

The cashier slid the cardboard tray with two tall plastic glasses across, gave Jim his change, and thanked him before turning to the next person in line.

Jim carried the tray to the counter, where beans, onions, jalapenos, and other condiments were located. Setting the tray on the counter, he handed Maria one of the glasses and filled his with unsweet tea. While she was filling her glass, he put small Styrofoam containers of each item from the condiment counter on the tray and waited.

"Ready?" he asked as Maria snapped a lid on her glass.

"Yup," she replied, shoving a straw through the hole in the cover.

As they exited the restaurant, Jim asked, "Do you want me to drop you off at your dorm, or do you still want to eat at my place?"

"I've decided to give you a chance to make up for your latest stupid remark over lunch at your place," she answered, smiling. "Besides, I don't have any bread for the sandwich."

When they reached the car, Maria opened her door and slid into the seat, saying, "Let me hold that. I don't want it sliding around on the back seat or spilling my tea."

Jim handed her the tray and closed the door before walking around the front of the car. Climbing in, he told her, "I'm glad you've decided to allow me to recover from my latest 'stupid' remark."

Starting the car, he continued, "I guess I'll have to be more careful when I say things, or you'll just have to excuse things I say when they come out stupid. Probably be better for you to overlook what I've said. I just never know when I may say the wrong thing. And, as you know by now, I can't keep my mouth shut sometimes."

Maria leaned over and kissed him on the cheek, saying, "I'll always excuse your remarks. I know you can't help it sometimes."

Sitting back smiling, she continued, "Besides, every now and then, I may act a little crazy, and you'll just have to put up with that!"

Jim smiled at her as he backed the little VW out of the slot and replied, "I guess we both may have to put up with a little odd behavior every now and then. But I'll reserve judgment until I see just what you mean by *a little crazy*!"

Chapter 6

When they got back to Jim's apartment, he placed the tray on the table while Maria pulled a couple of paper towels from the roll beside the sink. Putting them down, she got two of the plastic plates from the cupboard and, along with the knives, forks, and spoons, finished setting the table.

Once Jim took what was left of the loaf of bread from the refrigerator, they each took some of the brisket and made sandwiches and loaded their plates with the beans, two ribs, and what each wanted of the condiments.

Taking a bite of her sandwich, Maria asked, "Have you ever considered getting real dishes instead of these picnic things you have?"

Biting into a rib, Jim answered, "Thought about it, but these are free. If they get broken, I toss them out. An, they all go in the trash if I ever have to move."

"So," Maria asked, lifting a spoon full of beans that had small pieces of onion and jalapeno mixed in, "what do you hope to find out from your meeting with Mono-whatever?"

"Monogenic's," Jim corrected. "I'm hoping that they can tell me the disposition of the barley strain they patented."

"What if they won't tell you?" she asked.

"Not sure," Jim admitted. "But, why wouldn't they? Even if it's just something that they haven't used or failed in field tests, I think it wouldn't matter to them if I used that information."

"If it was never used, would that change your mind about using it in your paper?" she asked, sipping her tea.

"Probably," Jim answered. "But it's so late in the semester, I'd hate to start over on another topic."

"Maybe they could help you with something that they've developed and are using," Maria suggested.

"Possibly," Jim agreed. "If this turns out to be a bust, maybe they'll be glad to help with a successful project. If for no other reason than to have some friendly publicity from a Doctoral thesis."

"What if you took an application while you're there?" Maria asked, finishing her meal.

Getting up and taking her empty plate to the sink, she continued, "That way, maybe they'd be more open if they thought you might want to work for them."

"That's a thought," Jim said as he finished his last rib.

Maria reached around him to take his plate and said, "Just sit there while I rinse these off."

Jim turned slightly, and she kissed him quickly before returning to the sink. The sound of the running water was the only thing Jim heard as he continued to think about the upcoming meeting. He was surprised a few seconds later when Maria slipped around him and straddled him on his chair.

"Ready for dessert?" she asked as she put her arms around his neck.

Noticing the obvious lack of clothes she now had on, Jim smiled and asked, "No whipped cream?"

"Nope," she told him. "Just like good brisket, no extra seasoning required."

Jim stood with her arms around his neck and her legs around his waist and started toward the bedroom, saying, "I don't suppose you plan on making this a tradition, do you?"

"Nooners or desert?" she joked as they approached the bed.

Thirty minutes later, Jim rolled away from Maria, saying, "I've got to take a quick shower and put on some clean clothes before my meeting. If you want to shower here, you can either wait or join me."

Maria jumped out of bed and ran into the bathroom laughing, "*You* can either wait or join *Me*!"

Jim shook his head and smiled back, "I'll join, but this is just going to be a shower. Absolutely no hanky-panky!"

"Your loss!" she told him as she turned on the water. "You may never get the chance again."

Almost true to his word, Jim showered quickly with only minor playing around. That finished, he dried off and headed for his closet with a towel around his waist.

Maria was close behind while he was selecting one of the two remaining clean shirts. Pulling the towel from around him, she said, "You may not let me touch right now, but at least let me look."

"Be quick," Jim said as he slipped on the shirt. "I've got no time for nude modeling right now."

As he pulled on a pair of clean underwear, Maria complained, "You're no fun at all, Mr. Jackson. Absolutely no fun whatsoever!"

Jim smiled as he pulled on a pair of crisply starched jeans and told her, "If I'm absolutely no fun, why do you hang around me?"

"Just to see what stupid thing you say next," joked Maria as she headed for the kitchen to retrieve her clothes. "Good thing, too. You seem to say stupid things more often than you want to have fun!"

Jim grabbed his damp towel from the floor where Maria had dropped it, quickly twirled it, and snapped it at Maria's butt as she walked away.

Barely missing, he said, "And if this is what you mean by being a little crazy, I'm pretty sure I can put up with it."

As soon as Maria had her clothes on and headed to the car, Jim asked, "Do you still want to go to the dorm or what?"

"Dorm," Maria answered as Jim backed out of the parking slot. "I still need to put on some clean clothes. What are you going to do after your meeting?"

"Depends," Jim said as he pulled onto the road.

"Depends on what?" Maria said as she looked in the vanity mirror on the passenger side's sun visor.

"How long the meeting takes," Jim answered. "I'm hoping for at least a couple of hours. If it's longer than that, I'll probably quit for the day."

"What do you plan to do?" he continued as they approached her dorm.

"Probably go back to the library," she answered as he pulled up to the curb.

Leaning over to kiss her, Jim said, "I'll stop by there when I'm done. If you're still there, we'll talk. If not, I'll call you when I'm done."

"Sounds good," Maria told him as she opened her door. "Do you want to do anything later this evening?"

"Let's see how this goes with Monogenic's," Jim answered. "If it's good news, maybe a couple of beers to celebrate. If I get nothing, I probably won't be in the mood for much."

"Okay, let me know," Maria said as she got out and shut the door. "I'm also good at commiserating the depressed."

"Good to know," Jim said as she stepped away from the car. "I'll let you know as soon as I can."

Jim waved as he drove away, wondering what information he would get from the folks at Monogenic's and whether or not it would mean starting over on his thesis.

Chapter 7

Heading for Monogenic's on Research Parkway, Jim wondered if he should have put on a sports coat, maybe even a tie, to make a more suitable impression. Although this wasn't an interview, he still wanted to make a professional appearance, especially if he followed through on Maria's suggestion about asking for an application.

Parking at the location he had gotten from the computer, he was mildly surprised to see it was merely a suite in an office building. Opening the door, he walked to the lone desk in the small front office.

"May I help you?" the man behind the desk asked.

"Yes, sir," Jim answered, "I'm here to find out if the branch president will meet with me."

"Are you Jim Jackson?" the man asked.

"Yes, sir," Jim told him.

The man got up and came around the desk, offering his hand and saying, "Hi Jim, I'm Jerry Moss. We spoke on the phone earlier."

Jim shook his hand and said, "Yes, sir. Nice to meet you."

"Mr. Hawk told me to bring you right in," Jerry said, leading Jim through a door into the hall that served several offices on either side.

"That's great," Jim said, following him. "I didn't really expect him to be available right away."

"Not a problem," Jerry told him as they arrived at the end of the hall. "We always try to help students at A&M whenever we can. You did say that you were almost finished with your PhD, didn't you?"

"Yes, sir," Jim answered. "This is my last semester, I hope."

"Congratulations," Jerry said after knocking and then opening the door.

"Mr. Hawk," Jerry said, approaching the massive desk where a man dressed in khaki pants and a knit short-sleeved sports shirt was getting up. "This is Jim Jackson, the guy I told you about."

Mr. Hawk rounded the desk, extending his hand and saying, "Good to meet you, Jim."

Shaking the offered hand, Jim responded, "Thanks, Mr. Hawk. I appreciate you meeting me. Especially this quickly."

"No problem. And please, just call me Mike," he said.

Walking to a small conference area where five comfortable leather chairs were arranged around a small, short oak table, Mike said, "Have a seat, and let's see what we can do to help you. Jerry, why don't you join us as well."

Jim waited until both men were taking their seats and followed suit. Facing the two men across the table, Jim said, "Thank you again. I hope I'm not taking up too much of your time."

"Not at all," Mike said. "Now, let's see if I've got this straight. You're working on your Doctorial Thesis in

Molecular Biology and are interested in one of our products, right?"

"Yes, sir," Jim answered. "I'm especially interested in Barley MBM 106729."

"I don't recall that specific strain of Barley," Mike said. "Do you, Jerry?"

"No, sir. Not off the bat. But, if I may use your computer, I'll look it up," Jerry told him.

"Go ahead," Mike said as Jerry got up and walked to Mike's desk. "While he's researching that, why don't you tell me why this specific barley interests you?"

"Well, sir," Jim replied, "I was looking for a complex project that proved to be an asset to agriculture in general and, more specifically, would be able to sustain production in arid climates."

"How did you come by this particular one?" Mike queried. "Had you previously heard about it?"

"No, sir," Jim said. "I was using a search matrix that resulted in several hundred possibilities. This one just happened to be one of those searches. Then I noted that it was the combination of animal and plant."

"Ahh," Mike said, sitting back. "Just random selection. Were any of the others on the list our products?"

"Yes, sir. Several," Jim answered. "There were others from different companies, but the majority were patented by Monogenic's."

Mike nodded his head and said, "We do try to stay ahead of our competitors. That's not easy with the rapid advances in technology nowadays."

"I understand," Jim told him. "That's one of the reasons I got into this field. I believe that there is a great future in GMOs."

Jerry came walking back with a printout from the computer saying, "Here's what I've found on that barley."

Mike took the sheet and spent a moment looking at it before saying, "Now I remember this one."

Handing the sheet to Jim, Mike asked, "What has your research shown thus far?"

Looking at the paragraph on the sheet, Jim answered, "Not much, sir. I've found only the basics. Patent number. Product name. But what I'm looking for is what became of the project."

"Was there any information on that available?" Mike asked Jerry.

"No, sir," Jerry answered. "Other than what I showed you, the only information I saw was that we still hold the patent, but it never went into production."

"Any guess why?" Mike asked.

"No, sir," Jerry admitted. "However, there was a follow-on project that may have proven to be a better strain after field tests."

"That sounds reasonable," Mike said, nodding his head.

Turning to Jim, Mike continued, "That's one of the biggest problems we have. We spend years and countless dollars on a project that looks promising. Then, either another company beats us or comes up with something that does what we did even better. Gets frustrating."

"I imagine so," Jim agreed. "I certainly don't know the costs involved, but I do know they are substantial. Then, to have a competitor nullify all that work."

"Sometimes it isn't just a competitor," Mike responded. "Sometimes it's another project within house. We try not to overlap research, but occasionally, a project in an entirely separate area proves to be better at what we were trying to do."

"That's more often than you'd suspect," Jerry agreed. "We may be looking at drought resistance on one, and another one that we were researching protein levels proves to be more resistant to the drought than the first, and have the increased proteins as well."

"Hazards of the field," Mike said. "But, if we can get a better product, it doesn't matter how it came about. Even with all the science behind it, sometimes Mother Nature steps in and reminds us that she's still in control."

"Not to change the subject," Mike continued. "Have you given any thought to an internship?"

"Not really," Jim answered. "I've been pretty caught up with just getting the degree finished."

"I completely understand," Mike agreed. "However, if you're interested, we may be able to do two things here."

"What's that, sir," Jim asked.

"I was just thinking that if you wanted to continue your research on this barley, what better place than here?" Mike replied. "And, by working with us, you'd have legitimate field experience when you're ready to start looking for a job."

"That sounds good," Jim said, nodding his head. "But one of my biggest problems is a lack of time."

"Not a problem," Mike said. "I'm sure Jerry can structure it so that the only real time you spend with us would be about the same as you would be researching on your own."

"I'm sure I can manage that," Jerry concurred. "It might even mean less time total since you'll have access to the information we have. As well as other researchers we have on staff."

"That does sound promising," Jim said. "I can certainly see the advantages of having access to your files. That alone would save me hours of research at the library, even if the information is available there."

"And," Mike said, "if this particular barley doesn't meet your criteria, it would be easy to provide you the information on other strains. Or, possibly, even another product. We've made some rather phenomenal advances in our corn research."

"This all sounds fantastic," Jim told them. "Would it be possible to think about this for a day or so?"

"Not at all," Mike said, rising from his chair. "Like all good scientists, you need to evaluate every aspect of the problem before you make any conclusions."

Jerry and Jim both rose from their chairs and followed Mike toward the door as Mi.ke continued, "Jerry will give you an application as we leave. Not that you'll be viewed as an employee, but we do need to do certain background checks on anyone that has access to some of our proprietary information."

"Certainly," Jim said, following Mike down the hall.

At the front door, Mike turned to Jim, extending his hand, and said, "I've enjoyed meeting you, Jim. I hope you do give consideration to my proposal."

Jim shook his hand, saying, "I appreciate your time, sir. And I'll certainly give the internship considerable thinking."

Jerry came up behind Jim and handed him a pale green folder, saying, "Here's our standard employment package. Let me know if I can help with any questions you may have."

Jim took the folder, shook Jerry's hand, and said, "Thanks again, gentlemen. I'll be in touch with you within the next day or so."

"Our pleasure, Jim," Mike said, holding the door open. "I hope to see you again."

Jim nodded and headed down the sidewalk toward his car as Mike and Jerry watched.

"What do you think?" Mike asked when he was certain that Jim couldn't overhear their conversation.

"Not sure," Jerry answered. "For now, I'd say that it was just a fluke that he stumbled on that particular strain of barley."

"Could be," Mike said as he watched Jim get in the car. "But we can't afford to take any chances. Having him here as an intern will allow us to make sure he doesn't follow this any further than we want."

"Agreed," Jerry replied. "Out of all the GMO's out there, why'd he find this one?"

"That's what we need to find out," Mike said, opening the door to go back into the building. "If it was just a fluke, as you said, we need to try to redirect his research."

"Yes, sir," Jerry said. "I'll have one of the research assistants over at the lab start gathering information on something that we can provide when he hits the brick wall on this one. That should shift his attention away from this barley."

"Good idea," Mike agreed. "And I think we should provide a little incentive for him to accept the internship. Maybe offer him a salaried position while he's doing his research. Tell him that it's standard since we may benefit from his work."

"Yes, sir," Jerry said. "And, we'll also be able to argue that any work he produces belongs to Monogenic's. We can, therefore, control the content that would be made available to the public, including the thesis."

"I guess the only good thing we can say for now is that it was fortunate that you happened to be standing in for Barbara when Jim first called," Mike told him as they headed down the hall. "There's no telling what that brick-head would have told him."

"Maybe so," Jerry said, following Mike into his office. "But I'm sure she wouldn't have asked what project he was looking at."

"True," Mike agreed. "That little bit of info at least gave us enough time to doctor the computer files. Speaking of that, are you sure everything has been deleted from the unclassified files?"

"Positive," Jerry answered. "As far as any information on MBM 106729 is concerned, it dead ends immediately following unfavorable field tests on germination."

"Good," Mike said. "Stay on top of this one, Jerry. We can't afford any undesirable info to get into a public document."

"Will do," Jerry said as he turned to leave the office.

Chapter 8

Jim drove straight back to the campus and parked in the library lot. Taking the folder that Monogenic's had given him, he carried it and his briefcase into the library. Noting that he had left Maria slightly more than two hours ago, he went to Dr. Lindsay's office before he went to the computer room.

Standing in the doorway and knocking on the frame, Jim waited until Kay looked up from her phone call. Motioning him in, she returned to listening to the conversation on the phone.

A moment or so later, she spoke into the handset, saying, "Thanks, Gary. I appreciate your help."

"Well," Kay told Jim. "That was Gary from the US Patent Office. He had some interesting news."

"What's that?" Jim asked.

"It appears that your patent number still belongs to Monogenic's," Kay told him. "But Gary pulled some strings and found that there is an almost identical patent held by a small research company in South Africa."

"What does 'almost identical' mean?" Jim asked.

"I'm not entirely sure," Kay admitted. "Gary just said that comparing the technical data provided from the Monogenic's patent matches the one in South Africa perfectly."

"Interesting," Jim said thoughtfully. "Did he give you the name of the other company and the patent number?"

Kay picked up a sheet of paper from her desk where she had been taking notes and said, "Here is all the information that Gary could find."

Jim took the sheet and studied it for a second before asking, "May I keep this?"

"Of course," Kay said, nodding her head.

Kay paused for a moment and then said, "There's more."

Jim looked up to see her smiling and asked, "What's that?"

Taking a small stack of paper from her desk, Kay smiled and said, "Gary sent me all of the technical data that was provided in both of the patents."

"Holy shit!" Jim exclaimed as he took the stapled pages. "How'd you manage to get these?"

"Gary," Kay answered. "I told you he pulled some strings. Apparently, he knows somebody somewhere that knows somebody somewhere else. Bottom line---you're welcome."

"I don't know how to thank you, Dr. Lindsay," Jim said excitedly. "This may give me the end result of the barley I've been researching."

"It appears that there must be some cooperation between Monogenic's and the South African company," Kay said. "Maybe since Monogenic's doesn't appear to be using their patent here, they may have 'outsourced' the program."

"That's possible," Jim agreed. "Especially if this barley was developed for an area like where the South African company's located."

"At least now you have a few leads that may allow you to finish your thesis," Kay said, implying that she needed to get back to her main job. "If you need help again, don't hesitate to stop by."

"Certainly," Jim said, slipping the new papers into his briefcase. "You've been great! I can't thank you enough, Dr. Lindsay."

"Don't mention it," Kay said. "Especially anything about where this information came from. Gary was adamant about not revealing his sources."

"I understand," Jim said, turning to leave. "Again, thanks!"

Now looking forward to resuming his research, Jim hurried to the computer room. Not seeing Maria, he settled into a chair in front of a vacant computer and brought it online to begin.

Not knowing exactly where to start, he began by doing a search for the South African company. Typing 'Mombasa Research, Inc.' into the search bar, Jim waited for the data to appear.

Within a few seconds, the first information appeared on the screen. Reading it as it filled in, Jim saw that it was a small company located in Zwairiland. Minimizing the screen, he then typed Zwairiland into the search bar and waited.

When it appeared on the screen, Jim saw that it was a small country bordering the east side of Ethiopia. About the size of New Mexico, it was mainly an arid land with a large agricultural economy.

As he was taking notes about the climate and environmental conditions, Maria walked up behind him and put her hands on his shoulders, saying, "Here you are."

Jim turned and looked up at her saying, "Yup, still here."

Maria put her papers on the desk and pulled a chair from a vacant desk over to sit by Jim. "Anything new?"

"Lots," Jim said, looking from the screen to his notes. "I may have found the answer that I was looking for."

"What'd you find?" Maria asked, putting her arm around Jim's shoulders.

"I think I found where the patent went," Jim answered.

"Did you get that from Mono-whoever?" Maria asked.

"Monogenic's," Jim corrected her. "And no, they didn't give me this."

"Speaking of Monogenic's," Maria sarcastically said, "what did you find out from them?"

"Not much," Jim admitted, still concentrating on the flow of information on his computer screen.

"Did you ask for an application?" she asked.

"Nope," Jim said, filling another page with notes.

"Why not?" Maria asked.

"I'll tell you later," Jim answered, looking back at the computer.

Maria pointed at the screen and asked, "Where's that?"

"South Africa," Jim told her.

"Is that where the patent went?" Maria asked as she studied the information currently on the screen.

"I think so," Jim answered. "I certainly hope so."

The student at the adjoining computer logged out, picked up his books, and left. Sliding over to the now vacant computer, Maria logged on and glanced at Jim's screen.

Typing the search bar with Zwairiland, she soon had the same site Jim was studying.

Running her mouse around the pad, she kept clicking on areas until she had a map of Zwairiland displayed. "Hey," she exclaimed. "Did you know that this is right by Ethiopia?"

"Noticed that right off," Jim replied.

"Do you know what's important about Ethiopia?" Maria asked.

"Important in what respect?" Jim asked, still scrolling through the data on his screen.

"Important in the whole chain of human life!" she told him. "This is where the first homo sapiens started."

"Just how can you be so sure about that?" Jim asked, glancing at her screen.

"The DNA of every human can be traced back to this area," she explained. "Every race on the face of the earth can be traced back to a woman in Ethiopia."

Minimizing the screen, Maria switched to where she had been doing research for her paper. Several searches and even more refined searches finally pulled the information she was looking for.

"Here's what I wanted to show you," Maria said as she paused her mouse.

Jim leaned over and looked at the screen. "What are you showing me?"

"Homo sapiens idaltu," she told him. "They are the oldest known subspecies of today's modern man."

"They dated the fossils from about 160,000 years ago," she continued. "Modern anatomically man dates from about 130,000 years ago."

"And this information is important how?" Jim asked, returning to his computer.

"Just interesting," Maria said. "There have been terrible famines in this part of the world, and maybe that's why Mono--shittics is interested in the area."

"Monogenic's," Jim corrected her again.

Reaching into his briefcase, he handed her the folder he had been given after his meeting. "Read this," he said. "Maybe then you'll remember their name."

Maria quickly scanned the brochures and application forms before asking, "Didn't you just say you didn't ask for an application?"

"Didn't have to," Jim said, logging off his computer. "They gave it to me."

"Why?" Maria asked, still looking at the profile of the company in the brochure.

"I'll tell you over dinner," Jim told her. "If you're ready, log out, and we'll go somewhere to talk."

"Thought you'd never ask," Maria joked as she logged off and powered down her computer."

Chapter 9

Jim loaded all of the miscellaneous notes and papers into his briefcase and waited for Maria to gather all of her material. Rechecking that they had logged off the computers, they pushed their chairs beneath the desks and headed for the exit.

As they passed the librarian's office, Kay was walking out and asked, "You done for the day, Jim?"

Jim paused and answered, "Think so, Dr. Lindsay. Do you know Maria?"

"Don't think so," Kay told him.

Jim looked at Maria and said, "Maria, this is Dr. Kay Lindsay, the head librarian. Dr. Lindsay, this is Maria Pompillio."

Kay extended her hand, saying, "Nice to meet you, Ms. Pompillio."

"You too, Dr. Lindsay," Maria said, taking Kay's hand.

"Are you a student here?" Kay asked.

"Yes, Ma'am," Maria answered. "I'm trying to finish my Masters this semester."

"What's your major?" Kay asked.

"Archaeogenetics," Maria told her.

"Ahh," Kay said. "The tracing of our ancestors. Interesting."

"I enjoy it," Maria replied. "Sort of a coincidence that both Jim and I are studying related areas."

"Sort of," Kay admitted. "But you're tracing DNA backward through time while Jim's changing DNA forward."

Kay paused thoughtfully for a moment and continued, "Maria, have you considered what sort of changes to future DNA would mean to your ability to trace the lineage of either plants or animals?"

"No," Maria admitted. "I hadn't thought about that."

"Well," Kay wondered, "if some GMO is examined for ancestral origins, wouldn't the presence of an inserted gene skew your results?"

"Possibly," Maria answered. "However, I think that we could isolate the odd gene and still follow the strain backward."

"And, if the inserted gene was from a totally different species, we could discount it from the study," Maria concluded.

"I suppose you're right," Kay said. "But it makes for an interesting wrinkle if it happened. Doesn't it?"

"That sounds like a great idea for your Doctoral thesis, Maria," Jim said.

"If I get that far," Maria answered. "Right now, I'm struggling to get through the Master's program."

"I don't think you'll have a problem," Kay told her. "You seem to have a quick, intelligent response for off-the-wall questions."

"Being quick is one thing," Jim offered. "Being correct is quite another thing."

"An inquisitive mind is the big thing here," Kay admonished. "I'm sure Maria knows when to make a statement of fact instead of a supposition. And that's all we're discussing here. Kind of a 'what if?' thing."

"You're right," Jim agreed. "But for now, we need to head out for dinner."

Kay smiled at both of them and said, "Anyway, it was nice to meet you, Maria. Y'all have a nice dinner. Will I see you back here tomorrow, Jim?"

"Pleased to meet you, also," Maria said, shaking Kay's hand.

"I probably will," Jim told Kay. "I got a lot of new data and a few new places to look."

"Let me know if I can help. See you tomorrow," Kay said, heading back toward her office.

"Nice lady," Maria whispered as she followed Jim.

"Very," Jim answered as he held the door open for her.

"Where do you want to go?" Maria asked as they approached the car.

Opening her door for her, Jim suggested, "How about grabbing something from Arby's to eat at the apartment?"

"Sounds fine to me," Maria answered as she slid into the seat.

Jim rounded the front of the car, opened his door, and tossed his briefcase into the rear seat.

"Can we stop and get some ice cream?" Maria asked as Jim got in the car.

"What kind do you want?" Jim asked, seeing the begging look on her face.

"Blue Bell Pistachio Almond!" Maria said, clapping her hands together. "That's my favorite. Or, Rocky Road if they don't have the Pistachio Almond."

"I suppose we can look," Jim said, grinning as he started the car. "But, to be honest, I was hoping for some more of the dessert I had after lunch today."

Maria slapped his arm, saying, "That's all you think of, isn't it, Mr. Jackson?"

Backing the VW out of its slot, Jim replied, "Hey, that was your idea. Not mine! Remember?"

"Yes, I remember," Maria teased. "And, if you get me some Pistachio Almond, you just might, *might*, get that special dessert."

Jim laughed as he headed out of the parking lot, "Might?"

"That's what I said," Maria told him as they pulled onto University Drive. "I'll let you know after dinner."

"What if I'm full after the ice cream?" Jim joked as they approached Arby's.

"Then you better not eat the ice cream," Maria answered. "But, that's your choice. Pick one or the other."

"I can't have both?" Jim asked as he pulled into the parking lot.

"Not sure," teased Maria. "Maybe if you control your appetite, you might get both."

Once they had gotten their order and headed back to the car, Maria asked, "When are you going to tell me about that application?"

"I'll tell you when we get to the apartment," Jim told her as they got back into the car.

"Sounds mysterious," Maria said. "You told me you didn't ask for an application, yet you have one. Did you steal it?"

"Of course not," Jim said, heading for the grocery store.

"What then?" Maria wanted to know.

"I told you that I'd tell you over dinner. Just wait until we get to the apartment," Jim said, pulling into the parking lot.

Following Jim into the store, Maria continued, "Something sounds fishy here. You have something you didn't ask for. Something you didn't steal. Did they just have them lying around for anyone to pick up?"

"Nope," Jim answered, stepping into the grocery store. "Now, why don't you just drop it until we get home?"

"Fine," Maria pouted. "I'll wait. But there better be Pistachio Almond. If not, I'm not sure about that other dessert."

Arriving at the frozen food section, Jim asked, "What about if they have Rocky Road instead? You said that would be okay."

"Yes, that would be okay. Just okay," Maria teased. "But for what you've got in mind, I need Pistachio Almond."

Peering into the selection of ice creams, Jim stopped in front of one of the glass doors. Opening the door, he pulled out a green gallon container and said, "Looks like I get two desserts tonight!"

Maria shook her head and replied, "There's that other condition."

"What was that?" Jim asked, heading for the cashier.

"What if you're too full?" she reminded him.

"Not going to happen," Jim laughed as he paid for the ice cream. "Not going to happen."

Chapter 10

When they arrived at Jim's apartment, Jim carried the meals from Arby's, and his briefcase as Maria followed him with the ice cream. Sitting his briefcase down, Jim juggled the keys until he had the one for the apartment between his thumb and fingers.

Unlocking the door and walking in, Jim headed for the kitchen while Maria followed with Jim's briefcase. After setting the food on the table, he took the ice cream from Maria and placed it in the tiny freezer.

"Just sit that on the counter," Jim told Maria as she followed him.

"I'll get some napkins," she said as Jim rinsed out the glasses they had gotten from Dickey's at noon.

Taking a small bucket of ice out of the freezer, Jim asked, "What would you like to drink?"

"What do you have?" Maria asked as she ripped two sheets from the roll of paper towels.

"Dr. Pepper and water," Jim told her as he sat the glasses on the table.

"Dr. Pepper," she answered.

Jim took the two-liter bottle of Dr Pepper from the refrigerator and sat it on the table. Along with that, he took a small jar of horseradish from the shelf and took the lid off before placing it on the table.

Once he had filled the glasses with ice, Maria poured them full of Dr Pepper, asking, "Is now when you're going to tell me about that application?"

"Soon," Jim said as he sat and divided the roast beef sandwiches and curly fries between them.

Taking the top bun off his sandwich, Jim ladled a generous amount of horseradish across the thinly sliced beef.

"Any catsup?" Maria asked as she took her seat and spread a thin layer of the horseradish on her sandwich.

"Of course," Jim said, getting out of his chair. "One of the few vegetables I eat on a regular basis."

"Tomato is a fruit," Maria said as she took a bite of her sandwich.

"True," Jim said, returning with the half-full bottle of catsup. "But if you wouldn't put it in a fruit salad, it must be in the vegetable family."

"It's still a fruit," Maria quipped as she poured a puddle of catsup on the waxed paper that had once surrounded her sandwich. "Doesn't matter how you use it."

Jim sat and poured catsup on his sandwich wrapper saying, "Tomato, tomatoe, potato, potatoe, fruit, vegetable, it's still the only vegetable I eat around here."

After a few moments of enjoying their meal, Jim finally said, "The application."

"What about it?" Maria asked, around her mouth full of fries.

"They gave it to me," Jim answered.

"Why?" she asked, taking a sip of her drink.

"They offered me an internship," Jim said, wiping his mouth with the paper towel.

"What did you tell them?" she asked.

"I said I'd let them know in a day or two," Jim told her as he finished the last of the fries.

"I think that's great!" Maria exclaimed. "At least if you're there, you can have more access to the information on your barley project.

Jim leaned back and thought for a moment before answering, "Maybe. But something doesn't seem right."

"What do you mean?" Maria asked as she got up to clear the few things from the table.

"I'm not sure," Jim admitted. "Just a feeling I've had since I found out about the company in South Africa using their patent."

"What's so strange about that?" Maria asked, sitting back down at the table.

"To start with, why didn't they know that someone was using their patent?" Jim asked.

"Maybe they did," Maria said.

"No, at least they didn't tell me," Jim told her as he sat forward and placed his elbows on the table.

"Did you ask them?" Maria said, leaning forward.

"Pretty much," Jim told her. "I asked about the patent, and they didn't seem to remember it."

"That's not so strange," Maria argued. "As you said, they've got thousands of patents."

"True," Jim responded. "But when I asked about this one, they used the computer, and the information they gave me never mentioned it was being used in South Africa."

"Maybe since it was another company that was using it, they didn't track it," Maria suggested.

"I doubt it," Jim argued. "After all they spent in time and money, they would at least know what was going on with their product. Especially if they had outsourced the test trials."

Maria got up and walked to the counter where she had placed Jim's briefcase. Pulling out the green folder, she said, "Maybe you just didn't ask the right question."

"Possibly," Jim agreed. "But it was as if they were denying any information about it. If nothing strange was going on with this product, why didn't they at least tell me it was undergoing field tests in Zwairiland?"

Maria studied the brochure for a moment and asked, "What does that have to do with your accepting the internship?"

"Maybe nothing," Jim said, deep in thought.

"Well, I still think you should accept it," Maria said as she laid the brochure on the table. "It's entirely possible that they just didn't go into the right area of the computer."

"Possible," Jim replied. "The other thing that sort of surprised me was how easy it was to get to see the Branch President on such short notice."

"He may just have had an hour or so available," Maria countered.

"Maybe," Jim agreed. "But it's still unusual. Normally, I've had to schedule meetings days in advance."

"I still think you're overthinking this thing," Maria argued. "Can't you just accept that it was fortunate that he was able to see you? Besides, how could he have known that you were there about that barley?"

"I told him," Jim answered.

"When? When you got there?" Maria asked.

"No," Jim said. "I told the receptionist when I called for the appointment. As it turns out, he, the receptionist, was in the meeting with me and the president, Mike Hawk."

"Why is that strange?" Maria asked.

"Think about it," Jim said. "Since when does the receptionist stay for a meeting with the president? Not to mention, he, the receptionist, Jerry Moss, used the computer in the President's office to get the information on the patent."

"Still not that strange," Maria continued to argue. "Maybe he was there to take notes. Maybe he's more a personal assistant than a receptionist."

Jim reached over and took the brochure from in front of Maria and flipped through it quickly.

Sitting back, staring at the organizational chart, Jim said, "He's no receptionist. He's the Vice-president!"

"There," Maria said, crossing her arms across her chest. "That explains why he was there."

"Then why didn't he tell me who he was?" Jim asked, tossing the brochure on the table. "Why did he let me believe that he was just a low-level receptionist?"

"Did he ever say he was the receptionist?" Maria asked.

"No," Jim admitted. "I just assumed so after he answered the phone when I first called."

"There you go," Maria said, getting up. "You made an assumption based on a lack of information. As a Ph.D., you should know better. Ice cream?"

Chapter 11

An hour or so later, Maria lay with her head on Jim's chest and her arm across his stomach as she murmured, "That was better than the ice cream."

"Definitely," Jim breathed.

"Sleepy?" Maria asked.

"Not really," Jim told her as he kissed the top of her head.

"Want to get up?" she asked, hoping the answer was no.

"Nope," Jim told her. "I'm pretty happy right here."

Maria smiled to herself and then asked, "Want to talk about the internship?"

"Sure," Jim answered as she rolled onto her side.

"What's really keeping you from just saying yes?" she asked.

Jim thought for a moment and then answered, "I think it's that I believe they were trying to hide something from me."

"So?" Maria responded. "You're just some 'supposed' student that walked in off the street. As far as they know, you could be some industrial spy that's trying to get information."

"Possible," Jim admitted. "But wouldn't it have been just as effective to have told me that they couldn't discuss any of their proprietary information?"

"Maybe," Maria said as she leaned on her elbow to look at Jim. "Maybe they didn't want to make any assumptions until they verified your status."

Jim slid up in the bed and arranged his pillow behind his back. "Then why didn't they tell me that on the phone? Or when I first arrived?"

Maria slid up beside him and pulled the sheet over her breasts, saying, "Maybe they just wanted to see you. You know, in case they recognized you."

"The thing about that is that they never asked for my student ID," Jim told her. "That would've been one of the first things I'd do if some strange guy came asking questions," Jim replied.

"Maybe that's why they wanted you to fill out the application," Maria responded.

"Reasonable," Jim said, nodding his head.

Reaching down and taking Maria's hand, he continued, "That still doesn't explain why that Moss guy didn't introduce himself as the Vice President."

"Oversight?" Maria suggested.

"I doubt it," Jim countered. "Why would a VP want to be mistaken for a receptionist?"

"Maybe he didn't want to appear self-important," Maria rationalized.

"Either way," Jim told her, "I still have concerns about their lack of openness about the company in South Africa."

"Again, maybe they didn't want to give you any information about ongoing projects until they verified who you were," Maria repeated.

"It's still a lot of misdirection," Jim complained as he adjusted the sheet over his waist.

"What would it hurt to just fill out the application?" Maria asked, laying her head on Jim's shoulder.

"Nothing, I suppose," Jim admitted.

"Just because you give it to them doesn't mean you have to accept the internship," Maria reasoned.

"No," Jim agreed. "I could fill it out, turn it in, and then decide if I want to get involved with them."

"Not taking it might mean you have to change the direction of your thesis," Maria advised.

"That's the only reason I may want to pursue this thing," Jim said. It appears that I may have run out of options without their help."

"What was the name of the country where the patent is being used?" Maria asked.

"Zwairiland," Jim answered.

"Maybe I can do a little research on them," Maria said, thinking about the studies already done on the Ethiopian population's DNA.

"What good would that do?" Jim asked.

"I don't know," Maria answered. "Maybe just see if the area's people are closely tied to Ethiopia. That shouldn't take too much effort. Just some basic searching through the existing data."

"Why would that be important?" Jim queried.

"Again, I don't know," Maria answered. "I'm still not sure I'm heading in the right direction with the paper I'm working on. Maybe doing some research showing how more closely aligned the DNA is with populations geographically closer to Ethiopia."

"Wouldn't that be expected?" Jim asked. "I mean, I'd expect more variations the further you get from the origin. That is if Ethiopia is truly the origin."

"It is," Maria confirmed. "But it appears that the Middle East is where societies became more prevalent. Then, the trail leads north to Europe."

"If that's the case," Jim argued, "then Zwairiland would most likely show closer ties with the Middle East."

"Not necessarily," she countered. "There are more similarities among tribes within Africa than with Middle East populations. If the studies have been done, all I have to do is cross-reference one study against another to see if Zwairiland has closer ties to Africa or the Middle East."

"Sounds like loads of fun," Jim joked. "Nothing like following an old trail when you already know where it ended."

Maria playfully slapped Jim on the arm and countered, "Better than trying to get mice to breed cucumbers!"

"Barley," Jim corrected as Maria slid her hand under the sheet.

"No," she smiled. "This is definitely more like a cucumber."

As they both slid back down, Jim rolled over onto Maria and said, "Maybe the cucumber bred the mouse?"

"Smart cucumber," Maria whispered as she pulled Jim into her.

Chapter 12

The next morning, Jim woke feeling Maria's breasts pressed against his back. Her slight snoring sounded more like sighing as he lay there, relishing the comfort of having her cuddling against him.

As he eased away from her, Jim listened for any changes in her breathing. Trying not to wake her, he slid slowly out of the bed and tiptoed into the kitchen, picking up his hastily discarded underwear on the way.

Opening the refrigerator, he shook the orange juice container to estimate how much was left. Shaking his head that he hadn't gotten more when they stopped for ice cream, he poured a little into one of the glasses from the sink and sat it on the table.

Next, he took the near-empty can of Folgers Classic Roast from the cupboard and sat it beside the coffee maker. Dumping the old grounds in the plastic trash can, he rinsed the basket, poured what remained in the pot in the sink, filled it with water, and then poured it into the ancient Mr Coffee. Shaking what remained in the coffee can into the basket, he placed it into its holder and pressed the 'on' button.

Sipping his juice, he started reading the application. Not much different than others he had filled out for previous jobs. Standard boilerplate in most areas. After finishing his initial review, he took a pen from his briefcase and started filling in the open areas as well as he could.

He was on the last page when Maria slipped into the kitchen wearing another of his T-shirts. Kissing him on the top of the head, she opened the refrigerator, removed the orange juice, and reached for the other glass in the sink.

"Not much left," she remarked when the container dribbled forth its last drop.

"Nope," Jim said as he laid the application back on the table. "Looks like none left now."

Maria carried her glass to the chair opposite Jim and asked, "Do you ever just go grocery shopping?"

"Obviously not recently," Jim smiled at her. "Guess I need to do twice as much shopping when you're around."

"Would you rather I not be around?" Maria pouted.

"Not what I said," Jim countered. "Certainly not what I meant."

"Like I said earlier, you can say the stupidest things," she smiled.

"Tell you what," Jim said, taking his empty glass to the sink. "We'll go grocery shopping this afternoon.

Taking two of the three coffee cups from the otherwise empty shelf, he asked, "Coffee?"

"Please," Maria said as she reached over and picked up the completed application.

"Looks like you are taking my advice," she said as she tossed it back on the table.

Setting a cup in front of her, Jim replied, "I always take your advice, don't I?"

"I doubt it," she retorted. "But at least you kept your foot out of your mouth and didn't say something else stupid."

Taking his seat, Jim nodded and said, "I can learn. Slowly, maybe, but I can learn."

"When are you taking the application in?" Maria asked as she sipped her coffee.

"Still thinking about it," Jim answered. "I'll make my mind up by lunch today. I'd like to have an answer about the internship instead of just dropping off the application."

"Well, you know what I think," she said.

"Yes, and I'm starting to think that's a good idea," Jim responded.

Maria smiled knowingly and said, "It appears that you *can* learn. There may be hope for you yet."

For the next few minutes, they sat quietly, enjoying the coffee and each other's company. Finally, Jim rose and poured the remains of his cup into the sink. Rinsing it, he asked, "Done with yours?"

"Yes," Maria answered as she came up behind him.

Reaching around him to rinse her cup, she pressed her breasts against his back, putting one arm over his shoulder, and asked, "Doing anything special this morning?"

"Back to the library," Jim told her as he ducked beneath her arms. "I want to do some research on the company that's using Monogenic's patent."

"Do you need to go back to the dorm?" Jim asked as he walked into the bedroom with Maria close behind.

"That I do," Maria replied as she shoved Jim onto the bed. "But if you can't spare me 15 minutes right now, you may never get me out of the dorm again.

Jim smiled, shaking his head, and watched Maria pull the T-shirt off over her head. "The things I have to do," he complained as he lifted his hips and removed his underwear.

"Oh Lord, no," Maria laughed as she flopped onto the bed beside him. "Was that another stupid thing you just said?"

Chapter 13

Almost an hour later, Jim untangled himself from Maria's arms and legs, saying, "Now I've really got to take a shower and get to the library."

As he headed for the bathroom, Maria called out, "You can have it to yourself. This time!"

"Thanks," Jim replied as he started the water running.

"Just leave it on when you get out," Maria reminded me as she scrunched a pillow up under her head.

A few minutes later, Jim called, "I'm out!"

Maria sat up in bed, stretching, and said, "I'll be right there."

Jim returned to the kitchen after he'd gotten dressed and was reading the brochure when Maria walked in. Looking up, he asked, "Ready to go?"

"Might as well," Maria quipped. "I certainly don't want to give you any more 'things that you have to do'!"

Jim laughed as he put everything back in his briefcase and told her, "Some things that I have to do are enjoyable, some drudgery, but that last one was a pure delight. I'll do that one any time you ask."

Maria just laughed with him as she kissed him on the cheek, saying, "*Almost* a good recovery."

They were both silent during the short drive. Stopping at her dorm, Jim told her, "I'll be in the library until lunch. If you want, come join me."

"I'll be there as soon as I change clothes," she said as she took her notes from the backseat.

"Okay," he said as she got out of the car. "I'll try to save you a computer next to me."

Driving off as she waved goodbye, Jim started thinking again about the internship. He couldn't shake the feeling that he hadn't been told the entire truth about the barley strain. Something just didn't seem right.

Locating two adjacent computers, he placed his briefcase in one chair while he sat in the other. His new search would be trying to find any information on Mombasa Research. Maybe there he would find why they were using what amounted to either pirating the barley strain or some undisclosed corporate ties.

Within minutes, Jim found that Mombasa was a subsidiary of a much larger corporation headquartered in Ethiopia. Agrigenic was the name of the parent corporation for Mombasa.

Typing Agrigenic into the search bar, Jim found that they had offices spread across South Africa and were incorporated in the early '80s. Digging deeper and deeper into the computer information, Jim noticed very Western-sounding names as corporate leaders, especially when it came to the various laboratory locations.

Not surprising, he thought as he scanned the organizational charts. Obviously, the company had hired outsiders to head their labs. Maybe there weren't enough native people with the technological expertise to perform the gene splicing if that's what they were doing.

"Hey," Maria said as she walked up and took Jim's briefcase from the chair. "Any luck?"

"Some," Jim answered as he continued to make notes. "I've learned that Mombasa is part of a company called Agrigenic."

"Agrigenic?" Maria asked as she sat down. "Sounds like your Monogenic's."

"Lots of something-genic's out there," Jim explained. "A lot of companies have a 'genic' in their name to show that they are doing DNA work."

"I guess," Maria murmured as she booted up her computer and logged on.

Neither said much for the next few minutes as Maria scrolled through several screens. "Look at this!" Maria exclaimed.

"What?" Jim said as he glanced at her screen.

"This," she said, pointing to a list of numbers that meant exactly nothing to Jim.

"What does that mean?" Jim asked as he tried to see the title of the charts and graphs that preceded the numbers.

"According to the charts, Zwairiland has had a rather dramatic drop in population over the last 20 years," she explained.

"And that means?" Jim queried.

"Could mean almost anything," Maria said, trying to refine her search. "Could be normal migration. Could be the result of a prolonged drought or plague. Could be any number of things."

"What does that have to do with your DNA research?" Jim asked, returning to his screen.

"Nothing, as yet," Maria told him. "I haven't tried to cross reference Zwairiland and Ethiopia yet. I was just trying to get some information on the population over the last couple of centuries."

"What did you find out?" Jim asked, feigning interest.

"It seems that the population grew at a below-average rate since they broke away from Ethiopia shortly after the famines and the insurrections against communism," she answered. "Then, about 20 years ago, the population started really dropping."

"Strange," Jim concurred as he moved his mouse back and forth, clicking on various sites.

A few minutes later, Maria spoke again, "That's odd."

"What this time?" Jim asked.

"Every country in that region has had a rather static growth rate, except Zwairiland," she explained. "If the people were leaving at an abnormal rate, it should show in other countries increased population growth rates. It doesn't."

"What if the number of people that are leaving is so small that it wouldn't have much of a percentage change on the recipient country," Jim argued.

A few minutes later, she sat back, staring at the screen. Finally, she spoke, "It's the birth rate."

"Alright," Jim replied, still not grasping the significance. "Besides, what does that have to do with your paper on DNA That's more Sociology."

"I know," Maria said. "But civilizations don't just start declining. At least not in modern times."

"Here's another little tidbit of information," Jim said as he opened a new file.

"Apparently, there was a rather large oil reserve discovered in Zwairiland about 30 years ago," he continued. "As of yet, it hasn't been exploited."

"I'm going to dig into this a little deeper," Maria emphatically said. "Something's happening there that isn't quite normal."

"Speaking of normal," Jim announced as he finished his notes and logged off the computer, "Let's grab a bite to eat."

"Just a minute," Maria said intently, scribbling notes.

Finally sitting back in her chair, she announced, "I guess I'm ready. But I'm going to come back to this after lunch."

"Fine with me," Jim said as he stuffed his notes into his briefcase.

"What about you?" Maria asked as she slid her chair back under the desk.

"I'm going to stop by Monogenic's after I bring you back here," Jim answered as he headed for the exit.

"Are you going to accept the internship?" she asked, following him across the library.

"Yup," he said, holding the door open for her.

"What made you decide that?" Maria asked as they walked to the car.

"Pretty much what we talked about earlier," Jim answered as he held her door open. "I can't seem to get any further without their assistance. It's either that or find another project, and I've spent so much time on this one."

"Besides," he continued as he started the car, "I'm pretty sure that this one has been a success. Otherwise, why would another company be using it?"

Chapter 14

After a quick lunch at the nearby What-a-Burger, Jim drove back to the library and let Maria out. Waving goodbye as she headed up the sidewalk, he headed for Monogenic's.

Wondering how much of his research and the discovery of the patent held by Mombasa or the ties with Agrigenic he should reveal, he pulled into the lot in front of the office. Taking the completed application out of his briefcase, he headed inside.

The rather cute blond at the reception desk smiled as he walked up. "How can I help you, sir?"

"I came by to drop off an application," Jim answered.

"I can help you with that," she said, holding out her hand.

Jim handed her the application and asked, "Is either Mr. Moss or Mr. Hawk available?"

"I believe Mr. Moss is in his office," she said as she punched a couple of numbers on her desk phone. "I'll check."

Jim stood quietly while she smiled at him as she was waiting for the phone to be answered. After a few seconds, she picked up the application and said, "Mr. Moss, there's a gentleman out here who would like to see you."

"A Mr. Jim Jackson," she answered after a slight pause. "Yes, sir. I'll tell him."

"He'll be right out," she said, replacing the phone. "Would you like something to drink while you wait?"

"No thanks," Jim said, looking around the reception area.

Jerry came through the door a minute later, saying, "Hi Jim. Good to see you again."

Jim shook the outstretched hand and said, "Thanks, Mr. Moss. Good to see you, also."

"What brings you by today?" Jerry asked.

"Just dropping off the application," Jim answered. "I was also hoping you might have a few minutes."

Jerry turned to the receptionist and asked, "Could I please have the application, Barbara?"

Barbara handed it to him and smiled, "Anything else, Mr. Moss?"

"No, not that I know of," Jerry answered as he glanced at the papers.

"Why don't you follow me to my office, Jim?" Jerry asked as he turned toward the connecting door.

Jim followed Jerry down the hall and into an office just short of Mike's office, where they had met previously. Not as large as Mike's, it was still well furnished with two plush leather executive chairs arranged in front of a well-polished oak desk.

"Have a seat," Jerry said as he walked around the desk.

"Thanks," Jim said as he waited for Jerry to sit.

"What can I do for you today?" Jerry asked, taking his seat.

"Just a couple of questions," Jim said, sitting down.

"Shoot," Jerry said, leaning forward with his elbows on the desk.

"First," Jim told him, "I'd like to apologize for making an assumption the other day."

"What's that?" Jerry asked.

"I've got to admit that I thought you were a receptionist," Jim explained. "I didn't know you were the Vice President."

Jerry sat back smiling, made a small wave of his hand, and said, "No need. Sometimes, I forget that people from outside the organization don't know me."

"It's really a small office," he continued as he leaned forward again. "At times, any of us may be sitting in for Barbara if she's away from her desk. Please, think nothing of it. Hell, you may occasionally be asked to answer the phones if you decide to work with us."

Jim nodded and told him, "Thanks. I still feel bad about making that assumption."

"Speaking about working here," Jerry said as he picked up the application, "what have you decided regarding the internship?"

Jim thought for a moment and then answered, "I think it would be a good thing for me. Especially since I'm having problems getting any further information on the barley strain that we discussed the other day."

"But, there is one further question," Jim continued, trying to figure out how to ask the question about the two patents without letting Jerry know what he had learned.

"Ask away," Jerry said.

Jim paused for a moment, then asked, "Is it possible for another company to have access to one of your patents? Maybe in another country?"

Jerry sat back in his chair and frowned slightly as he asked, "What do you mean? Are you asking if another company or country can steal our patent and use it?"

"Yes, sir," Jim answered.

Jerry steepled his fingers and told him, "That's possible. Other nations have been violating our patent laws or copyright laws for ages. Is there anything specific you have in mind?"

Jim thought for a moment and then answered, "No, sir. I was just wondering how secure your patents were. It just occurred to me that if another company or country got access to your research, they could benefit from it."

"Possible, as I said," Jerry replied. "But, in the case of our genetic material, the patent doesn't specify the exact genes we use. Nor does it provide data about where in the host DNA we insert it. Does that make sense?"

"Yes, sir," Jim agreed. "I guess I thought it might be like the copyright thing. Once it's written, it can be copied exactly."

"Not that easy with our GMOs," Jerry told him. "You'd have to have the entire methodology to duplicate our product. And that isn't always included in the patent."

"That answers my question," Jim said, nodding his head.

"Good," Jerry said, smiling. "Now, what about the internship?"

"If the offer's still good, I'd like to take it," Jim answered.

"Excellent," Jerry said, standing up. "I'll have to review your application. Maybe do some background checks. But I don't foresee any problems."

Rounding the desk, he continued, "I'm sure Mike will be pleased to hear that you'll be working with us."

Jim stood and took Jerry's outstretched hand, saying, "Thanks, Mr. Moss."

"Please," Jerry said, shaking Jim's hand, "just call me Jerry."

"Yes, sir," Jim said as they headed out of the office.

When they reached the reception area, Jerry said, "I'll be getting back to you in the next day or so. We'll work out a suitable work schedule for you."

"That's great," Jim said, shaking Jerry's hand again. "I look forward to hearing from you."

"We'll definitely be in touch," Jerry said as he opened the door for Jim. "Have a good afternoon."

As soon as Jerry saw Jim drive away, he turned and headed back to his office. Picking up his phone, he called Mike's office, asking, "Got a minute?"

Nodding his head, he replaced the phone and took Jim's application as he left his office.

Knocking on Mike's door, he waited until he heard the invitation to come in. Stepping into the office, he held out the application and said, "He's agreed to work with us."

Motioning to a chair, Mike took the application and glanced through it. Setting it on his desk, he asked, "What are your thoughts now?"

Jerry leaned back and said, "I still think this is the best approach."

Pausing for a few seconds, he continued, "But he did ask one question that bothers me."

"What's that?" Mike asked.

"He asked if another company could be using our patent," Jerry answered.

"Do you think he's discovered anything?" Mike asked, afraid of the answer.

"Not sure," Jerry admitted. "The question was rather generic, but it made me wonder if he knew something."

"I don't know how he could possibly discover our other operation," Mike said, somewhat relieved. "There's no information tying us to any operation that involves 106729."

Jerry frowned and replied, "I hope you're right. I know we've never published anything that involves our South African 'partner.' It still worries me that he may have stumbled onto something."

"That's exactly why we wanted him here in the first place," Mike said. "Now it's even more important to keep an eye on him and redirect his research."

"I agree," Jerry replied.

"How's the research on an alternative project for him coming?" Mike asked.

"Not sure," Jerry admitted. "I just sent the request over to the lab yesterday."

"Maybe you better drive over there and make sure we get this done," Mike ordered as he stood. "And get someone reliable to do the background on Mr. Jackson. I want to know this man as well as I know my own brother."

"Yes, sir," Jerry said, standing. "I'll take care of it."

Chapter 15

Jim drove straight back to the library and parked. Grabbing his briefcase from the rear seat, he hurried up the walk. The whole way over, he had been thinking about Jerry's explanation regarding another company using their patent. Or another country.

Entering the computer section, he spied Maria in the back row with an empty seat beside her. When he got there, he tossed his briefcase on the desk and logged onto the computer.

"How'd it go?" she asked as she scribbled notes on her pad.

"Fine, I guess," Jim answered.

Taking her eyes from the screen, she asked, "What do you mean, fine?"

Jim typed Mombasa Research into the search bar and waited as he explained, "I accepted the position, and Jerry told me that as soon as he could run some background checks, he'd call."

"Is that it?" Maria asked as she resumed scrolling through the data on the screen.

"No," Jim admitted as the site he was looking for appeared on the screen. "I also told him that at first, I thought he was a receptionist."

"What did he say about that," Maria wanted to know.

"Some mish-mash about forgetting that everyone didn't know him and that everyone answers the phone sometimes," Jim explained.

"That sounds plausible," she told him. "Anything else?"

"I also asked about the patent thing," Jim told her.

"And?" she queried.

"He told me that even if another company or country got the data that was in the patent, they wouldn't be able to duplicate it," Jim said, scrolling down the screen.

"Do you believe him?" Maria asked, turning to look at him.

Jim paused for a moment and told her, "I'm not sure."

"Why not?" she asked, paying close attention.

Turning in his chair to face her, he said, "I'm still not convinced that Mombasa didn't get their patent from Monogenic's. But I'll admit that I can't disprove Jerry's answer. Yet."

"So, what's your plan now?" Maria asked, still looking at him.

"I think I may need to ask Dr. Lindsay for some help again," he told her. "If her friend in the patent office will talk to me, maybe I can clear up this little issue."

Jim turned back to his computer and found the patents section under Mombasa. Sitting back in his chair, looked at the list and said, "They've only got one patent registered."

Maria looked at Jim's screen and asked, "Is that the same as Monogenic's?"

"Yeah," Jim replied as he gathered his notes. "I'll be right back."

Pushing his chair back, Jim hurried toward the front, hoping that Kay would still be in her office.

Knocking on the door frame, Jim waited until Kay looked up and then asked, "Got a minute?"

Kay laid her pen on the desk and said, "Sure, Jim. Come on in and have a seat."

Jim took one of the chairs in front of her desk, asking, "Would it be possible for me to speak to your friend in the patent office?"

"I guess," she answered. "Is this about the information I gave you yesterday?"

"Yes, Ma'am," Jim said. "I just need to know if it's possible for another company or country to duplicate patented GMOs."

Reaching for her phone, Kay replied, "I think he'll be able to answer that. I'll ask him if he'll speak with you."

Jim waited while she dialed and listened for someone to answer. Then Kay said, "Good afternoon, Gary. How are you today?"

After a couple of seconds, she continued, "I'm fine, too. Thanks for asking. The reason I'm calling is to see if you'd talk to the young man I told you about yesterday."

Nodding her head, Kay said, "Thanks, Gary. I'll put him on."

Handing the phone to Jim, she whispered, "His name is Dr. Howard."

Jim took the phone and spoke, "Good afternoon, Dr. Howard. I'm Jim Jackson, a Ph.D. student here at A&M."

Jim listened for a few seconds and then asked, "Sir, I was wondering if a company's patent could possibly be duplicated. Specifically, if there is enough data contained within a GMO patent to enable another company to exactly duplicate it?"

Listening for an answer, Jim picked up his notes and then said, "Thanks. One further thing, if you don't mind."

Hearing the response, Jim continued, "Would it be possible for anyone you know who has access to the patents of another company to talk to me?"

A moment later, Jim explained, "I'd like as much detail, specifically the genes inserted and where within the DNA chain, it was inserted. That is if that information is available."

Listening, Jim then said, "No, sir. This isn't about an infringement suit. It's just research on my part for my Doctoral Thesis."

"Yes, sir," Jim said a moment later. "I do appreciate your assistance and I'll wait for your answer."

Handing the phone back to Kay, Jim said, "Thanks, Dr. Lindsay. I'll be back in the computer section for the next couple of hours if you need to find me."

Kay waited until Jim was out of her office before speaking into the phone, "What do you think, Gary?"

"No," Kay said after a second, "he's just trying to determine if the patent we discussed is an exact match for the other one you gave me. I think he's hoping that it is so that he can follow the barley strain from conception to conclusion."

"He's been working on this project for quite a long time, and he hopes it proves the value of GMOs," Kay continued. "I don't think there's anything subversive or secretive about it. Just research to validate his thesis."

"Thanks, Gary. I'll wait for his call," Kay said before replacing the phone.

When Jim got back to his seat, he put his notes on the table and resumed searching Mombasa's data.

"And?" Maria asked, glancing at him.

"Not sure," Jim said as he made more notes about the chief officers from Mombasa's organizational chart. "Dr. Lindsay will let me know if there's any further information from her friend at the patent office."

"Want to know what I've found?" Maria asked, turning in her seat.

"Sure," Jim said as he was finishing his list of names.

"Something, I'm not sure what has reduced the birth rate in Zwairiland from a historical average of over 25% to less than one percent," she explained.

Surprised, Jim asked, "That's a rather dramatic decrease, isn't it?"

"I'll say," Maria continued. "What's even more interesting is that it's only during the last 20 years or so."

"Any ideas?" Jim asked as he returned to Monogenic's site.

"Not yet," Maria told him. "But, the initial data points to an entire generation not being born."

Just as Jim started to ask her another question, Kay walked up and said, "Jim, there's a gentleman on the phone for you. If you'd follow me, please."

Jim rose to follow Kay and told Maria, "I'll be right back."

Chapter 16

Jim followed Kay back to her office and waited for her to check that the caller was still on the line. "He's right here," she then said before handing the phone to Jim. "I don't know his name," Kay whispered with her hand over the phone. "Please don't ask either."

Jim accepted the phone and said, "Hello."

Listening for a second, he continued, "Yes, sir. My name is Jim Jackson, and I'm a Ph.D. student at Texas A&M."

Again, he waited while the caller talked. "No, sir," Jim said. "This is just to verify some data on my thesis. As far as I know, it'll never leave the campus."

Jim smiled at Kay and waited again before saying, "The only purpose of making sure these two patents are identical is to give me the data on crop production, thus showing that a specific GMO will succeed in an environment that otherwise couldn't sustain agriculture at the required production rate for the population."

"Yes, sir," Jim finally said. "Thank you for your time."

Jim hung up the phone and stared at it for a moment before looking up. "Thanks, Dr. Lindsay," he finally said.

"Did you get what you needed?" she asked.

"Yes and no," Jim answered. "He said that since there could possibly be some minor differences in the two patents or changes since the patents were issued, he can't guarantee that they're identical. However, everything within them is a perfect match."

"What do you plan to do now," Kay asked, concerned that Jim was running out of options and time.

Jim smiled at her and answered, "Keep plugging, I guess. I've accepted an internship at Monogenic's, and maybe that's where I'll find the answer."

"Well, good luck," Kay consoled him. "I do hope you can find the answer there. I'd hate for you to have to change this late in the game."

"Me too," Jim replied as he turned to leave. "But, either way. Thanks for your help."

"Anytime," Kay said, returning to her work.

Jim returned to his computer and stared at the screen as Maria sat looking at him. She finally said, "From the look on your face, I'd guess that you didn't get any good news."

"Kind of," Jim said as he thought about what he could do next. "I didn't get an entirely positive answer, at least not one that I could defend with certainty."

"But," he continued as he resumed his search on Monogenic's site, "I have enough confidence in them being the same that I'll keep on it."

"Maybe if they, Monogenic's, give you the internship, they'll be more open about it," Maria suggested. "At least they should know you're not trying to steal their material or something."

"I guess," Jim said as he started searching previous years' Monogenic's organizational charts. "We'll just have to wait to see if they accept me and then if they'll let me have access to the data I need."

For the next couple of hours, they both concentrated on their separate issues. Jim copied the names of all of the officers for each previous year until he reached the company's original incorporation.

Logging off, he asked, "Much longer?"

"About done," Maria answered. "I've just about got all the information I need. Then, hours and hours of looking at it to see if there's something I've been missing."

When she finally logged off, Jim asked, "Want to come over after we go to dinner?"

"I don't think so," Maria answered as she collected her notes. "I think I need to spend the night at the dorm. That way, I won't be distracted as I try to make sense of this crap."

"I understand," Jim said disappointedly. "What would you like for dinner?"

"I don't care," Maria told him. "You pick."

"How about Mexican?" Jim asked as he finished putting his notes in his briefcase.

"Sounds fine," Maria said, pushing her chair in.

When they got to the restaurant, neither was very talkative as they ate their meals. Other than an occasional smile and a little small talk, both of their minds were on the specifics of their discoveries. Or lack thereof.

As Jim pulled up in front of the dorm, Maria turned to look at him. Shutting off the motor, Jim asked, "Anything wrong?"

"No," she said, shaking her head. "I just can't shake the feeling that the problem with that birth rate indicates something very abnormal. I've never heard of that unless there's been some cataclysmic environmental event."

"Maybe they just quit having sex," Jim joked. "Maybe they wanted a night in the dorm."

Maria gave him her best 'go to hell' look and asked, "Just what do you mean by that?"

Realizing that he had once again made a stupid remark, Jim tried to recover by saying, "Just joking! I don't know. Maybe there's something that's reduced the testosterone level. Maybe all the women are ugly. I don't know!"

"And just what has that got to do with the dorm?" Maria demanded, crossing her arms.

"Nothing," Jim answered contritely. "It was just a stupid remark because I'm disappointed that you're not coming over."

"Yes, very stupid," Maria scolded him. "Believe it or not, I do have other things to do besides spending all of my time with you."

"I know," Jim sheepishly answered. "Again, it was just a stupid remark."

Maria waited silently for a couple of minutes and then finally said, "Alright, let's just drop that. I do have a lot of work to do on this paper. Plus, there's studying for my classes. I certainly don't need any additional worries about your stupid remarks."

Jim smiled slightly and agreed, "I understand. We both need to spend a little more time on why we're here. We'll have plenty of time together later."

Jim watched her shuffling her papers and finally asked, "Still pissed?"

Maria sighed and finally said, "No. I guess I've just got too much on my mind right now."

Jim smiled and said, "I know. Like I said, there's always later. But, if you need a break later this evening, maybe a quick beer, give me a call. I'm sure after a couple of hours of looking at all this organizational crap, I'll need one."

Maria leaned over and kissed him, saying, "Me too, probably. We'll see."

As she opened her door to get out, she asked, "What's your schedule tomorrow?"

"I've got two classes in the morning," Jim answered. "Then, unless I hear from Monogenic's, I guess I'll go back to the library."

"I've got three," Maria told him. "But, if you'd like, I'll meet you at the library around noon. We can have lunch."

"Sounds good," Jim said, relieved that things were heading back toward normal in their relationship. "I'll be there."

Maria gave him a quick kiss and got out. Jim watched her all the way to the entrance to her dorm before starting the car. Driving away, his thoughts turned to the dilemma he was facing in proving the Zwairiland program was the same as Monogenic's abandoned program.

Chapter 17

Jim had been home for a couple of hours when the phone rang. Hoping it was Maria calling to get together for a beer, Jim answered hopefully, "Hello."

The look of disappointment was plain on his face when he heard the male voice ask, "Is this Jim Jackson?"

"Yes," Jim replied. "Who is this?"

"This is Jerry Moss. How are you doing?"

"Good, Mr. Moss," Jim said. "What can I do for you this evening?"

"Well, Mr. Hawk, ask me this afternoon if you'd come to a decision," Jerry answered. "I told him that you'd agreed to come to work with us."

"Then, I told him that we were just waiting for the background checks," he continued.

"Yes, sir," Jim said. "I understood that."

"Well, anyway, Mr. Hawk said that he didn't think we needed to wait for the checks to be completed," Jerry explained. "He'd like for you to come in tomorrow if that's convenient."

Jim thought for a moment and said, "Yes, sir. I can come in around two o'clock if that's alright."

"Two would be fine," Jerry told him.

"Is tomorrow going to be my first day as an intern?" Jim asked.

"I suppose you could call it that," Jerry answered. "Mainly, it's to see if we can develop a schedule around your classes and any other time constraints."

"Also," he continued, "we'd like to show you our lab facilities, let you meet some of the people you will be dealing with, you know, sort of a guided tour."

"That sounds fine," Jim replied.

"Great," Jerry said. "I'll see you tomorrow."

"Yes, sir. And thanks for the call," Jim told him.

"You bet. Good evening!" Jerry said before hanging up.

Jim replaced the receiver and stared at it for a moment, not knowing whether to be suspicious or glad that he might get to find the answers to his questions sooner than expected.

Sitting at the kitchen table, Jim pulled his notes from his briefcase and spread them out. Lining up the Mombasa charts in chronological order, he studied the names. Nothing jumped out at him other than the obvious Western-sounding names he had noticed before.

Next, he arranged the charts of Monogenic's in the same way. Starting at the first list of names, he traced some of them across the time span until they disappeared.

Most of them appeared to remain within the organization and be promoted to areas of greater responsibility. A few disappeared after a co-worker was promoted, then another, and sometimes a third. These, he guessed, left because they weren't getting promoted. Or were fired.

The one thing he wished he had listed was the names of all of the lab personnel. Also, the organizational charts of the subsidiaries are located around the world, but that would be too time-consuming.

Realizing that it was probably too late to expect Maria to call, Jim decided to head back to the library to see if he could get another hour or so on the computer.

As he was walking in, he saw Kay turning out the lights in her office. Stopping, he said, "Late evening, Dr. Lindsay?"

"A little," Kay replied as she walked toward him. "You're coming in rather late, aren't you?"

"Yes, Ma'am," Jim admitted. "I was hoping to get a little more information on the officers and lab personnel at Monogenic's."

"Any people you're especially interested in?" Kay asked.

"Not yet," Jim told her. "I'm basically trying to find anything that connects Monogenic's with Mombasa."

"Still hoping that the patents are the same," Kay said knowingly.

"Yes, I'm afraid that I am," Jim told her.

"Have you thought about having someone from our computer sciences section do a search for you?" Kay asked.

"What do you mean?" Jim asked, unsure of what she was getting at.

"They have programs that can search multiple documents looking for matches," Kay explained.

"They may be searching for a certain word, maybe a phrase, just about anything," she continued.

"What would be the point of that?" Jim asked.

"It's pretty common for language people to find if certain phrases are common within different cultures," she explained. "Of course, you have to translate the phrase into each of the languages you're looking at."

"Do you think they could do that with names," Jim asked hopefully.

"Certainly," Kay said, turning back to her office. "Come with me for a second, and I'll see if we can save you some time."

Flipping on the light switch as she walked to her desk, she told him, "The right computer guy can do in minutes what would take you days."

Waiting for her to dial the number she obviously knew by heart, Jim asked, "Do they charge much for this service?"

Smiling, Kay said, "Not me. We'll just call this 'library business' this time. Okay?"

Speaking into the phone, she asked if anyone was available to run the word match program. Hearing there was, she turned to Jim and asked, "Do you have the lists with you?"

"Most of it," Jim answered. "I was going to get the rest of it this evening and work on it tomorrow."

Speaking into the phone, she asked, "If I give you the name of two companies, can you do name searches to see if any people are, or have been, in both?"

Hearing that they could do it, she thanked them and said she would be by in a few minutes.

"Let me have what you've got," Kay said, hanging up the phone. "And they'll need the names of the companies as well."

Jim sat his briefcase on the chair beside him and dug around for his notes on Mombasa and Monogenic's. Handing them to Kay, he asked, "Would it also be possible to add another company to their search?"

"I suppose," Kay said, accepting the loose papers. "Why? I thought you were just interested in these two."

"It just occurred to me that the tie, if there is one, maybe with Mombasa's parent company," Jim explained as he searched for the sheet where he had noted Agrigenic.

"Here it is," he said as he handed Kay the sheet. "I'd like to see if there are any ties between Agrigenic and Monogenic's."

"What about ties with Agrigenic and Mombasa?" Kay said, looking at Jim's scribbled notes.

"That would probably be more likely since they're both part of the same organization," Jim told her. "But, if it isn't too much trouble, sure. I just don't want to make this too difficult."

"There's nothing a computer nerd likes better than a programming challenge," Kay laughed. "I'd be willing to bet that if you added three airline companies, two hotel chains, and a dog grooming business in Arkansas to the mix, it would make their day."

Glad to know that numerous hours of tedious cross-checking names was going to be done for him, Jim smiled and said, "Thank you. Again! You've saved me a lot of time."

"Not a problem," Kay said, ushering Jim out of her office.

As she was turning off the lights, Jim asked, "When do you think they will have their results?"

"Knowing them, I'll probably swing by and get it in the morning," Kay answered. "Are you still going to use the computers tonight?"

Following her toward the exit, Jim said, "No. That was the only reason I was here tonight."

"Any plans now that you've got a few spare hours?" Kay asked, walking out the door that Jim was holding open.

"I may swing by and see if a friend of mine would like to celebrate my good fortune. Maybe a beer or two," Jim answered, following Kay down the sidewalk.

"Wouldn't be a certain Maria that I met the other day, would it?" Kay asked as she searched for her keys.

"Just might be," Jim said as Kay unlocked her car door.

"Well, she certainly is cute," Kay said, placing Jim's notes on her dash. "You guys go have some fun tonight, and I'll have these tomorrow morning when you stop by."

"Thanks again, Dr. Lindsay," Jim said as she started the car. "I'll be by as early as I can."

As soon as Kay pulled away, Jim hurried to his car and headed for Maria's dorm.

Chapter 18

When Jim arrived at Maria's dorm, he parked and walked into the lobby, knowing that there would be someone there that would either lead him to her room or go get her.

As if good luck had decided to follow him, he spotted Maria sitting on one of the many couches. She had her legs curled beneath her as she intently read one of the pages of notes he had watched her make earlier this afternoon.

Noting that she had put on fresh clothes, he had walked almost to her before she noticed him. "Hey," he said, continuing the last few steps to the couch. "Mind if I sit down?"

Maria picked up the few pages that were on the cushion beside her and said, "Sure. What brings you here this late?"

Jim sat beside her and answered, "I just came from the library. I was intending to spend the next couple of hours researching organizational charts, personnel listings, you know, boring stuff."

"And why aren't you still there?" Maria asked, sitting all of her notes on the table beside her.

"I got some unexpected help," Jim told her. "Dr. Lindsay is asking someone in the computer science department to run the lists using some magic program they have that will do it overnight."

"That's great," Maria said, smiling. "I guess that means you'll have what you're looking for tomorrow."

"I believe so," Jim replied. "And one other thing."

"What," she asked.

"I got a call from Jerry Moss, you know, the Vice President of Monogenic's," Jim said. "He said that I should come in tomorrow for my orientation."

"What about the background stuff?" she asked.

"Apparently, the president, Mr. Hawk, said there was no need to wait for it to be completed," he explained.

"I guess that means they must trust you," Maria said, nodding her head.

"I suppose so," Jim said. "Anyway, I was hoping that we could go grab a beer and celebrate. That is if you are through studying for the evening."

"I can do that," Maria answered. "It might even be good to talk to you about what I'm looking at."

"I don't know how much help I'll be," Jim told her. "But I'll at least listen and try to help."

"Okay," Maria said, getting up. "If you'll hold my notes, I'll run up to my room and grab a couple of things."

"No problem," Jim said as she handed him several loose pages, a pen, and a yellow legal pad.

"Be right back," she called over her shoulder as she headed for the door that separated the lobby from the rooms.

Jim watched her disappear and then started looking at the top sheet of the stack she had given him. Although sociology definitely wasn't his specialty, he was very familiar with analyzing data.

One thing that was readily apparent from her notes was that there was a huge difference between the birth rates of neighboring countries. Outside of Zwairiland, the graphs she had hastily sketched showed an almost straight line across every year that had historical data available.

Zwairiland showed an almost identical lineup until 20 or so years ago. This was pretty much as she had told him earlier, but looking at the graphs, he understood why she was interested. Sometimes, a picture *is* worth a thousand words, Jim thought.

"Ready to go?" Maria asked, coming through the door.

"Sure," Jim said, rearranging her papers and handing them to her as she walked over to the couch.

Standing, Jim said, "I see what you're talking about. The population or birth rate thing."

"Odd, isn't it?" she said as she followed Jim toward the exit.

"Definitely," he told her as he held the door open.

Once in the car, they made the short drive to a small pub off campus frequented mainly by college students. Once inside, Jim led the way to a booth at the rear where they could have some privacy. As Maria was putting her notes on the table, a young lady arrived to take their orders.

"Two Buds," Jim told her. "Bottles, please."

As she walked away, Maria asked, "Are you excited about tomorrow?"

"Yup," Jim said, smiling at her. "Mainly because a lot of tedious, boring crap is going to be done for me."

"I meant the internship thing," Maria said.

"That too," Jim admitted. "I know I won't learn much tomorrow, but Jerry said we'll go to their lab. That's what I'd really like to see anyway. That's where the heart of the work is done, and that's where I hope to be when I finally finish this scholastic crap."

As soon as the beers were delivered, Jim asked, "What did you want to talk to me about?"

Maria leaned over and told him, "I've done a little research on Zwairiland and as much of their history as I could find."

"What did you learn?" Jim said, taking a sip of his beer.

Maria sat back, holding her beer, and said, "Zwairiland was once just one of several tribes that populated South Africa. Sometime centuries ago, one of the more aggressive tribes started 'acquiring' its neighboring tribes."

Taking a drink, she continued, "There had been minor skirmishes over the years, disputes over shared hunting grounds, raids on each other for food or animals, but nothing more than happened here in America between the Indian tribes. Sometimes, they even intermarried despite their disputes."

"Then," she said, "one formerly single tribe conquered most of the others and became what we now call Ethiopia. Being much larger and stronger, they 'annexed' Zwairiland as their final consolidation."

"But," she continued, "Zwairiland always tried to break away and become an autonomous country again. The biggest problem was that they lacked the strength to fight for their freedom, and their constant petitions for separation went unheeded by the government."

"I guess that's what led to their separation after the famine," Jim said, nodding his head.

"Somewhat," Maria told him. "But that was only part of it. Now, this is just my assumption, but it fits what happened. I think that with the insurrection that took place with the communists, along with the famine, the Ethiopian government was either glad to get rid of an argumentative group or didn't have the votes necessary to prevent their succession."

"What does any of this have to do with the birth rate thing?" Jim asked.

"I don't know," she admitted. "But I find it very strange that the one country that broke away from Ethiopia is the only one that seems to have the drop."

"That is strange," Jim agreed. "But I don't see any way that Ethiopia could cause it. Unless they were kidnapping all of the women of childbearing age, and that surely would have been noticed."

"I know," Maria said, finishing her beer. "But there's got to be a reason that just one country has this issue. I can't help but think it has something to do with Ethiopia."

"You could be right," Jim said, smiling at her. "Not to change the subject, but do you think we can continue this discussion at my place?"

Maria shook her head and answered, "Mr. Jackson, I think this was all a ploy to get me to come home with you all along. Wasn't it?"

"Maybe," Jim said as he rose and placed some money on the table. "I still think we could discuss this just as well at my place. And maybe I'll come up with the solution later in the evening. You wouldn't want to miss that, would you?"

Laughing, Maria stood up and told him, "I'm pretty sure I know what 'solution' you'll come up with. But I know you're trying to make up for your last stupid remark."

"It's sure a good thing I'm a forgiving girl," Maria continued as they headed for the door.

"It sure is," Jim agreed as they left the pub. "It sure is."

Chapter 19

The following morning, Jim tried to untangle himself from Maria's arms and legs without waking her. Slowly removing her arm from across his chest, he laid it on the sheet that covered most of her. Sliding out from beneath her leg that was exposed, he slipped out of the bed and tiptoed into the kitchen.

Opening the refrigerator, he saw exactly what had been there the previous morning: a couple of cans of Budweiser, a half-empty bottle of Catsup, a few slices of stale bread in the wrapper, and some unidentifiable items long overdue for the garbage. There was also that long-forgotten carton of milk hiding in the back of the top shelf. And a few slices of pizza still in the now grease soaked box.

Checking the cupboard, he spotted a small jar of instant coffee. Shaking his head, he silently vowed to do the shopping he had been putting off for way too long. Filling the Mr Coffee with tap water, he turned it on and waited for the water to pass through the empty filter.

When enough had re-entered the pot, he poured it over the spoonful of freeze-dried crystals he had placed in a cup he had lifted from the sink and rinsed. Taking it to the table, he sat down, looking at the notes he and Maria had continued to discuss for a short period when they got to the apartment.

Trying to make some sense out of the data, Jim again wondered if there might be some tie between Mombasa, Agrigenic, and Monogenic's. Even if there was, he just didn't think that would be relevant to the birth rate issue.

The creaking of the floor caused him to look up as Maria came in wearing nothing but another of his T-shirts. "Morning," she said as she took a cup from the sink.

Jim watched her as she attempted to pour coffee into the cup. Seeing nothing but clear water, she frowned at him and asked, "No coffee?"

Jim lifted his cup, pointed it at the jar of instant coffee, and answered, "Just this."

Maria took the spoon from the counter and stirred some of the brown crystals into her partially filled cup. "You've got to get to the store," she reminded him as she added more water from the pot.

"I know," Jim said, smiling as she sat across from him. "And I guess I need to buy more T-shirts as well."

"You just can't help it, can you?" she said, shaking her head.

"What, not shopping?" Jim asked.

"No," she said, sipping the foul brew that imitated coffee. "Making stupid remarks."

"What this time?" Jim asked with a quizzical look on his face.

"The T-shirt remark," Maria chastised. "I just can't believe that you'd say something about me wearing your clothes after spending the night. How stupid! You should be telling me how good I look in it instead of whining about me wearing it!"

"Maybe I meant that I should buy more so you'll stay more often?" Jim tried.

"Quit digging," Maria said. "When you find yourself in a hole, quit digging!"

Jim sat quietly for a moment and then said, "I'll never win this, will I?

"Nope," Maria said, rising from her chair. "But it's what I've come to expect from you. You're awful smart in some ways. But you're dumb as a blonde in others."

Jim sat with his head down as she passed. Kissing the back of his neck, she said, "Don't worry about it. I know you mean well and.....if I didn't like you....never mind. Let's get out of here."

As soon as Jim let her out at the dorm, he drove straight to the library. Heading for Kay's office, he silently hoped that there were no names that appeared on both, or all three, companies.

Seeing her working at her desk, Jim knocked softly and waited for her to look up. "Good morning, Dr. Lindsay," he said as she waved him in.

Taking a short stack of computer printouts from her desk, Kay said," Good morning, Jim. I suppose this is what you've come for?"

Jim took the papers from her hand and quickly flipped through them. "Yes, Ma'am," he said. "You don't know how much I appreciate this."

Waving him out, Kay merely said, "Not a problem. If you get stuck again, don't hesitate to stop by."

Jim took the papers and hurried to the computer section. Once there, he saw what he both hoped for and dreaded at the same time. Seeing several names that were at both Monogenic's and Mombasa was surprising. Not surprising was the number between Mombasa and

Agrigenic. But the biggest surprise was to see a couple that appeared in all three.

As he was starting to log onto the computer, he glanced at the clock on the wall just above the door. Seeing that he had only 10 or 15 minutes before his next class, he retrieved the papers from the desktop and headed back to his car to get his briefcase.

For the next three hours, Jim tried to pay attention to the professors as they delved into the mysteries of genes and DNA. Scribbling notes and underlining those things that he guessed would be on the exams, as well as some that he needed to research more, Jim was mildly surprised when the last class came to an end. That left barely five minutes before he had promised to meet Maria at the library.

Grabbing his briefcase from beneath his seat, he stuffed his notes inside and headed out of the classroom. Once out of the building, he walked as fast as he could down the sidewalk without appearing to be in a hurry. The two-block walk took slightly more than five minutes, but Maria wasn't in the computer room when he entered.

Taking a seat, he removed the computer printouts and sat staring at them. Finally logging on to the computer in front of him, he picked the first name from the Mombasa list that was common with Monogenic's and Agrigenic's.

Using the Mombasa site, he queried the organization chart to see if he could get any further information on the man's past. No luck. The site merely told of his position within the organization and how many other positions he had held while there.

He was just about to enter another name when Maria walked in and stood behind him. "What-cha doing?" she asked looking at the screen.

"Trying to get some background on the names that appear on both companies. Especially those that show up on all three," Jim explained.

"What if they're just common names? Like John Smith," Maria asked. "Isn't that possible?"

"Possible," Jim admitted as he logged off. "But molecular biology is still a rather small field. To have the same name appear on different companies' organizational charts would be quite a coincidence."

Gathering his material and stuffing it back in his briefcase, he continued, "Maybe between Mombasa and Agrigenic, that wouldn't really surprise me. But not Monogenic's, too."

"Anyway," he said, "I've got a little over an hour before I have to be at my orientation. Ready for lunch?"

"Yes," Maria said, following him out of the room.

As they drove toward Arby's, Maria asked, "Are you going to ask about this when you go for your orientation?"

"Nope," Jim said, pulling into the small parking lot. "There's too much that I don't understand yet. And, you know the old adage, never ask a question unless you already know the answer."

Chapter 20

After lunch, Jim dropped Maria off at her dorm and drove to Monogenic's. On the way, he tried to organize his thoughts about what he knew and what he didn't know. Not really a suspicious person by nature, all of his studies and training made him look closely at anything that might have more than one possible outcome.

Pulling up to the office building, he decided to leave his briefcase and notes in the car and just accept at face value everything they showed him or told him. There would be plenty of time to verify or disprove at a later date. Today, he was just a receptacle for information.

"Mr. Jackson," Barbara said as he walked in. "Please wait a moment while I let Mr. Hawk and Mr. Moss know you're here. I know they're expecting you."

She pressed a couple of buttons on her phone and spoke quietly. Hanging up, she told him, "Mr. Moss will be right out."

A moment later, Jerry came through the door saying, "Hello, Jim! Looks like you're right on time. Punctuality is a trait we require here at Monogenic's, and it appears to be one we don't have to stress with you."

Shaking Jerry's hand, Jim replied, "No, sir. Too many years of meeting deadlines or classes. Guess it's a habit to be on time."

"Good," Jerry said, leading Jim down the hall. "Mike's waiting for us in his office. Would you care for something to drink?"

"No, thanks," Jim answered as Jerry knocked on the door to Mike's office.

Not waiting for the response, Jerry opened the door and announced, "Jim's here, right on time."

Mike rose from behind his desk, saying, "Good to see you, Jim. Please, both of you, have a seat."

As Jim took the chair across the table from them, as he had before, Jerry asked, "Do you have anything this afternoon that would have any bearing on our tour?"

"No, sir," Jim answered. "My schedule is completely clear."

"Good," Mike said. "Jerry's got a pretty tight 'show and tell' schedule set up this afternoon. But, if at any time you need to be somewhere else, just let him know. We can always pick up where we left off either tomorrow or another day."

"Thanks," Jim told him. "Unless this is going to be more than six or seven hours, I'm all yours."

"Well, let's get started then," Mike said, nodding his head. "First, let's look at the overall organization. As you know, our main goal is to provide the finest agricultural products that science can develop."

"To this end, we spend millions on research and testing before we ever offer a new product to the market. Sometimes it takes years, especially when we're delving into an untried area," Mike continued.

"That's not to say that most of our research is that long," Mike explained. "When we're just crossing a certain plant, such as wheat, with another, such as rye, the process can be much shorter. Probably less than half the time and at only a fraction of the cost."

"But even then," Jerry added, "it may be years of testing in the field before we truly know if we've hit upon the right combination."

"True," Mike agreed. "But in the meantime, we're still producing a viable product and get some financial benefits from the crops we grow."

"What about long-term effects?" Jim asked. "I guess I'm asking if a GMO, or just cross-pollinated plant, can possibly morph into something that has adverse characteristics."

Jerry and Mike exchanged quick glances, and then Mike answered, "Possible. Especially when grown in an area where there are numerous other varieties of plants, we can't control where the wind blows the pollen, and yes, it's entirely possible for some of the pollen from our plants to affect another. Or 'rogue' pollen enters our fields."

"But," Jerry added. "That problem rarely impacts more than a small percentage of the crop. Mainly on the outskirts of the field."

"And that's true of any plant," Mike said. "It's the way a lot of the hybrids on the market came about. Unintended cross-pollination. But the odds of anything detrimental developing are astronomically against it."

"Mother nature has her own methods of ensuring the survival of each species," he continued. "Regardless of what we do, she has the final say."

"Now," Mike said, picking up a folder from the table and handing it to Jim, "this includes more in-depth data on the complete organization and information on our successes. Of course, this isn't information we give to the general public, but it's all available elsewhere. This will just save you the time of looking for it."

Jim took the folder and glanced inside quickly, saying, "Thanks. I've been doing a little research on the organization and this'll hopefully tie up any loose ends I've been looking for."

Jerry and Mike again exchanged quick glances before Jerry said, "Well if you have no further questions, I've got us scheduled at the lab in 15 minutes."

"No, sir," Jim said, rising from his chair as Mike stood. "I'm ready to go see where you make the magic happen."

Smiling, Mike extended his hand and said, "If you do have any questions later, just ask Jerry, and he'll answer them. I hope you enjoy your tour."

"I'll meet you in front," Jerry said, holding the door open for Jim.

Watching until Jim exited the hall, Jerry closed the door and asked, "What do you think he meant about adverse effects?"

"I'm not sure," Mike said with a worried look on his face. "Could be nothing. The other thing that concerns me is his in-depth interest in the organization of the company."

"I agree," Jerry told him. "By the way, our corporate security has found nothing yet that would indicate that we have a problem."

"How thoroughly are they digging?" Mike asked.

"Very," Jerry answered. "Although we can't access his activities at the school, we've searched his apartment and placed a few transmitters inside. Also, the phone."

"If he discusses anything there, we'll know," he continued.

"Anything else?" Mike asked.

Jerry looked at his watch and replied, "They placed a locator beacon on his car as soon as he left the reception area coming back here."

"They were also going to look at any material he'd left in his car," Jerry continued as he headed for the door. "We won't get anything on that until later this afternoon."

"Good," Mike said as he turned for his desk. "Stop by after you finish this afternoon."

Turning, he told Jerry, "Put a transmitter in his car as well. I want to know every time he talks to anyone. I just wish we could monitor his conversations at the school as well."

"I'll take care of it," Jerry said, heading for the door.

Chapter 21

Jerry led Jim to a new Chevrolet Suburban, sitting in a reserved slot directly in front of the office. The glare from the sun on the dark black paint made Jim squint as he waited for the passenger door to be unlocked.

Opening the door as he heard the thunk of the lock releasing, he slid into the leather seat. "Buckle up," Jerry reminded him as he started the engine. "Can't have you getting hurt on your first day on the job."

Jim pulled the strap from over his right shoulder and snapped it into place. Glancing around the car, he couldn't help but notice that all of the windows were very darkly tinted. Probably more than the law allowed.

Jerry flipped on the air conditioner and glanced at Jim, saying, "The tint keeps it lots cooler especially when it's sitting in the sun out at the lab. Or in some dusty corn field in the middle of BFE."

Jim smiled at the colloquialism and asked, "You take this out on field visits?"

"Occasionally," Jerry answered as he backed out of the parking spot. "Mostly the lab, though."

Heading west through town, Jim couldn't remember seeing any information about where Monogenic's labs were located. Several minutes later, they arrived at a series of white buildings that appeared to be warehouses of some sort.

Pulling into a reserved slot in the large parking lot, Jerry said, "Here we are. Doesn't look like much from the outside, but we have one of the most advanced labs in the world here. And, we have others located around the world almost as good."

Jim unbuckled his seatbelt and climbed out, looking at the huge buildings. Nowhere was there any sign denoting what was happening inside, nor who owned the property.

Jerry locked the car with the remote and headed up the sidewalk to the single door into the first building. Stopping beside the keypad, he punched in a series of numbers and waited for the click as the door unlocked.

As the door automatically shut and locked behind them, Jerry led Jim to a single desk in a small room where a uniformed security guard was rising from his seat. "Afternoon, Harold," Jerry said. "I need a pass for our newest member."

"Yes, sir," Harold said, reaching for a sign-in log. "Is this the same person whose info you sent over yesterday?"

"Yup," Jerry said as he signed in. "Mr. Jim Jackson."

Harold sat down and opened the top drawer of the metal desk. Pulling out a laminated card with Jim's name printed above the Monogenic's logo, he said, "Right here, Mr. Moss."

Jerry took the pass and handed it to Jim, saying, "Keep this clipped to your shirt while you're in any of these buildings. We'll have a new one made as soon as we get your picture taken. In the meantime, this one will suffice as long as you're escorted by company personnel."

Jim clipped the pass to his shirt pocket and accepted the pen from Jerry. As he was signing his name below Jerry's, he noted that each entry and exit had a time written beside it.

"Thanks, Harold," Jerry said as he headed to the single door several feet behind the desk. Waiting for the guard to buzz them in, Jerry said, "We can only go to the non-sterile areas today. But we'll be able to see into some of the labs from the hallway."

Stepping through the door was like entering another world, Jim thought as he followed Jerry down an extremely wide hall. Everything was a brilliant white, an almost glaringly lit, and not a smudge or dust particle to be seen.

"This is our infirmary," Jerry said as they approached a window that looked into a large room with row upon row of green growing things. "In here, we can simulate almost any region in the world to see if our babies are viable."

Waving through the window at a man in a white smock, Jerry then pointed to the door and headed toward it.

"That's Dr. Fields," he said, waiting for the door to open. "He's the head of both this area and product testing."

Jim almost broke out laughing as he said, "Dr. Fields, head of field testing. How coincidental is that?"

Jerry merely smiled and said, "You're not the first one to find that amusing, but Dr. Fields doesn't."

"Sorry," Jim said contritely as the door opened.

"Mr. Moss," Dr. Fields said, greeting him. "What brings you to our little neck of the corn patch?"

"Dr. Fields, I'd like for you to meet Jim Jackson," Jerry said, introducing them. "Jim's finishing his doctorate in molecular biology over at A&M. He's going to be sort of an intern with us until he graduates."

"Welcome, young man," Dr. Fields said, grasping Jim's hand. "Glad to have you."

"We'd like a quick walk through some of your current tests," Jerry said as they headed toward the first row of plants.

"Surely," Dr. Fields said. "We are currently evaluating the growth rate of this particular strain of corn. Right now, we are simulating the average temperature, rainfall, sunlight, and soil conditions from mid-Iowa."

As they went from row to row, he continued, "Each row has a slightly different soil composition, and we vary the amount of moisture provided by differing amounts as you go from section to section of the row."

Jim had noticed letters every 20 feet or so on each of the numbered rows. "Do you have the ability to recreate the same water composition from each area?" he asked as they walked along.

"Good question," Dr. Fields said, nodding his head. "You've found a smart one, Mr. Moss. Most people wouldn't know the difference between Texas well water or Missouri rainfall."

"We can, to a certain extent," he continued. "But the real tests will be in the exact location. We can simulate here all we want, but until it's actually grown in the target environment, we don't really know for sure."

After several minutes of information about how the facility modified the climate in the room to simulate the test area, Dr. Fields led them back toward the door and asked, "Are there any more questions, young man?"

"No, sir," Jim said, taking the outstretched hand. "I appreciate your time."

"My pleasure," he replied. "Stop by any time. Good to see you again, Mr. Moss."

Jerry smiled and nodded, saying, "Thanks, Dr. Fields."

As he followed Jerry down the hall, Jim asked, "How many fields do you have around the world?"

"Several that we own," Jerry said. "But mostly, we lease the land or pay farmers to grow our crops."

"That way," he continued as he stopped beside another door, "we can test our products in numerous locations at the same time in a multitude of locations."

Pressing a buzzer on the door frame, Jerry finished by saying, "Most of the time, we just offer the farmer an amount that he would have gotten if you averaged his last ten years of produce. If there are additional expenses, such as specific fertilizers, herbicides, or insecticides, we reimburse him.

After touring the next massive room, Jerry led him through most of the rest of the building. Now, almost five in the afternoon, Jerry said, "That's about all of the areas we can let you in for now. Ready to head back?"

"Sure," Jim said as they returned to the security desk to sign out. "How much more is there to see?"

"Oh, not a lot," Jerry said as they headed for the exit door. "At least not in this area, but the rest of it is where we actually develop the seeds that travel through the rest of the facility and, hopefully, into actual field tests."

Unlocking the car, he told Jim, "With some luck, we'll have your background check done in another day or two. When that clears, we can grant you access to the more restricted areas."

"I'm looking forward to it," Jim said as he buckled his seatbelt.

Chapter 22

As soon as they arrived back at the office, Jerry asked, "What's your schedule look like for tomorrow? Maybe we can get you into the restricted areas if enough of the background checks have been completed."

"I've got one class at two in the afternoon," Jim answered. "I plan on spending the morning in the library studying or researching a few things from today's classes."

Closing his door after getting out, Jerry said, "Okay, why don't you give us a call around noon tomorrow, and we'll see where we stand with your clearance."

Jim shut his door, walked around the front of the car, and shook Jerry's hand, saying, "Yes, sir. I'll do that. And thanks for the tour today. Very impressive."

"Think nothing of it," Jerry said, laughing. "If you think today was impressive, wait until you see the labs. Some truly amazing things are taking place there."

"I look forward to it," Jim said as he headed for his car.

Jerry watched as Jim got in his car and started the engine. With a wave, he walked the short distance to the entrance and went in. Checking once more to ensure Jim had left, he headed straight to Mike's office.

Knocking on the door frame, he saw Mike talking to their Chief Security Officer, Rocky Ford. Mike motioned for him to come in as he was telling Rocky, "Thanks for the report. Keep on it. We may have a bigger problem than I originally thought."

"Yes, sir," Rocky said. "I'll be sure to let you know if we find anything else."

"Good," Mike said, standing from behind his desk.

Mike waited until the officer had left the office and said, "Please shut the door, Jerry."

Jerry closed the door and then took a seat in front of Mike's desk. As soon as he was seated, Mike handed him a file saying, "Here's the preliminary report."

Jerry skimmed each page and handed it back, saying, "Nothing much in here."

"No, this is just to keep in our files to fulfill the background check," Mike said as he took the file back and sat it on the desk.

"The real information is in this one on our Mr. Jackson," he continued, handing another file to Jerry. "This one will be destroyed as soon as we resolve the issue."

Jerry sat back, reading each page, occasionally glancing up at Mike. Finally, he said, "Looks like we've got a bigger problem than we initially suspected."

Taking the file back, Mike said, "Looks that way."

Mike put the file in a drawer, locked it, and went around the desk. "At least we know that he has no verifiable information. For now, all he has are suspicions and data that can't be connected with us."

"How much does he know about the project in Africa?" Jerry asked.

"Not much," Mike replied. "He's learned the name of the company, but I don't see how he can tie them to us."

"How did he learn their name?" Jerry asked incredulously.

"Not sure," Mike admitted. "We just know he's visited their site several times over the last couple of days."

"And he's been on Agrigenic's site as well," he added.

"What's he been looking at?" Jerry asked.

"Mainly organizational charts," Mike told him. "I think he's looking for a connection, but there isn't anything on record. Even the board of directors and stockholders have no common links, except between Mombasa and Agrigenic."

"That'd be normal," Jerry said. "I don't see how he can make any inference tying them to us based on their corporate structure."

"I don't either," Mike agreed. "But he must suspect something, or he wouldn't be spending this much time on it. How'd the tour go?"

"Fine," Jerry answered. "Of course, we didn't get into the more sensitive areas. I told him we had to wait for his background check."

"Have you gotten anything done on an alternate research project for him?" Mike asked.

"Yes, I've assigned Larry Mallory to do a complete history and have it in the files," Jerry answered.

"Who's Larry Mallory?" Mike asked.

"He's been with us for about five years," Jerry said. "He came to us with a master's degree and the intention of returning for his Ph.D."

"Where's he been working?" Mike asked.

"He's one of the lab assistants in the genetic section," Jerry answered. "He basically records data, takes care of the odds and ends that take too much time for our bio-engineers, and consolidates follow-up reports on field testing."

"What program is he compiling the data on?" Mike asked.

"He picked 'Corn RVM 4335624', Jerry told him. "And I agreed."

"What's the reason for this one?" Mike asked.

"Well, it's a very complex GMO," Jerry explained. "It uses genetic material from bacteria, rodents, and soybeans. Not to mention, it's been in the field for over seven years without a single complaint."

"What was the purpose of the original concept?" Mike asked.

"We were looking for a fungi-resistant strain that had an increased protein ratio and rapid maturity," Jerry explained. "This particular strain did more than meet our expectations, and it also demonstrated a remarkable tolerance to mild drought."

"What about production rates?" Mike asked, nodding his head.

"We can provide data that supports at least a seven percent increase in corn production," Jerry told him. "In years with above average rainfall, it goes up to over 10%."

"Sounds good," Mike agreed. "Make sure that Mr. Mallory doesn't push this too hard. We don't want Jim to think we're forcing something on him."

"No, sir," Jerry explained. "Larry will have several programs to show him. Most of them are mildly successful. Some have been terminated due to enhanced follow-on strains. But this one will stand out since it fits what Jim seems to be looking for."

"When do you expect him to be back?" Mike asked, walking back around the desk and taking his seat.

"He's supposed to call around noon tomorrow," Jerry replied. "What do you want to tell him about the background checks?"

"Tell him that they're complete and that we'll grant him full access to our facilities," Mike answered. "Then we'll assign him to Mr. Mallory. Speaking of Mallory, are you 100% sure we can trust him?"

"Yes, sir," Jerry told him, nodding his head. "Larry knows that any problems will be laid squarely at his feet. And his future with Monogenic's hangs in the balance."

"Fine," Mike replied. "I want someone else over there keeping an eye on both of them anyway. Nothing too obvious. Just sort of watching where they go and what files they use. You know. I just want a heads up before anything gets out of hand."

"Understood," Jerry told him. "I've already mentioned to Dr. Thompson, the lab chief, that I was assigning a special project to Larry and asked him to keep an eye out."

"By the way," Jerry said, turning for the door. "Anything of interest from Jim's car?"

"Not yet," Mike said, picking up the phone. "Security found a lot of notes and things in his briefcase. They took photos of every page and are getting them developed. I expect a report from them later this afternoon."

"I'll let you know what we find when I see the results," Mike concluded as he started dialing the phone.

Chapter 23

Jim glanced over at his briefcase as he headed back toward the campus. Frowning, he didn't think he'd left it lying just as it now lay. He never locked his car; he never thought he had anything inside worth stealing.

When he pulled into the library parking lot and killed the engine, he reached over and pulled the briefcase toward him. It was still latched, but it was never locked, either.

Opening it, he just saw loose sheets, the brochures, a yellow legal notepad, a couple of pens, pretty much what he'd placed in it. Pulling out the computer sheets that had run the personnel from all three companies, he shook his head at his stupidity for leaving his briefcase in the car. Especially these sheets that would show how far he'd been digging.

Then there were the notes on the patents, both Monogenic's and Mombasa's. Another stupid thing to leave where someone could find it. "Maybe Maria's right," Jim said aloud to no one but himself. "Maybe I do some pretty stupid things!"

Heading straight for the computer section, he hoped he'd find Maria there. They hadn't made any definite plans for this evening. Not even tentative plans. He just hoped she'd be there. After all, it was past most class times, maybe, except for a few labs.

Not seeing her, he decided to continue his search on a couple of key personnel from Mombasa and Agrigenic. Maybe some of the names were common, but he'd bet that at least one of them would match.

Almost an hour later, he found three names that belonged to the same people at Mombasa and Agrigenic. He'd pulled up everything he could find on them, and it was certain--they were indeed the same people.

Now, looking at the names that were on Monogenic's and Agrigenic's, he eliminated both rather quickly. Since these were the same names he'd seen on all three, he verified that the name associated with Mombasa was the same person from Agrigenic. But it definitely wasn't the same person from Monogenics.

Out of ideas, Jim logged off and replaced everything in his briefcase. Now faced with a complete strikeout on the personnel angle, the only thing left that appeared to be a tie was the patent. And he didn't know how he could go any further in that direction.

Walking out of the library, Jim wondered if he wasn't seeing things that weren't there. No personnel connections with South Africa. Mike and Jerry had told him that there were no connections between the companies. And the patent thing could be just a coincidence or a typo.

As he approached his car, he heard a shout. Turning his head, he saw Maria coming up the sidewalk, waving her arm. Waving back, he waited until she was close and then asked, "Late classes?"

"Sort of," she said, leaning over to kiss him on the cheek.

"Care for some pizza and a beer?" Jim asked as he walked to the passenger side of the car.

"Sure," Maria said as she got in. "I've got some important information to talk about anyway."

"Probably go better over beer and pizza anyway," Jim said as he slid into his seat and started the car.

Heading toward Pizza Hut, Maria asked, "How'd it go with Mono-whatever?"

Smiling at her obvious attempt to get him to correct her, he answered, "Not bad. They've got a massive complex just outside of town. You'd never suspect that it contains one of the most advanced molecular biology facilities in the country."

"From the outside, it looks like several warehouses," he continued as they parked at the Pizza Hut.

"Want to come in while I wait?" Jim said, opening his door.

"Sure," Maria answered, climbing out of the car.

Once they'd placed their to-go order, they took an empty booth to wait. "One odd thing," Jim said right after they sat down.

"What's that?" Maria asked as she took one of Jim's hands.

"I can't be sure, but I think somebody looked in my briefcase," Jim told her.

"What makes you think that?" she asked.

"Just little things," he admitted. "It wasn't quite where I left it in the seat, nothing specific. Mainly just a feeling."

"You're seeing too much. Maybe it slid around on the drive over there. Maybe you hit a pothole. Maybe you stopped too quickly," Maria countered. "You've just had a suspicious nature about this company ever since you found that another company, half a world away, has a similar patent."

"Maybe so," Jim admitted. "Maybe I'm so frustrated at being this close and not finding out what happened to that barley strain. Not to mention all the time I've wasted if I can't prove its value."

"Well, that's the reason you decided to work with Mono-something, isn't it?" Maria asked, smiling. "Maybe they'll give you the answer."

"Maybe," Jim sighed. "But they haven't given me any hope so far."

"When are you going back?" Maria asked as they heard their names being called to pick up the order.

"I'll call them tomorrow," Jim said as he paid for the pizza.

"Oh, do we need to stop for beer?" Maria asked as she got in the car, and Jim handed her the box.

"Yup," Jim answered as he climbed in. "And groceries, but not today."

"Why not?" Maria asked as he backed out of the parking slot.

"I'd rather relax with a pretty lady," Jim said as he headed for the closest grocery store that sold beer.

"Still trying to make up for stupid remarks," Maria joked. "But it's working. How can I hold a grudge when you feed me hot pizza and cold beer? You sure know the way to a woman's heart, Mr. Jackson."

Jim laughed and reminded her, "And you have a forgiving heart, Ms. Pompillio."

"That I do," she agreed. "That I do."

"I'll be right out," Jim said, stopping in front of the sliding glass doors. "Anything else while I'm in there?"

"Well, if you mean to keep me hostage overnight, you better get some orange juice and some coffee," she told him.

"And I thought I just told you that I didn't want to do grocery shopping this afternoon," Jim said as he slammed his door.

"And I thought you wanted me to spend the night!" she yelled as he walked away.

A few minutes later, Jim returned with a sack and slid them into the backseat. "I've got everything you asked for," he said as he started the car.

"You don't know what I'm going to ask for later," she joked.

"Ice cream," Jim said. "Pistachio almond."

"Probably," she answered, nodding her head. "Maybe a good dessert after that."

"If I'm not too full," Jim joked as he pulled into the lot beside his apartment.

"You better not be," Maria laughed as she carried the pizza and followed Jim up the walk.

Chapter 24

Mike was in his office doing routine paperwork when Rocky tapped on the door. Looking up, Mike motioned him in while he finished signing the last few orders for supplies.

"Anything interesting?" Mike asked, sitting back in his chair.

Rocky handed a thick envelope over and answered, "A few things. I'll wait until you've had a chance to look the photos over."

Mike opened the envelope and let the stack of pictures slide onto his desk. Looking at each one, he saw nothing that he didn't already know or suspect until he picked up the last two.

Holding them up, he asked, "This was in his brief-case?"

"Yes, sir," Rocky answered. "I put them on the bottom so you'd see them last. I was pretty sure they'd be the ones you'd want to talk about."

Mike set the pictures down and frowned. "So, somehow, he's learned that there's a similar patent being used in Zwairiland. That's probably why he asked that question about another company using our patents."

Picking up the phone, he dialed Jerry's office and waited. "You better come in here," Mike said before hanging up.

Two minutes later Jerry walked into the office asking, "Find something?"

Mike handed the photos to him and waited. When Jerry looked up, Mike asked, "What do you think?"

"I think he knows too much," Jerry answered.

"I agree, somewhat," Mike replied.

"What do you mean, somewhat?" Jerry asked incredulously. "He knows about the patent!"

"Maybe," Mike said, getting out of his chair. "So he knows there's a 'similar' patent being used in Africa. He knows that Mombasa's using it. He knows that Agrigenic is the parent company of Mombasa."

Motioning for Rocky and Jerry to take a seat, Mike sat across from the indicated seats and continued, "He still can't tie Monogenic's to either company. He can't prove their patent is a duplicate of ours. Bottom line, nothing has changed."

"How'd he find out about the Mombasa patent to start with?" Jerry asked. "I just don't think that was random luck."

"Doesn't matter," Mike said, shaking his head. "Where he got his information is irrelevant as long as it didn't come from us."

"I just wish we could tap into the school's computers," Jerry remarked. "At least then we'd know where he's searching."

"Can't be done," Rocky interjected. "If he had a computer at home, we could do it. There's absolutely no way to hack into their system without getting caught."

"Doesn't matter," Mike said. "As long as we can monitor what he does at home or in his car, we'll find out soon enough what he's been doing."

"Speaking of his home and car," Rocky interjected, "he has a girlfriend named Maria Pompillio. Apparently quite close. As a matter of fact, she's over there right now."

"Has he said anything to her?" Jerry asked.

"Not as far as we know. At least not since we bugged his car," Rocky answered. "Just normal hormonal college kid stuff."

"What do we know about her?" Mike asked.

"Nothing. Yet," Rocky answered. "I started a background check on her when we learned they were seeing each other."

"When do you expect to find out if she's involved with Jim's project?" Jerry asked.

"Day or two," Rocky answered. "For now, we know she's a student working on her Master's Degree in Archaeogenetics and lives in the dorm when she isn't spending the night at Jim's."

"If they're colluding on this, we'll hear about it through the bugs we put in his apartment," Rocky explained. "We may even get that tonight or tomorrow."

"What should we do about the Mombasa patent thing?" Jerry asked. "Should we devise some story about sharing it or that they're doing our field research or something?"

"Absolutely not," Mike told him. "We set the stage when he first asked about it, and we didn't give him any information. If we admitted to something else now, it would make him even more suspicious."

Mike rose from his chair and concluded, "All we can do now is react. We've taken every precaution we can. We have to stick to the original plan unless we get any information that dictates a change. Rocky will continue to monitor his car and house. He'll also get some information about this Maria girl. Mallory will try to steer him away from the barley program. Until something changes, we stick to the plan."

As Jerry and Rocky rose, Mike said, "Thanks for the good work, Rocky. Call me if you get anything else. If you think it's important, call me at home. Thanks for coming in."

Nodding, Rocky headed for the door as Mike said, "I want to make sure we get Jim over to the labs tomorrow. I want to keep him as close as possible to keep an eye on him."

"I'll do what I can," Jerry said. "I think getting a chance to look at the actual GMO process will encourage him to spend as much time as he can in the lab."

"Just don't forget that he's no dummy," Mike reminded him. "I can deal with his suspicions about the patents. Not a real problem. Even if he were to learn they're identical, no biggie. As long as he doesn't find out the results of our initial lab testing, I'm not terribly concerned."

Heading for the door, he continued, "I want you to double check that all of the lab reports on that are destroyed and any information available is as benign as possible. As long as it appears to be normal protocol, and there's nothing anywhere that can show we knew about the adverse side effects, we can deny anything even if it were ever discovered."

"I'll head over there tomorrow morning," Jerry said as he followed Mike down the hall. "I'll personally check all of the paper files and computer data to show that it was dropped shortly after it was developed."

"Stay on top of this, Jerry," Mike warned as they approached the exit. "This could mean not only our jobs but some serious criminal charges from either country. It would probably be an international charge as well."

"Understood," Jerry solemnly said. "For the next few weeks, or until Mr. Jackson drops this, I'll be in his hip pocket."

Chapter 25

Jim and Maria spent the evening just sitting around, eating pizza, drinking beer, and relaxing. After going to bed early, Jim was awake well before the sun came up. Sneaking out of the bed, he padded into the kitchen and started a pot of coffee while he waited for Maria to wake up.

Opening his briefcase, he still had the feeling that something was amiss. Maybe Maria was right. Either way, it didn't matter right now.

For the next hour, he re-read his notes, occasionally making additional notes on different pages, trying to find any connections. Nothing, absolutely nothing that could be verified. Finally, in desperation, he shoved everything back into the briefcase and decided that the important thing was to see if he would learn anything at Monogenic's.

After filling his cup and another for Maria, he walked quietly into the bedroom. "Maria?" he whispered, only slightly loud. "Are you awake?"

"Mmmm," was all he heard as she rolled toward where he had slept.

Sitting the cups on the nightstand, Jim slowly started pulling the single sheet down from her back. Still mostly asleep, she tried to pull it back up. Again, Jim started pulling it down. It was almost uncovering her butt when she lifted her head and looked over her shoulder at Jim's grinning face.

"I hope you have a good reason for waking me up so early," she mumbled as she pulled the sheet back up over her shoulders.

"Hot coffee?" Jim offered.

"Nope," she said as she buried her head in the pillow.

"Pistachio almond?" he joked.

"Not in the mood for dessert right now," she told him.

"What are you in the mood for," Jim asked hopefully.

"More sleep," she told him. "Now go away and leave me alone."

"Okay," Jim said as he picked up the two cups. "If you change your mind, I'm sulking in the living room."

Jim walked into the small living room and sat the coffee cups on the table in front of the couch. Sitting down, he switched on the TV and made sure the volume was as low as possible yet still where he could hear it.

The early news programs offered nothing that interested him, so he started surfing the channels. Filled with numerous marketing channels, he finally returned to the news and watched it as he sipped his coffee.

Just a few minutes later, Maria came out wearing a T-shirt and sat down beside him. "I guess I'm awake," she said as she laid her head on his shoulder.

"Good," Jim said as he kissed the top of her head. "Would you like some coffee now?"

"Please," she answered as she snuggled against him.

"Then you've got to let me get up," Jim told her.

"Then no, no coffee. More snuggle," Maria said, sliding her arm across his stomach.

"We could have done this better in bed," Jim said. "Much better."

"No, then you'd have wanted something else. I just want to snuggle," she told him.

"Probably," he admitted. "But that's your fault." "My fault?" Maria asked, raising her head to look at him.

"Yup," Jim said, grinning.

"How do you figure that?" Maria asked.

"You're too cute to resist," Jim answered. "A mere mortal man like me can't be held responsible. Since I'm not responsible, it must be you."

"Am I supposed to take that as a compliment?" she asked.

"Of course," Jim said as he smiled at her. "It's either a compliment or another of my stupid remarks. Your choice."

Maria laughed and told him, "I better take it as a compliment. You make way too many really stupid remarks, and this one's close, but I'll give it to you. Now, where's my coffee."

Jim got up as she sat up and reached for the now cold cup on the table. "Be right back."

As he poured the cold coffee down the drain, he noticed some white, chalky dust on the countertop. Wiping it with his hand, he wondered where it came from. It looked sort of like that fake cream that comes in packets.

Shaking his head, he refilled the cup and headed back to Maria. "What's on your agenda today?" he asked, handing her the cup.

"Not much," she said, taking a sip. "What about you?"

"One class at two, then maybe some time at Monogenic's," Jim answered. "That's if my background checks are done."

"I don't have to be in class until 11," Maria told him. "How about breakfast at IHOP?"

"Sounds good to me," Jim answered. "But, I need to get a couple of hours in at the library. And I need to call Monogenic's around noon."

"Why don't you call them now while I get dressed?" Maria asked, setting her cup on the table.

"I think they wanted me to call later so they would have more time for the checks to be done," Jim guessed.

"Maybe they'll know now," she insisted. "Can't hurt. You can always call again later."

"Sure," Jim agreed. "Can't hurt."

"Nope," Maria said as she got up. "You just listen to me, and you'll probably do alright."

"Always," Jim said, picking up the phone. "I always listen to you."

"You just don't sometimes hear me," she said, heading for the bedroom. "Or you just hear what you want to hear."

"What did you say?" Jim teased as he waited for the phone to be answered. "I didn't quite hear you."

Maria turned half around and flipped him the finger saying, "Listen to this, asshole!"

As Maria came back into the room, Jim was just hanging up the phone. "What'd they say?" she asked.

"Everything's done," Jim answered. "They said that I can have access to the labs this afternoon. If I have time after class."

"Great," Maria said. "Maybe they'll have some more information on your rodent rice."

"Barley, but that'd be nice," Jim told her as he got up. Taking the two empty cups into the kitchen, he continued, "And maybe Santa Claus will come early this year. Maybe the Easter Bunny and the Tooth Fairy will be there, too."

"Don't give up hope," she said, following him. "Maybe they have some files somewhere that weren't on the computer. Maybe they looked up the wrong thing the other day."

Grabbing his briefcase, Jim replied, "I don't think a company with as much attention to detail as a GMO requires would lose data like that."

"You never know," Maria said as they headed for the door. "Look at all those Presidential tapes or memos that seem to get lost. Or miss filed."

"Or lied about," Jim replied as he opened the door.

Chapter 26

"What're you going to do about your research?" Jim asked as they pulled up to IHOP?"

"Not sure," Maria answered as Jim killed the engine. "I still need to do some comparisons. What I'd like to find are DNA similarities in the region. Then I can make a better analysis of the differences based on more than just the area."

"Plus, it's more in line with your major instead of your minor," Jim said as he opened his door. "I'd guess that whoever approves your thesis wants it somewhat on subject."

"True," Maria agreed. "I'll dig around a little more at the library. If I can't find some link to abnormal DNA or another reason for the decline, I may switch topics."

They'd just finished eating and were heading back to the campus as Rocky was knocking on Mike's door, asking, "Got a minute?"

"Come in, Rocky," Mike answered. "Got anything new?"

"Nothing concrete," Rocky said, shaking his head. "Just that Ms. Pompillio is looking at something to do with DNA."

"What's her degree in?" Mike asked.

"Archaeogenetics," Rocky answered after checking his notes.

"That's not surprising, then," Mike told him. "She's studying human DNA. It has nothing to do with GMOs."

"Okay," Rocky said, nodding his head. "It just caught my attention."

"What have you learned from your bugs?" Mike asked.

"Not much," Rocky admitted. "The only thing we've heard that has any bearing on the subject was a casual mention of missing data."

"What was said?" Mike asked.

"Ms. Pompillio just made some remark about the possibility of misplaced files," Rocky explained. "It was in reference to what she called 'Rodent Rice,' which I took to mean our barley patent."

"Probably," Mike agreed. "What were they talking about when she made that reference?"

"Just that Mr. Jackson was granted access to the labs," Rocky explained. "And that he might be able to get some information here."

"What does that have to do with misplaced files?" Mike asked.

"Maybe nothing," Rocky admitted. "But you wanted me to report any references to the patent, and this seemed to be along those lines."

"What was Mr. Jackson's response?" Mike asked.

"Something about losing data on GMOs would be about as likely as Santa Claus, the Easter Bunny, and others," Rocky told him. "The last thing he said about it was that there was a greater possibility of being lied to than having missing files."

"Okay," Mike said. "Anything else?"

"No, sir," Rocky said. "Do you mind if I ask what his interest is in a product that we aren't actively using?"

"We're just concerned that he may be trying to pirate our research for some other purpose," Mike lied. "Nobody has shown interest in that patent for years, and all of a sudden, here comes a Ph.D. student digging into it. That's all."

"Okay," Rocky said, preparing to leave. "It's just that we've never dug this deep to check out anyone else. Anyway, I'll get back to you if I hear anything else."

"Thanks," Mike said, picking up a sheet of paper. "I talk to you later."

As soon as Rocky was seen leaving the hall, Mike called Jerry into the office. "Yes?" Jerry said, coming through the door.

"Have you heard if Jim's coming in today?" Mike asked.

"Not for certain," Jerry answered. "He has an afternoon class, and he said he'd try to come over after that."

Mike rose from his desk and motioned for Jerry to have a seat by the table. Sitting down, he continued, "Jim made some remark this morning about being lied to. It's more important than ever that no information other than what we've told him is ever discovered."

"I understand," Jerry said, nodding his head. "I had Dr. Thompson direct another audit of the data we collected and forward it to me today. If he can't find anything other than what we've left in the system, then I don't see how anybody could find it."

"Good," Mike said, nodding his head. "Now, all we need to do is get Jim over to the lab, give him a quick tour, introduce him to Larry, and see what develops."

"I'm hoping that Jim calls back as soon as he's out of class this afternoon," Jerry told him. "I've made sure that both Larry and Dr. Thompson will be available late this afternoon in case it's late when Jim calls."

"By the way," Mike said. "Rocky asked why we're digging this deep on Jim."

Surprised, Jerry asked, "Why's he interested?"

"He just thought that it was unusual to go to this much trouble for a routine background check," Mike answered. "I told him we had some suspicions about corporate espionage. And, if anyone else asks, that's the story."

"Sure," Jerry agreed. "As far as the lab people are concerned, they're under the impression that Jim's nothing more than a student researching GMOs, and we're just trying to help him."

"Excuse me a second," Mike said as the phone on his desk rang.

"Yes?" he said into the phone.

"Put him on," he told Barbara. Putting his hand over the mouthpiece, he said, "It's Jim."

"Hello, Jim," Mike said when the call was transferred. "How are you today?"

Listening for a moment, he said, "That's great. When can we expect you?"

"Fine," Mike said, "I'll tell Jerry to set the tour up for this afternoon. How about one o'clock?"

"Great, see you then," Mike said before hanging up.

Walking back to his seat at the table, Mike said, "His afternoon class was canceled. Will Mallory and Thompson be available that early?"

"I'll make sure," Jerry said, nodding his head. "There shouldn't be any problem since they know the tour was scheduled for this afternoon anyway."

"By the way," Jerry asked, "anything on Jim's lady friend?"

"Not so far," Mike answered. "She's aware of Jim's research, even jokes about it, calling it 'Rodent Rice,' but I don't think she's very interested other than in passing."

"Are we still checking her out?" Jerry asked.

"Other than the standard checks, no," Mike said as he rose. "Unless she shows more than minor curiosity about what her boyfriend's doing, I don't see the need."

"Have you thought about having Mallory pursue a 'friendly' relationship with Jim?" Jerry asked as he stood up.

"Not really," Mike told him. "If it develops, that's a plus for us. But other than making sure he assists Jim as much as possible, it might seem suspicious to push it in that direction. We want Mallory to think this is just routine assistance to students from A&M."

"Of course," Jerry said as Mike sat down at his desk. "I'll call the lab and give them a heads-up for an earlier-than-planned tour."

Chapter 27

Jim dropped Maria off at the dorm and drove to the library. Knowing that she would be in class until he had to attend his own, there would be little chance of seeing her again this afternoon since he didn't know how long he'd be at Monogenic's.

As he was heading to the computer section, Dr. Lindsay came out and called, "Hey, Jim. Gotta minute?"

"Sure, Dr. Lindsay. Whatcha need?" Jim asked as he walked toward her.

"I just got a phone call from Dr. Marshall that your two o'clock class has been canceled," she told him. "If you see any of the other students around, pass the word."

"Sure," Jim told her. "Say, do you mind if I use your phone right quick?"

"Not a problem," Kay said. "You can use the one at my secretary's desk. I've got a few calls to make right now, but I'll tell her that it's okay."

"Thanks," Jim said as he followed her toward her office.

When the secretary nodded and handed Jim the phone, Kay waved goodbye and entered her office, shutting the door behind her.

As soon as the receptionist at Monogenic's came on the line, Jim asked for Mr. Moss. A few seconds later, he heard Mr. Hawk answer. Once they had set the time for him to arrive and start the tour, Jim hung up and carried his briefcase into the computer section.

After he logged on, he tried to think of anything he hadn't already tried to get more information on Monogenic's patent. If it was the same as the Mombasa patent, then it must have been developed for arid climates.

Even if it might never be useful, he typed Zwairiland into the search bar and quickly navigated to the climatology section. Making notes of annual rainfall, average temperatures, and any other relevant data that might reveal a reason for a GMO in that area, he tried to come up with a theory.

If, and that was a very big if, he could find out the specifics of why MBM 106729 had been developed, and if, just as big an if, it matched what he knew was the environment of Zwairiland, then he had a baby step toward proving to himself that there had to be some tie.

Checking the clock on the wall, he quickly logged off and shoved his notes into the rapidly filling briefcase. Thirty minutes was plenty of time to drive through What-a-Burger and grab a quick burger before he needed to meet Jerry at the office.

Tossing his briefcase onto the passenger seat, he headed off campus and got his usual cheeseburger with everything on it, including jalapenos, fries, and a Dr Pepper. Holding the drink between his legs, he put the torn sack on his briefcase and opened the wrapper on the burger. Pouring the fries onto the makeshift plate, he headed toward Monogenic's.

When he pulled up and parked, the burger was gone in huge bites, and most of the fries had disappeared as well. Leaving the mess to clean up later, he took his drink and headed for the door.

As he entered, Barbara said, "Good afternoon, Mr. Jackson. Mr. Moss said for you to go back as soon as you get here."

"Thanks," Jim said before he took a final sip of his drink. "Is there somewhere to put this?"

"I'll take care of it," Barbara answered as she rose from behind her desk.

Handing her the almost empty container, Jim said, "Thanks again."

As Jim walked down the hall toward Jerry's office, he wondered why he had never seen any of the other offices open or seen anyone else around. Upon reaching Jerry's open door, he knocked and waited for Jerry to replace the phone.

"Come on in," Jerry said as he hung up. "Have a seat. I was just on the phone with our lab chief and told him we'd be coming over."

"Thanks," Jim said as he took one of the chairs arranged in front of Jerry's desk. "I wasn't sure if things would be ready since I'm about four hours early."

"Not a problem," Jerry told him. "Is there anything you'd like to know before we head over there?"

"No, sir," Jim answered. "I can't think of anything."

"Good," Jerry said as he stood up. "We might as well get going. I think you're going to enjoy today's little tour."

"I've assigned one of our lab assistants, a fellow by the name of Larry Mallory, to take care of you when you get a chance to spend some time in the lab," Jerry told him as they headed up the hall.

"Is that where I'll be working?" Jim asked as they entered the reception area.

"Certainly," Jerry said, holding the door open. "Isn't that what you wanted? Get a chance to see how all your education is applied in real life?"

"Yes, sir," Jim said as he waited for the passenger door on the Suburban to unlock. "I just never expected to be there."

"Where did you expect to be?" Jerry asked as soon as they were in their seats.

"I don't know," Jim admitted. "Maybe with Dr. Fields. Maybe in the office with you and Mr. Hawk."

"Waste of your talents," Jerry said as he backed out of the reserved space. "Besides, I think you'd find our office boring. And watching plants grow would be even more so."

Pulling into his parking slot when they got to the laboratory complex, Jerry said, "We'll be taking your picture today for your ID. Then we'll have to wear what we call a sterile suit when we enter the genetics section."

"Yes, sir," Jim said as they entered one of the buildings that they hadn't been in yesterday. "We have to wear them in some of our lab classes."

As Jerry was signing in, he told the security guard to get a temporary pass for Jim and to notify Personnel to send someone over with a camera for the permanent ID.

Jim took the pen from Jerry and signed the next line on the page. He was surprised to see that there were at least 50 names above his on the page that had signed in, and only one had signed out.

"Lots of people," Jim remarked as he accepted the temporary pass and clipped it to his pocket.

"Takes lots with all the projects we're working on," Jerry said as they were buzzed into the main facility.

Opening the first door on their right, Jerry said, "We'll get into our suits here. These are all a micro-fiber material that won't shed nor produce any static electricity, as are the booties and the skull cap."

When they stepped into the small room, Jim saw stacks of overalls, booties, and caps on three tables along one wall. Following Jerry to the overalls, he selected the next one down in the stack and stepped through the legs before zipping it up. After slipping the paper booties over his boots and putting what looked like a shower cap on, Jim followed Jerry back into the hall that led to the labs.

"You'll be leaving your suit in the room across from where we dressed when you leave this afternoon," Jerry said, walking down the hall. "Larry will make sure you're taken care of and start teaching you the protocol for working in this facility."

Again, as with the other buildings he had previously seen, this one was immaculate. Even though the floor appeared slick and shiny, the soles of the booties didn't slip or slide as they moved almost soundlessly to the door where Jerry stopped.

Entering a code, the door buzzed, and Jerry swung it open into a small glass enclosure. Jim could tell from the breeze coming from overhead that another effort at sterility was being used. A few seconds later, the door into the actual lab buzzed, and Jerry pushed it in.

"In addition to everything else, this room has positive pressure to make sure no outside contaminates can enter," Jerry told him as Jim looked around the room.

"Here comes Larry now," Jerry said as a white-suited man approached.

"Mr. Moss," Larry said as he extended his hand. "Good to see you, sir. And I guess this is the new intern, Mr. Jackson."

"Yes, it is," Jerry replied. "Jim, this is Larry Mallory. He'll be your guide, mentor, and almost boss for the next week or so until we get you checked out on our procedures."

"Nice to meet you, Mr. Jackson," Larry said, extending his hand.

"You too, sir," Jim replied, shaking Larry's hand. "And it's just Jim, please."

Laughing, Larry said, "Fine, Jim. And please, just call me Larry as well."

Chapter 28

The rest of the afternoon passed quickly as Larry showed Jim where each of the various labs was performing gene extraction or insertion. Jerry followed them around most of the time but was missing more and more often as the day progressed.

"How do you determine which specific gene to extract?" Jim asked as they watched through a window as several white-garbed people worked with electronic microscopes and robotic equipment.

"They've got maps of the DNA of just about everything they work with," Larry explained. "They can identify a specific gene of, say, a strand of corn DNA. Then, depending on what they're trying to do, they may pull out the gene that gave the corn some resistance to fungi and insert it into another strain of corn that wasn't resistant."

"What's the success rate?" Jim asked as the people behind the glass went from station to station.

"Pretty high," Larry answered. "I've been here over five years, and I'd say that over that period, it's been close to 90%."

"Amazing," Jim said. "I'm surprised that it's that high."

"Well, success can be measured in several ways," Larry explained. "Just because they had success in inserting the gene doesn't necessarily mean that the final product will prove successful."

"If they were trying to improve protein levels, that may be successful," he continued. "But it may also transfer some undesirable trait, such as stunted growth."

"I guess that would mean a smaller plant with higher protein," Jim theorized.

"Exactly," Larry said, nodding his head. "Then, you've got a smaller grain with a higher protein, but pound for pound, you may even lose when it comes to food value."

"Do they take the higher protein strain and try to splice a 'growth' gene back into it?" Jim asked.

"Sometimes," Larry said. "But, most of the time, it's several months or years until they determine that the program didn't produce the desired result."

"Are there any problems with harmful effects on either animals or humans?" Jim asked.

"Not really," Larry told him. "We do extensive testing on lab animals before we introduce it for production."

"So, the chance that a specific strain of, say, rice could ever enter the food chain if it adversely affected either man or cattle would be nil?" Jim asked.

"Exactly," Larry said, nodding his head.

"What happens to the animals if they've been fed a strain of corn or barley that caused some problems?" Jim asked.

"Usually, the problems correct themselves after they're taken off of the engineered grain," Larry answered. "Very seldom does a GMO have lasting effects if it's removed from the test animal's diet."

"What happens to the GMO that caused problems?" Jim asked.

"Basically, it's abandoned as a product, and the specific techniques and genetic makeup are filed for future reference," Larry explained. "That way, if some genetic engineer tries that combination again, the computer will automatically cross-reference to the master files and let him know it was a failure."

"Can they still use it by changing some other set of genes?" Jim asked as they moved to watch another set of people working in a different lab.

"I suppose," Larry admitted. "But each program must be approved by our chief, Dr. Thompson, and then the protocol is sent to Mr. Hawk for approval."

"I didn't know Mr. Hawk knew much about the science of GMOs," Jim said.

"Oh, he's not a molecular biologist," Larry said. "But he has to look at the funding, chance of success estimates, time to production estimates, and a lot of other factors."

"Then, if he approves it, it's forwarded to the big scientist in the sky," Larry continued.

"Who's the 'big scientist in the sky'?" Jim asked.

"The head dog of science at Monogenic's," Larry answered. "The guy up at corporate headquarters in Austin."

"So, he gets to approve any new project?" Jim asked.

"No, he only gets to reject or recommend a new program," Larry said. "He forwards his approval up to the people, like Mr. Hawk, that look at funding and so forth."

"Each branch, like us, has the authority to perform research within certain constraints," Larry said. "The scientists here may do initial testing, just to see if they can splice a gene into the DNA, but further experimentation takes approval from higher up."

"Getting back to rejected programs," Jim asked, "is there any chance that one might slip through the cracks?"

"What do you mean by that?" Larry asked.

"I mean, what if a program was rejected because of some minor adverse side effect, like stunted growth," Jim continued. "Is it possible that another biologist with the company could develop it anyway?"

"Not possible," Larry said. "As I told you earlier, the results of the original program are filed and will automatically be attached to any new program that's entered for consideration."

"What if they wanted to produce it anyway?" Jim asked.

"They'd never get approval," Larry said emphatically. "Dr. Thompson would never let it go upstream. And, even if it slipped by him, there's Mr. Hawk and the others at corporate that would get the same 'failed program' notice. Can't happen."

"Sounds like it takes several layers of approval for a new strain to ever get into production," Jim said just as Jerry rejoined them.

"What layers of approval are you talking about?" Jerry asked.

"Jim was just asking about what happens to any project that failed after initial testing," Larry answered. "I was telling him about how Dr. Thompson, Mr. Hawk, and the guys in Austin have to approve any new program."

"Anything specific you'd like to ask about?" Jerry asked, looking at Jim.

"Not really," Jim answered. "I was just wondering how you kept from duplicating a program that had already been attempted and failed."

"I'm sure Larry explained how our computer system cross-references any new procedure that's under consideration," Jerry said. "There's absolutely no way we would ever go to the expense or waste any effort on a project that has already failed. Too many levels of scrutiny."

Jim nodded his head and said, "I understand. It must take a team of computer specialists to develop programs that can match so many variables in genes, DNA of so many plants, or animals, and not miss something."

"That it does," Jerry said. "The main computer is in Austin, and I think the staff that keeps it running has more people than we have in research."

"That must be expensive," Jim commented.

"Very," Jerry said. "But, when compared to the expense of duplicating failed programs, it's minor. If you'd like a tour there someday, we can certainly arrange that. Or, you can see a minor part of it back at our office."

"You have the same computers here?" Jim asked.

"Yes, but only to a small degree," Jerry answered. "We only need the capacity to look at our programs. If it passes us, then we send it to corporate. They have the data from every branch around the world."

"That's why they get the final approval," Jim said, nodding his head. "They have all the information from other branches that may have tried what you're attempting."
"Exactly," Jerry said, checking his watch. "But I'm afraid we need to be getting back. The photographer from the ID section is supposed to be waiting with the security guard by now. Then, you and Larry can coordinate your schedules for further visits."

Jim turned to Larry and said, "Thanks for your help, Larry. How do I let you know what my schedule is for when I'm available to come back?"

Larry shook Jim's hand and answered, "Just let Mr. Moss or his secretary know. They can notify me, and I'll be available."

Jerry shook Larry's hand and said, "Thanks, Larry. I'll let you know when Jim wants to come back."

Once they had returned to the front of the building, they removed their overalls, booties, and caps. After placing them in the marked containers for later cleaning or disposal, they returned to the security desk.

Once Jim's picture was taken, Jerry thanked the photographer and signed out. "Your ID will be at my office tomorrow morning," he said as Jim signed out. "Just stop by or call when you know when you'd like to come back out here."

"Yes, sir," Jim said as he followed Jerry to the exit. "I'd really like to get involved with the actual splicing process, if possible."

"No problem," Jerry said as he walked to the Suburban. "I'll talk to Dr. Thompson, and we'll find a new program and see if you can assist in its development."

"What about seeing our computer section?" Jerry asked as they headed back to the office.

Jim smiled and answered, "Not really. I'm interested in making things, not so much in the minutia of recording it."

Jerry laughed and said, "You gotta be a computer nerd to enjoy that, I guess. Well, to each his own, I suppose."

Chapter 29

When Jim got in his car and left, Jerry headed for Mike's office. Knocking on the door frame, he waited until Mike waved him in. Mike finished his phone call and asked, "How'd it go?"

"Fine," Jerry answered. "Only one thing that I overheard would be of interest."

"What's that?" Mike asked, rising from his chair.

"It concerned Jim asking about computer systems for tracking programs," Jerry answered as he followed Mike to the chairs around the short conference table.

"Go ahead," Mike said as he sat down in the leather chair.

"He just questioned how we kept failed projects from being attempted again," Jerry said as he took a chair across the table. "It was sort of strange, considering he has absolutely no interest in data systems or any computer work that isn't directly related to the research."

"What'd you tell him?" Mike asked.

"Larry had already explained the overall system, how each new proposal's run through the system to see if it's been tried before," Jerry explained. "I just told him that each branch has its own program, and if it passes scrutiny there, it's sent to Austin."

"Doesn't sound too threatening," Mike said. "Maybe he's just interested in knowing how we keep from duplicating another lab's work."

"Could be," Jerry said, nodding his head.

"Rocky had his car searched again after you left," Mike announced, changing the subject.

"Find anything?" Jerry asked.

"No, really," Mike answered. "There was a new set of notes about Zwairiland. Mainly about climatology."

"I still don't like him looking for anything having to do with MBM 106729 or Zwairiland," Jerry replied. "If he finds a single tie, we could be in for major problems."

"I know," Mike told him. "But we can't do any more than we've already done. Anything other than trying to shift his interest when he keeps running into a brick wall about our   patent."
"That's what concerned me when he asked about abandoned or failed projects," Jerry admitted. "I was just worried that he might want to use the computers to find out what happened to it after it was dropped here."

"I don't think that's a concern," Mike said. "If, as you've said, the computers and other files have been sanitized, there's nothing that can be found. He still hits the brick wall."

"Dr. Thompson assured me that there was nothing in the files past what we've let remain," Jerry said. "However, he did wonder what had happened to the patent since it was never put into production."

"Logical question," Mike replied. "But I'm sure he's seen several promising projects killed by either me or Austin. If he asks again, just tell him it was a corporate decision."

"Well, at least that's true, as far as any available data would show," Jerry agreed. "I also took a look at the corn strain that Larry's been preparing. Looks good, as far as meeting Jim's objectives are concerned."

"Just make sure it isn't too 'convenient,'" Mike said. "I sure don't want Jim to think this is an attempt to redirect his attention."

"Understood," Jerry assured. "The data's all available to anyone in the research department. It's not a 'package' deal that's been prepared. Larry just did the research according to our criteria and knows exactly where to point Jim when he decides to go in that direction."

"Good," Mike said, rising from his chair. "When's Jim going back to the labs?"

"Not sure," Jerry answered as he stood up. "I'm trying not to seem too interested in how he manages his time with us. But I think we piqued his interest enough that he'll take every advantage he has available to work over there."

"Is Dr. Thompson assigning anything to him?" Mike asked as he rounded his desk and sat down.

"We discussed it somewhat, nothing too specific," Jerry answered. "I just asked him to keep an eye out for any new projects that might interest Jim."

"How does he plan to use Jim," Mike asked as he pulled a stack of papers to the center of his desk.

"He'll treat him as a new hire lab assistant," Jerry replied. "Let him watch, explain the procedures, maybe let him try some basic extraction or insertion. I just want him involved enough that he'd rather be doing hands-on work instead of going through files or asking questions."

"Good plan," Mike said as he picked up his pen and began to sign the requests in front of him. "Let me know when Jim calls back to schedule his visits."

"Yes, sir," Jerry said as he headed for the door.

Chapter 30

Heading back to the campus, Jim noticed the clock on the bank's sign showing that it was shortly after five. He remembered that Maria had said that she had an 11 o'clock class, but wasn't sure what she had after that.

His best guess for now was to try the library. If she wasn't there, he'd go to her dorm. It wasn't so much as to tell her about his time at the lab, although he wanted to. It was more that he just enjoyed being with her.

"Funny," he thought, *"I've never really enjoyed being around a girl before, except for the obvious reasons. Why's this one different?"*

More students were leaving the library at this hour than seemed to be going in. Watching them leave, Jim decided that he'd been spending too much time on the computer here. So far, it had netted him very little over the last several hours. If anything new was to be learned about Monogenic's patent, it would be at the lab.

Reaching for his briefcase, he realized that he needed to get the trash from his lunch out of the car before he went anywhere with Maria. Using the original, now torn, sack that had held his meal, he picked up every fry or crumb and wadded it up.

Carrying the trash to the first trashcan he came to, he tossed it in and brushed off his hands. Sniffing his right hand, he couldn't help but notice the smell of stale fries and mustard.

His first stop in the library was the Men's room, where he tried to wash the smell from his hands. He wondered if the odor had been there when he went to the lab. He didn't remember it, but if it was, it was never mentioned. Still, he'd make sure he washed his hands before his next visit. What-a-Burger was good, but the lingering smell on his hands needed to be avoided around the professional scientists in the lab.

Coming out of the Men's room, he headed back to the computer section. Not seeing Maria, he reversed direction and started for the exit. Once outside, he glanced again searching for Maria among the students that were in the area. No luck.

Getting back in his car, he headed for her dorm, hoping that she was there. Of course, she hadn't said anything about being available this evening, and they hadn't made any plans. But, still, he wanted to see her.

Pulling up to the dorm, he parked on the street and headed up the walk. As he approached the door, another student he recognized from one of his classes was coming out. "Hey, Julia," he said. "Any chance you can do me a favor?"

"Sure," she replied. "What do you need?"

"Can you check to see if Maria Pompillio is in her room?" he asked.

"Do you know which room she's in?" Julia asked.

"No, sorry," Jim answered.

"I'll just check the register," Julia said as she turned around. "Why don't you wait in the lobby? I won't be but a couple of minutes."

"Fine," Jim said as he followed her into the building. "Just tell her Jim's here if she can meet me."

"You got it," she said as she opened the doors leading to the rooms.

A few minutes later, Julia came down and told him, "She said she'd be right here."

"Thanks," Jim replied as Julia headed out of the door.

Several minutes later, Maria came through the doors and walked across the lobby to where Jim was sitting. "Hey," she said, "how'd the tour go?"

"Fine," Jim said, standing up. "I was just hoping that you'd be available for dinner tonight, and we could talk about it then."

"Sure," Maria said. "But I've got to come back tonight. I'm trying to finish a paper for one of my classes."

"Do you have to do it tonight?" Jim asked as he opened the door for her.

"Oh, yes," Maria answered as she headed down the sidewalk to Jim's car. "It's due tomorrow. I'd planned on doing it a couple of days ago, but I sort of got distracted."

"So, I'm a distraction," Jim joked as he opened the passenger door for her.

"Sort of," Maria said as she started to get in the car.

Staring at his briefcase, she asked, "Do you want me to sit on it or move it?"

Jim answered, "Just toss it in the backseat."

When she picked it up, she then asked, "What about these fries? Are you saving them for me?"

Jim looked over her shoulder and noticed a couple of fries on the seat that had been beneath the briefcase. "I'll get them," he said as she stepped back.

"You should be more careful with your food," Maria said as she got into the car.

Jim closed her door and walked around the car to get into the driver's seat. "I don't know how those got there," he said as he started the engine.

"Didn't you buy them today?" Maria asked.

"Yes," Jim answered as he pulled away from the curb.

"That explains the mystery," Maria said knowingly.

"Not really," Jim said as he headed off the campus.

"Why not?" Maria asked.

"Yes, I had fries," Jim explained. "I stopped at What-a-Burger and got a cheeseburger, fries, and a Dr Pepper. As usual, I tore the sack open and poured the fries onto the sack, so I wouldn't have to keep digging into that little sack they come in."

"And you dropped a couple," Maria interrupted.

"Nope," Jim said as they headed for the little Bar-B-Q restaurant they both liked. "I made sure not to spill them. Everything was on the open sack when I was driving over to Monogenic's."

"Don't tell me this is like the other day when you thought your briefcase had been moved," Maria asked.

"Sort of," Jim admitted. "I just don't see how a fry could end up under the briefcase unless it was moved."

"Maybe it slid off the sack while you were driving," Maria suggested.

"Then, it would have been on the seat beside the briefcase," Jim reasoned. "Not under it."

"Are you becoming paranoid?" Maria asked as they pulled into the almost full parking lot.

"No, of course not," Jim said, finally finding a place to park.

"What then?" she asked as he killed the engine.

"I don't know," Jim admitted, turning to look at her. "It's just that two times in a row, something seems amiss. And both times after I've been to Monogenic's."

"You want to know what I think?" Maria asked as she opened her door.

"What?" Jim asked as he climbed out of the car.

"I think you're still suspicious of that company because you can't get the information you want from them," she said, slamming her door. "I think you're just frustrated and see some, I don't know, some conspiracy!"

"I never said that," Jim replied as they headed toward the restaurant.

"No, you never said it," she told him. "But you think they're lying about their patent, and you have no real evidence. You think they're screwing with your briefcase, and you have no evidence. I think this has become an obsession with you, and you refuse to admit it."

Jim was silent as they arrived at the entrance. "You want to know what I think you need to do?" Maria said as she went through the door Jim was holding open.

"Go ahead and tell me," Jim answered as he followed her inside.

"Get another project," she told him. "Give up on this one. It's driving you crazy!"

Chapter 31

Once inside the restaurant, Jim and Maria were escorted to one of the few open tables. As the hostess started to seat them, Jim saw a fellow student sitting alone at an adjacent table. "Hey, Brett," he said. "How's it going?"

"Fine, Jim," Brett said, standing up. "What about you?"

Shaking Brett's hand, he said, "Good. Same old thing, hours of fruitless research. By the way, I'd like for you to meet Maria."

"Hi, Maria," Brett said, taking her hand. "Good to meet you. Say, why don't you guys join me? Give us a chance to catch up."

Jim turned to the hostess and asked, "Would it be all right if we sat here?"

"Sure," she said. "I'll send a waitress right over."

Jim pulled out the chair for Maria to sit on Brett's left, and he took the one across the table. "Still on track to graduate this semester?" Jim asked as he sat down."

"I sure hope so," Brett answered. "The last three classes are going well, just some lab work that's kicking my ass."

"Brett's getting a Ph.D. in Pharmaceuticals," Jim explained to Maria. "We had many of the same classes back when we were working on our Master's."

"Aren't there a lot of differences in molecular biology and being a pharmacist?" Maria asked.

"Pharmaceutical, making drugs, not the pharmacist that fills a prescription," Jim informed her.

"That's okay, I've heard it before. But, not as much difference as you'd think," Brett answered. "Especially these days. There's even a field called pharming that closely parallels Jim's molecular biology."

"Farming?" Maria asked. "Shouldn't that be more in the agriculture field?"

"Not farming," Brett corrected. "Pharming, with a 'p.' Specifically molecular pharming."

"What does that mean?" Maria asked as the waitress came to the table.

"Go ahead and order," Brett said. "We'll enlighten you while you're eating unless you're sick of hearing about molecules, genes, proteins, or whatever Jim talks about instead of normal conversation."

"He does go on about his precious genes," Maria said as she ordered ribs, beans, and a Budweiser.

Jim shook his head as he ordered brisket, fried okra, and a Budweiser. "It's just as interesting as trying to find some DNA link with some subhuman from the past," Jim said as the waitress left.

"What's your major?" Brett asked, taking a sip of his Heineken.

"Archaeogenetics," Maria answered.

"Ahh," Brett said, nodding his head. "You two are a perfect match, then."

"What does that mean?" Maria asked.

"You know, Yen and Yang, fire and water, positive and negative," Brett explained. "You're looking backward for answers, and Jim's looking forward. Both using genetics. Opposites attract sort of thing."

"Oh, we're opposite, all right," Maria laughed. "He says stupid things, and I let him know."

As the beers were delivered, Jim asked, "What's the latest in your genetics stuff?"

"Quite a bit," Brett answered. "They've been using a gene from bacteria to produce a treatment for non-Hodgkin's lymphoma. They used to use plant genes, known as Plant Derived Proteins or PDP, but that caused a lot of uproar from some far-left activist groups."

"Why would people get upset about finding a cure for any disease?" Maria asked.

"It's not the cure they're pissed about," Jim answered. "It's the same in any GMO field. They're worried that some strains of GMO will harm the consumer. Whether it's a new strain of corn or a weed that's used to produce new drugs."

"That's right," Brett agreed. "Especially if the GMO is widely used, such as thousands of acres of corn in Iowa. Their biggest complaint is that pollen from the GMO will pollute a non-GMO. Maybe spreading proteins or antibodies through unintended cross-pollination, soil pollution, or water runoff."

"How do you get around that?" Maria asked as their food arrived.

"With plants, the companies mainly use greenhouses," Brett answered. "The problem with that is the limited production due to acreage requirements."

"Is that why you're looking into bacteria?" Jim asked, picking up a piece of fried okra with his fingers and popping it into his mouth.

"Exactly," Brett said as he resumed eating his ribs. "Very little space required, and it can be done in a sealed environment."

"Why don't you guys in the rodent rice field do that?" Maria asked, looking at Jim.

"Big difference," Jim explained. "They need only small amounts of the genes while we are trying to increase production. They're trying to find cures for diseases while we're trying to solve the famine problem."

"What's 'rodent rice'? Brett asked.

"It's not rodent rice," Jim said, smiling. "Maria thinks it's funny to change the name of my thesis project. It's actually a patent that Monogenic's developed combining a specific gene from a mouse with barley DNA."

"How's that coming?" Brett asked.

"Not well," Jim admitted. "The patent was issued, but there's no information available that I've found so far that it ever went into production."

"Is that unusual?" Brett asked, sipping his beer.

"Apparently not," Jim said, taking a bite of his brisket. "The people at Monogenic's say there're lots of strains they develop that never make it into production."

"Same in Pharming," Brett agreed. "Sometimes it works in testing, but it becomes either too expensive for production or doesn't work as well with humans as it did with the test animals."

"How'd you get Monogenic's to talk to you about their patents anyway," Brett asked as he wiped some grease from his fingers.

"Oh, he's got an internship with them," Maria said. "That probably means he'll have even less time with me than he does now."

"Never," Jim said, smiling. "If this works out, I may have even more time for you to listen to my stupid remarks."

"Speaking about unused or failed patents," Brett interrupted. "There was a program a few years ago that produced a contraceptive from corn."

"Oh God," Maria exclaimed, sitting back. "First rodent rice and now contraceptive corn. What's next, make plant people?"

"What happened to that?" Jim asked, suddenly interested.

"I think it's still being studied," Brett answered. "But, like some of the other programs, it caused such an uproar that it's been relegated to greenhouses."

"Can you imagine how that could be used?" Maria asked. "Nature's way of solving an overpopulation problem."

"Or creating un-population," Jim said as the thought about Zwairiland's population decline occurred to him.

Chapter 32

As they finished dinner, Jim got Brett's phone number and promised to give him a call later in the week for a beer. After all the goodbyes were said, Jim and Maria headed to the car.

"What was that 'un-populate' comment about," she asked as they walked through the almost empty parking lot.

"Nothing," Jim answered. He didn't want to voice his suspicions yet. Not until he found the tie between Monogenic's and Mombasa, if it existed.

"I've still got to go back to the dorm," Maria said as Jim opened her car door.

"I know," Jim said, closing the door after she got in.

"Maybe tomorrow night," Maria told him as he got in. "But I've got to finish my paper tonight."

"That'd be great," Jim agreed as he started the car. "What's your schedule tomorrow?"

"Two classes," she answered. The first one's at 11 and the other one's at 2. I should be free after four o'clock."

"I've got one at nine in the morning," Jim told her as he headed out of the parking lot. "I'm going to call Jerry after that and see if I can get some time in at the lab."

"You really like that lab stuff, don't you?" Maria asked as they drove back toward the campus.

"Yup," Jim said, turning onto the street that would take them to Maria's dorm. "It's the reason I got into this field. I hate research if it doesn't lead to something productive."

"I guess that's why you're so upset about that patent thing," Maria said as he pulled to the curb.

"I'm not upset," Jim argued. "It's just that I hate wasting time on things when I've got so much to do to graduate this semester."

Jim killed the engine and sat quietly for a moment before saying, "I was going to call Brett later, but if it's all right with you, I'd like to get with him tomorrow evening."

"Oh?" Maria asked, surprised that he'd rather see Brett than her.

"I mean, I'd like for us to meet with him," Jim corrected when he saw the disappointed look on her face. "You know, just a couple of hours for beer."

"I guess that'd be all right," she said. "Why the sudden urge to meet with him? Is it something to do with that contraceptive corn thing?"

"Sort of," Jim said as he opened his door. "I'm just interested in how they do their genetic work. More to see if our procedures are similar."

"You men and your genes," Maria pouted as Jim opened her door.

"I thought you liked my jeans," Jim joked as he held her in his arms.

"I like to get you *out* of your jeans," she said as she kissed him.

"I may, just may, let you do that tomorrow," Jim smiled as she headed toward the dorm.

"Here's to your jeans, or genes, whichever way you want to take it!" she said as she flipped him the finger.

Waiting until she opened the door to the dorm, Jim got back in the car and headed for home. There was nothing more he could do tonight, but he renewed his interest in getting more information on the Monogenic's patent.

It was just too much of a coincidence that a similar patent was being used in a country that was experiencing a drop in birthrates. It obviously wasn't the strain of corn they'd been discussing.

But, if it can be done with corn, it could probably be done with barley. If he could find the tie between the companies, the next question was why. What interest would Monogenic's have with controlling birthrates in a South African country?

Early the next morning, Rocky was waiting in the reception area when Mike came in. "Good morning, Mr. Hawk," he said, rising from his chair.

"Morning, Rocky," Mike said as he headed for the door leading to the hall. "What brings you in so early this morning?"

"I've got what could be bad news," Rocky said as Mike flipped on the lights in the office.

"Have a seat," Mike said, heading for the chairs.

As soon as Rocky had sat down, Mike asked, "So, what's the bad news?"

Rocky pulled a sheet of paper from the inside pocket of his sports coat and handed it to Mike. "This is the transcript of a conversation we recorded from the transmitter in Jim's car last night."

Waiting until Mike looked up, he continued, "It's not the entire thing; there were some references to other things, mainly boy-girl things, that we didn't transcribe. But the things I thought were important are included."

"What's this about the briefcase?" Mike asked. "Do you think he knows we've searched it?"

"He doesn't know, but he's certainly suspicious about something in that area," Rocky said, shaking his head. "Especially since it's been noticed both times we looked in it."

"How could you be so careless?" Mike demanded. "I thought you guys were supposed to be professionals."

"I know," Rocky confessed. "We were careless. The guy that was assigned to photo the material in the briefcase is new and got sloppy. It won't happen again."

"It better not," Mike said, fuming at a potential discovery of their activities. "As a matter of fact, any further 'inspecting' of his car will only be done by you, personally! Understand?"

"Yes, sir," Rocky said, accepting the chastisement. "I'll let everyone in the department know that no physical inspections or intrusions will be done without me being there."

"All right," Mike said, still upset about what should have been an easy task. "Now, what's this corn comment about?"

"I don't know," Rocky admitted. "I was hoping that it might mean something to you. We only thought it a strange comment, and I wanted to make sure you saw it."

"Was anything else said about it?" Mike asked.

"No, sir," Rocky told him.

Mike got up and headed for his desk, saying, "I want to hear those tapes."

Rocky stood standing by his chair and said, "Yes, sir. I'll have them here in less than an hour."

"Do that," Mike said as he picked up the phone.

"Better get in here," Mike said into the phone as Rocky walked down the hall.

Jerry walked in, asking, "Something wrong?"

Mike remained seated and handed Jerry the transcribed conversations and waited until he had a chance to read them. "What do you think?"

"Rocky's people screwed up," Jerry answered.

"Taken care of," Mike said. "I meant about the corn comment."

"I have no idea," Jerry answered. "It could mean anything."

"Just what's that supposed to mean?" Mike said, still angry. "I want to know if you think Jim's referring to the patent. That it was patterned after the corn project?"

"I don't see how we can assume that he'd have the slightest idea about what that corn did. He's been looking at the barley version," Jerry said, shaking his head. "He'd have to know more about that project than is written anywhere. Hell, there's not even a single person left here, besides you and I, that even knows what MBM 106729 did."

"Maybe you're right," Mike said. "But, now more than ever, make sure he's under constant watch. And I don't want him to have access to any of our computers."

"Understood," Jerry said. "I'll take care of it. And, since he told Ms. Pompillio that he was planning on spending the afternoon at the labs, I'll have everything arranged when he calls after his class."

"Do you think you need to stay with him at the lab?" Mike asked.

"No," Jerry replied. "That would probably make him think he's under surveillance, as suspicious as he seems to be."

"Your decision," Mike said as he took the transcript from Jerry's hand. "But, if there's any further inference to this patent or the corn, I'll have to make a call overseas."

"I'll make sure," Jerry said as he headed back to his office.

Chapter 33

As soon as Jim finished his only class for the day, he put his briefcase in the little trunk located in the front of the car. After shutting the hood, he put a small strip of cellophane tape on the seam between the hood and body on the passenger side.

Not sure if anyone would look there, or had ever really looked at his briefcase, at least this was a change that might confirm that someone, Monogenic's was interested in what he was doing.

Instead of calling, he decided to just drive to the office and see if Jerry had anything to tell him before he went to the labs. He hated being suspicious about the company. They were what he thought he wanted. Improving people's lives through GMOs.

The Suburban was in its slot when he pulled in the parking lot. As he walked into the reception area, Barbara said, "Good morning. Here to see Mr. Moss?"

"Yes, please," Jim said, waiting for her to make the usual phone call to see if he was available.

"Go on back," Barbara said, smiling as she hung up the phone.

"Thanks," Jim said as he opened the door to the hall.

Knocking on Jerry's open door, Jim waited for him to look up before saying, "Good morning, got a minute?"

"Come on in," Jerry said, rising from his chair and rounding the desk. "Sort of surprised to see you this morning."

"I just finished class and thought I'd drop by to see if it's okay for me to go to the labs this afternoon," Jim said. "Also, you said my ID would be here this morning, and I'll probably need it."

"That you will," Jerry said, turning toward his desk and picking up the phone. "Barbara, would you please bring Mr. Jackson's ID to my office?"

Hanging up and turning back to Jim, he said, "It'll be here in a minute. Just keep it with you from now on, and you can go directly to the lab without stopping by."

"Thanks," Jim said. "Do I need to coordinate with Larry for my visits?"

"More or less," Jerry said as Barbara came to the door.

Taking the ID from her, he said, "Thanks, Barbara."

Jerry looked at the ID for a second and then handed it to Jim, saying, "Standard mug shot. It doesn't matter if it's a driver's license or anything else. They all seem to make you look like a face you'd see on a wanted poster in the post office."

"Not very flattering," Jim admitted as he put the ID in his shirt pocket.

"Back to the coordinating with Larry," Jerry said as he leaned against the front edge of his desk. "I'd like for you to pretty much stay with him for the first few days. After that, if you're working on something else, or if Dr. Thompson has anything for you to do, just let him know your schedule."

"Of course," Jim said, nodding his understanding. "Any other advice for me?"

"No," Jerry said, straightening up. "Just go over there and see what you can learn."

"Hell, you may even have some new techniques fresh out of the textbooks," Jerry joked as he ushered Jim out of the door. "Stop by occasionally and let me know how it's going."

"Yes, sir," Jim said as he turned to head up the hall.

Once back in his car, Jim knew that he needed to grab something to eat before going to the lab. Remembering that there was a Burger King on the way, he decided that it would be the quickest way to grab a bite. "And wash your hands!" he said to the empty car as he pulled out of the parking lot.

When he arrived at the lab, he parked in the first open slot he saw in the small sea of cars. 'No reserved slot for the new guy,' he thought as he killed the engine. Walking around to the passenger side, he made sure the strip of tape hadn't come loose during his drive from the campus. Still there.

Opening the door to the building, Jim saw Larry standing, talking to the security guard. "Hey, Larry," he said as he walked over to the desk, pulled his ID from his pocket, and pinned it to his shirt.

"Good afternoon," Larry said as he watched Jim sign in. "Jerry said you were coming in and asked me to meet you out here."

"Hope I didn't keep you waiting," Jim said, putting the pen down. "I stopped off for a quick lunch."

"Not at all," Larry said as he led the way to the door that led into the labs. "Where'd you eat?"

"Burger King," Jim said, following Larry into the dressing room. "Not my favorite, but it fills my stomach."

"I know what you mean," Larry said, pulling on his overalls.

Jim dressed as he had been shown and then followed Larry into the room that blew any debris from them before entering the hall that connected the various labs.

"By the way," Larry said as he entered the code into the box beside the door, "the code is 5532 for this door in case I'm not here when you come back on your own."

"I thought I'd show you the connecting tunnel for the buildings first," Larry continued as they walked.

"Tunnels?" Jim asked.

"Yup, they run from each building to the next one," Larry explained when they reached the end of the hall. "That way, they can move things from one place to another without having to go outside."

"Why not just have a connecting walkway above ground?" Jim asked as Larry punched the down button on the elevator.

"Don't know," Larry answered as the doors slid open. "This was here when I got here, and I never thought to ask why."

"Anything else down here?" Jim asked as the doors opened onto another sparkling hall.

"Somewhere down here are the heating, air conditioning, the compressors that supply the positive pressure systems, maintenance, and so forth," Larry said as they walked along the hall.

"Amazes me how clean even this floor is," Jim remarked as they arrived at another elevator.

"Probably takes an army of cleaners," Larry said, pushing the up button. "And gallons and gallons of floor cleaner and wax."

As they stepped out of the elevator, Jim realized that they were in a different building other than the two he had seen on his other visits.

"What's in this building?" Jim asked as they walked down the hall.

"More labs," Larry said as they looked through the large windows that separated the labs from the hall. "These are for small animal testing."

As they walked along looking in the windows, Jim asked, "Where do they test the large animals, like cattle?"

"I believe they have a facility up north somewhere," Larry said. "I've never been there."

As they came to the end of the hall, Larry asked, "What would you like to do now?"

"I'd like to go back where we were yesterday," Jim said. "I'm more interested in the plant section."

"No problem," Larry said, heading back toward the elevator. "That's sort of my specialty too. I finished my Master's in molecular biology a few years ago and planned on getting my Ph.D."

"What happened?" Jim asked as they rode the elevator down.

"Ran out of money," Larry admitted. "I still plan on getting the degree, but until then, this is a good place to work, and what I've learned here will probably help me with the classes."

The rest of the afternoon went quickly as Larry introduced Jim to several of the scientists, and they discussed their projects.

Just as they were getting ready to leave, Dr. Thompson came out of one of the labs saying, "Excuse me, are you, Mr. Jackson?"

"Yes sir, I am," Jim answered.

"Good, I was told you were here today, and I've got a project you may be interested in," Dr. Thompson said. "Would you like to hear about it?"

"Of course, sir," Jim answered.

"Can you be here tomorrow morning, say eight o'clock?" he asked.

"I'll be here," Jim said.

"Fine, I'll see you then," Dr. Thompson said. "Have Larry bring you to my office as soon as you get here. Okay, Larry?"

"Yes, sir," Larry said, nodding his head.

Dr. Thompson turned and walked away as Larry said, "Well, you may get involved in a project quicker than you thought."

"I'm glad," Jim said as Larry started down the hall. "Sightseeing is fine, but I'd rather be working in the lab with the genes."

"You'll like it," Larry said as they entered the room to strip off their overalls. "I'll see you tomorrow morning."

Happy that he was going to get involved so quickly, Jim almost forgot to look at the piece of tape when he got to his car. It was there, but half of it was now under the hood instead of where he had placed it.

"Son-of-a-bitch," he thought as he got in the car. "Now there's no doubt. Someone's keeping an eye on me. I just wish I knew why."

Chapter 34

Jim drove back into town and arrived at the campus just after five o'clock. He wasn't sure where Brett lived or what his schedule was. Nor was he sure where Maria might be right now. The best place to start would be the library.

Seeing Dr. Lindsay's car still there, he parked and removed his briefcase from the trunk. Before shutting it, he pulled off the tape and wadded it up. Pausing at the first trash receptacle, he tossed it in before continuing up the sidewalk.

Walking to Dr. Lindsay's office, he knocked on the open door and waited for her to notice him. "Good afternoon, Dr. Lindsay," he said when she looked up.

"Good afternoon, Jim," she said, sitting back in her chair. "What can I do for you today?"

Jim stepped in and asked, "I'd just like to use your phone again, if I may."

"Of course," Kay said. "But please use the one on my secretary's desk. And, in the future, just ask her."

"Thank you," Jim said, mildly chastised. "I didn't mean to disturb you, and there was no one at her desk. I didn't want to use the phone without permission."

"No problem," Kay said. "She knows you're allowed to use it. If she's not there, go ahead and make your call."

"Thanks again," Jim said as he turned and left the office.

Sitting his briefcase on the secretary's desk, he took the slip of paper from his billfold and dialed Brett's number. Letting it ring several times, he gave up and replaced the handset.

Walking back to the computer section, he hoped he'd find either Maria or Brett in there. As he entered, he saw both of them sitting side by side, looking at their computers. "Hey guys," Jim said as he walked up.

"Hi, Jim," Maria said, looking up at him. "How'd the visit go?"

"Fine," Jim said, sitting his briefcase on the table between their computers.

"Anything interesting?" Brett asked, still scrolling down his screen.

"Pretty much," Jim said as Maria reached over and took his hand. "What are you guys looking at?"

"I've been chasing population numbers most of the time," Maria said, smiling at him. "Brett's been looking at something he wants to show you."

Jim looked at Brett's screen and asked, "Whatcha got?"

"You remember that corn we talked about last night?" Brett said, turning to look at Jim.

"Yes," Jim answered.

"Well, I decided to do a little research on it," Brett said. "Just to see if I could find it, who developed it, what happened during testing, and what became of it after the field tests showed the adverse effects."

"Find anything?" Jim asked, looking at the screen.

"Pretty much everything that I was looking for," Brett said, picking up his notes. "Here's all of the information I've gotten so far."

Jim looked at the top page of the legal pad and scanned the scribbled notes. Just as he started to hand the pad back to Brett, he took another look and said, "I think I've seen this company's name somewhere before."

"All of your companies have similar names," Maria said as she logged off her computer and gathered her notes.

"I still think I know this company," Jim said. "How much longer do you need here, Brett?"

"I'm about done," Brett answered. "What'd you have in mind?"

"How about we head to that little pub over on University and grab a couple of beers?" Jim said. "There's a couple of things I'd like to share with you about what I've been running into on my thesis."

"Sounds good to me," Brett said as he made some final notes and logged off his computer.

"Me, too," Maria said as she got up and kissed Jim on the cheek. "Two handsome men buying me beer. What girl could refuse that?"

As they headed for the exit, Jim asked, "Mind if we use your car, Brett?"

"Sure," Brett answered as he held the door open for Maria and Jim. "I'm parked just down the street."

"So, tell me about your afternoon," Maria said as they merged with the other students going to and fro on the sidewalk.

"You remember how you accused me of being paranoid?" Jim said as they followed Brett.

"I still think you are," Maria said, taking Jim's hand.

"I now have a reason to be," Jim said, turning to look at her.

"What?" Maria asked, surprised.

"I know someone is checking my briefcase," Jim said as Brett stopped beside an open-topped Jeep.

"I'll tell you on the drive," Jim said as Maria climbed into the rear seat.

"What's this about?" Brett asked as he got into the driver's seat.

"Long story," Jim said as he handed Maria his briefcase and closed his door. "I've just noticed a couple of little things since I've been going over to Monogenic's."

"Like what?" Brett asked, starting the engine.

"He thinks someone's looking in his briefcase," Maria volunteered.

"Yes, I do think that," Jim said emphatically as they pulled away from the curb. "And today, I put it in the trunk instead of leaving it in the seat."

"What does that change?" Maria asked. "You still can't prove someone's looking in it, even if it's in the trunk."

"Not necessarily so," Jim countered, shaking his head. "This time, I placed a little strip of tape on the hood to see if anyone opened it."

"And?" Brett said as he turned onto the University.

"It was pulled loose on the bottom and beneath the hood when I came out of the lab," Jim said.

"Maybe it blew there as you drove," Brett volunteered.

"Nope," Jim said. "I checked it before I went into the lab. It was just as I put it."

"Okay," Maria said. "So someone opened your trunk. Maybe they were looking for a spare tire."

"For an old VW?" Jim asked incredulously. "I doubt that. I think they didn't see the briefcase in the car, so they checked the trunk."

"Why would someone want to look in your briefcase?" Brett asked as they pulled into the parking lot. "I can't imagine anything important in a student's notes."

"That's what concerns me," Jim said as he climbed out of the car.

"Want to leave your briefcase here?" Maria joked as she got out. "Maybe the CIA or FBI is trailing us and can't wait for you to leave so they can get all the classified stuff you have. Maybe the Russians! Oh my God! Not the Russians!"

"Wise ass," Jim said, taking the briefcase from her. "Now, who's saying stupid things?"

Chapter 35

After being seated and ordering their beers, Brett turned to Jim and said, "Why don't you start at the beginning and fill me in."

"Sure," Jim said as they waited for the waitress to return. Glancing around, he slightly lowered his voice and told Brett everything that had happened since he first called Monogenic's and was offered an internship during his initial visit.

When Jim had brought him up to date, he continued, "And, after last night, I've been thinking that there may be a connection to the strain of corn that caused sterility and the radical drop in the birthrate in Zwairiland that Maria noticed."

"How can you make that connection?" Brett asked as the beer arrived. "That seems to be trying to make random events fit a preconceived idea."

"That's what I've been trying to tell him," Maria said as she leaned forward with her elbows on the table.

"I know, I know," Jim said, sitting back in his chair. "But there are just too many coincidences."

"Maybe so," Brett said, "but you still have no connection between Monogenic's and Mombasa. Or any proof that the patent Monogenic's holds is the same as the one Mombasa has."

"Nor do you know that Mombasa is even using their patent," Maria argued as she sipped her beer.

"Damn it! I know that," Jim said, getting frustrated. "But why won't Monogenic's tell me what happened to their patent. If they have data showing that it was rejected for any reason, it should be available."

"Have you asked since they first talked to you about it?" Brett asked.

"No," Jim admitted. "I was hoping that I could learn something from the people at the lab. Plus, if I'm correct, I don't want them to know that I'm still digging around looking for it."

They sat there for a few minutes until Jim asked, "Why did you decide to look into the corn thing?"

"I just wanted to see what happened," Brett answered. "More curiosity than anything. But, it's sort of in line with a project I've been working on."

"What project?" Maria asked.

"Trying to develop a cost/benefit analysis for the industry as a whole," Brett answered. "There were a lot of companies that went bankrupt after a GMO crop of soybeans was harvested, and the seeds that didn't get picked up sprouted the following year. These GMO plants were harvested with that year's normal crop."

"When it was discovered, the company was fined hundreds of thousands of dollars and spent millions in cleanup costs," Brett continued. "That drove many companies out of business and damn near destroyed the GMO industry."

"What's different today?" Maria asked.

"First, there's a very strict protocol regarding field production, including the measures required following harvest," Brett answered. "And, as you would guess, there's much tighter control by the FDA on where tests can be conducted and what GMOs can be field tested."

"So, you don't think there's any connection between Maria's research and any GMO?" Jim asked.

"I'm not saying that," Brett answered. "But, until you can prove some connection between a GMO and the birthrate issue, I think you're wasting your time."

"I agree," Maria said, nodding her head and looking at Jim. "I think you ought to drop this patent thing, get another test that you can prove, and move on."

"Maybe you're right," Jim admitted. "True, I have no proof that a GMO caused the problem in Zwairiland. I have no proof that Monogenic's has any ties with any company in either Ethiopia or Zwairiland. I have no proof that anything unethical or unlawful was done. Bottom line, I have no proof of anything other than I'm chasing a patent that goes nowhere."

"Exactly!" Maria triumphantly exclaimed. "Now, what do you plan to do?"

"Keep looking," Jim said stubbornly. "I don't care if I don't have proof right now. I'll keep going to Monogenic's and see if anything turns up. If not, in a couple of weeks, I'll see if they can give me a program that did prove beneficial."

"Oh, I almost forgot," Brett said, taking a folded sheet from his shirt pocket. "You wanted to see this."

Jim took the sheet and again saw the company name he thought he recognized. Opening his briefcase, he pulled the list of Monogenic's offices, subsidiaries, and contracted laboratories from the loose pages. Running his finger down the names, he found what he was looking for.

"Found it," he exclaimed. "Here's a connection!"

Jim laid the two sheets side by side on the table and pointed to the identical names of them. "There," he said proudly as he sat back and held his beer bottle.

Maria looked at where Jim was pointing and agreed, "Same names. Do you think they're the same company?"

Brett pulled the sheets in front of him and said, "I think so."

"So, what do you think now?" Jim asked.

"Two things," Brett answered. "First, this company's program is a corn GMO, and you're looking at a barley GMO."

"Same procedures can be used," Jim interrupted.

"Probably," Brett said. "But the important thing here is that this company no longer exists."

"What do you mean?" Jim asked.

"Exactly what I said," Brett continued. "That company went out of business shortly after the tests on the corn showed the sterilization problem."

"Probably because they lost so much money on it," Maria volunteered.

"Could have been," Brett said, nodding his head. "That was about the same time as the soybean thing."

"But they had the tie with Monogenic's," Jim argued. "Monogenic's would have the patent."

"Not necessarily so," Brett said. "The company was under contract but may own the patent."

"But, if they were under contract with Monogenic's, Monogenic's would own the patent since they were working for them," Jim argued.

"Again, not necessarily so," Brett repeated. "If the corn project was outside of their contract, maybe an in-house program, or for another company, it wouldn't belong to Monogenic's."

Jim sat back, knowing Brett was right. "Damn, I thought I had found a connection," he finally said.

"Exactly what have you done to try to find this connection?" Brett asked.

Jim told him about the computer sciences people running the officers from the companies trying to find a match and that there wasn't one.

"Have you thought about looking deeper than the officers?" Brett asked, sitting his empty bottle on the table.

"What do you mean?" Jim asked, signaling for three more beers.

"Maybe an employee of one of the companies became an officer of another," Brett suggested.

"I don't think any of these companies are going to divulge information on their employees," Jim said. "The officers are a matter of public record. Not the employees."

"What if I know a guy that can get that information for you?" Brett asked as the waitress set the bottles on the table.

"How can he do that?" Maria asked, reaching for a bottle.

"He has his ways," Brett said, smiling as he got his beer.

"Who's this guy?" Jim asked.

"He was a student here a couple of years ago," Brett said. "A computer science major."

"What happened?" Maria asked.

"He got caught using the school's computers to hack into their records," Brett answered. "And, needless to say, the school recommended he leave."

"Where's he now?" Jim asked.

"Still here in College Station," Brett answered. "As a matter of fact, I use him for some of my research."

"How does that mean he can find employee information that's not made public?" Maria asked.

"Oh, like I said, he has his ways," Brett said, smiling. "I forgot to mention that he bypassed all of the school's firewalls, security systems, everything."

"How'd he get caught?" Maria asked.

"Bad luck," Brett said. "It just happened that someone from the computer science division was using a satellite station and noticed something unusual. Then they looked at the security cameras in the room where he was and saw what he was doing."

"Tough luck," Jim said. "But do you think he can hack into these companies' computers and get that information?"

"I'd bet on it," Brett said. "When do you need it?"

Smiling, Jim said, "A week ago."

"How far back do you want?" Brett asked, sitting his beer on the table.

"Can he get the entire history?" Jim asked.

"Probably, if it was ever in their computer files," Brett said, standing up. "Not to spoil the party, but I need to get going."

Maria and Jim took one final drink and set their bottles down before standing up. "What's this going to cost me?" Jim asked as he tossed some money on the table.

"I'll find out," Brett said as they walked toward the exit. "Probably not much. My friend's family is rather well-off, and he mostly does this just to prove he can."

Walking to the Jeep, Brett said, "I'll let you know tomorrow if it can be done and when he can get the information."

Chapter 36

"I'll drop you off at the dorm," Jim said as Brett drove away.

"What if I don't want to go to the dorm?" Maria asked seductively.

"Where do you want to go?" Jim asked, knowing the answer.

"Shopping," Maria said as Jim held the car door open for her.

"Groceries, I'd guess," Jim said, shutting the door.

"Do you have a list?" Maria asked as he got in.

"Not a chance," Jim answered as he started the motor.

"How do you know what you need?" she asked as Jim pulled out of the library parking lot.

"I have a special gift," Jim said as he headed off campus.

"And that is?" she asked.

"I can tell by looking at an item if I want it," Jim answered as he pulled onto University Drive.

"How's that working for you?" she asked.

"You're here, aren't you?" Jim teased as he looked at her.

"Oh, you're funny! You're a funny man," Maria asked, laughing at him.

Maria leaned over and kissed him, asking, "How do you know that you got me because you wanted me or that I got you because I wanted you?"

"Don't care," Jim replied. "Just doesn't matter who wanted who as long as I got what I wanted."

Their light banter lasted through the drive until they pulled into the grocery store parking lot. "Seriously," Maria asked, "do you know what you need?"

"Of course," Jim said as he opened his door. Rounding the front of the car, he opened her door and told her, "Coffee, milk, bread, lettuce, baloney, mayo, mustard, catsup, three cans of oysters, butter, a box of plastic utensils, orange juice, and some Dr Pepper."

"No ice cream?" Maria asked as Jim got a shopping cart that hadn't been shoved back into the line of carts.

"Plenty left," Jim answered as he headed down the first aisle.

"You sure?" she asked, raising her eyebrows.

"Yup," Jim said as he pulled a carton of orange juice from the refrigerated section. "What do you think about what Brett suggested?"

"That's your call," Maria answered. "I'll go along with anything that either lets you finish this obsession or ends it. I just hate to see you chasing something that so far is a dead end."

"I agree," Jim said, nodding his head. "But, like I said, I'll stay on it for a couple of more weeks. If Brett's friend comes up with no ties and I can't find anything at Monogenic's, then I'll change projects."

"Will that give you enough time to finish a completely new thesis?" Maria asked as she followed Jim down another aisle.

"Sure," Jim said, taking a gallon of milk from behind the glass door. "But it'll mean that I've either got to get an extension or bust my ass at the library every second I'm not in class."

"Try for the extension," Maria said, patting Jim on the butt. "I'd hate to see this busted. Unless I get to bust it!"

After checking out at the register, Jim took the two sacks of groceries and headed for the exit. Almost to the door, Maria said, "Stop! You forgot the oysters."

Jim laughed and said, "I don't think I'll need them yet. Maybe if I have to avoid you for a month while I redo my entire thesis, then I'll get them before you come over."

"What makes you think I'll wait a month for you?" Maria asked as they walked to the car.

"You'll want to," Jim said as he put the sacks in the rear seat.

"Pretty sure of yourself, aren't you?" she joked as she opened her door and got in.

"Sure," Jim said, starting the engine. "Where else do you think you'll find someone that'll say stupid things and keep you in Pistachio Almond?"

Laughing, Maria answered, "There are plenty of stupid men around, in fact most of them."

"But what about the ice cream?" Jim asked as he pulled back onto University Drive.

"I was getting my own ice cream before you came along, Mr. Jackson," she said. "I'm sure I can go to the store and get more if I want it."

"You may find the ice cream, but I doubt if you'll find the dessert," Jim teased as they pulled into his apartment.

"Please grab my briefcase," Jim asked as he took the groceries from the back seat.

"You don't want to leave it here for the Russians?" she asked, getting the briefcase. "Or maybe put it back in the trunk for them to find again?"

Jim lifted one of the bags and raised a single finger to her as she shut the car door. "Let the Russians find this!"

Jim unlocked the apartment door and held it open for Maria, asking, "Would you mind baloney sandwiches tonight?"

"I sort of figured that when you recited your grocery list," Maria said as she tossed Jim's briefcase on the couch.

"Will you make them?" Jim asked, putting the sacks on the counter.

"Sure," Maria said as Jim started taking everything out of the bags. "How do you want yours?"

"Everything I bought," Jim said as he started putting each item in the refrigerator."

"Even the butter, orange juice, and Dr. Pepper?" she asked as she opened the loaf of bread.

"Okay, everything but those," Jim said, putting the coffee into the cupboard.

"All right," she said as she spread two slices of bread with mayo. "But you better take the coffee back out of the cupboard. You didn't include that in the exclusions list."

Jim kissed the side of Maria's neck and said, "You sure can be a wise ass, can't you? You know what I meant."

Maria continued making the sandwiches as Jim opened the package of plastic utensils and poured them into a drawer. "Do you really think Brett can get the information you're looking for?" she asked as she carried the sandwiches to the table.

"He seems sure," Jim said, taking two Dr. Peppers from the refrigerator and setting them on the table.

Getting a small bucket of ice from the freezer and two glasses from the cupboard, he set them on the table and continued, "If his guy can get the information, and if there's a connection, and if--"

"And if, and if, and if," Maria said, picking up her sandwich. "Let's forget about your stupid patent for the night. You've got a lot of *homework* to do tonight, and I don't want you to be distracted."

"Forgotten!" Jim said smiling as he took a bite of his sandwich.

Chapter 37

The next morning, Rocky arrived at Monogenic's early to give Mike his briefing on what they had collected on Jim's activities the previous day and night. As Mike entered, Rocky stood and followed him into his office.

"What have you got for me today?" Mike asked as he went to his desk and sat down.

"Not much, I'm afraid," Rocky answered. "Only one new issue and a possible repeat of an old one."

"Let's start with the new one," Mike said as he logged onto his computer.

Rocky pulled his notebook from his jacket pocket and said, "There was a mention of someone named Brett. We hadn't heard that name before, and it had something to do with him getting some information for Jim."

"That could be any sort of information," Mike said. "What was the context?"

"Nothing," Rocky answered, shaking his head. "As I said, Ms. Pompillio just asked if he, Jim, thought Brett could get the information he was looking for."

"Okay," Mike said. Pausing while he opened a program on the computer, he continued, "What's the possible repeat?"

"I don't know for sure," Rocky answered, "but there was a mention of Russians looking at his briefcase."

Mike looked up and asked, "Russians?"

"Yes, sir," Rocky said, nodding his head. "That's what was said."

"Rather strange, don't you think," Mike said. "What was the context?"

"Again, just sort of out of the blue," Rocky told him. "But there was a mention of them looking in the trunk of his car."

"Do you think he knows that we opened the trunk?" Mike asked, getting worried.

"I don't see how," Rocky told him. "I was there and made sure everything was replaced exactly as it was when we opened the trunk."

"Best guess?" Mike asked.

"I'd say that Jim told her about putting the briefcase in the trunk so no one would see it," Rocky theorized.

"Probably," Mike said, scrolling through the email on his computer. "Anything else?"

"Same stuff on their overactive libidos'," Rocky answered.

Mike sat back and looked at Rocky for a second, and said, "Was there anything new in the briefcase?"

"No, sir," Rocky said. "Any new notes were just the same as the old ones."

"Alright, I'll accept your theory of why the trunk was mentioned," Mike said, looking hard at Rocky. "But, just in case, let's leave his briefcase alone for the next few days."

"Yes, sir," Rocky nodded his head and agreed.

"Now, this Brett guy," Mike said. "Make sure we pay attention to any conversation or reference about him and his information."

"Yes, sir," Rocky said. "Anything else, sir?"

"Not that I'm aware of," Mike said, returning to his computer.

As Rocky was leaving Mike's office, Jim arrived at the labs a few minutes before eight and parked. Tossing his briefcase in the trunk and putting a new strip of tape on the hood, he clipped his ID to his pocket and walked to the entry.

As he entered, he saw Larry sitting on the edge of the desk, talking to the same guard that'd been there the previous day. "Good morning," Jim said as he stopped in front of the desk and signed in.

"Good morning," Larry said, standing up. "Ready for your first day of real work?"

"Eager," Jim said, following Larry to the dressing room. "Do you have any idea about what project I'll be working on?"

"No," Larry admitted as he dressed in fresh overalls, booties, and cap. "I haven't seen Dr. Thompson since we talked to him yesterday."

When both were properly dressed, Larry asked, "Remember the code?"

"Sure," Jim said, stepping up to the pad. Pushing the code 5532 into the pad, the familiar buzz came, and Jim opened the door.

"Great," Larry said as he entered the hall with Jim. "I'll take you to Dr. Thompson's office and let you go. If you get done early and want me to show you anything, his office will contact me."

"You said you were still planning on getting your Ph.D.," Jim said as they walked down the hall.

"Yup," Larry said as they passed one of the large windows, looking in at the white-coated people working inside. "When will you finish?"

"Hopefully, in a couple of months," Jim answered. "Four classes and my thesis are all that remain."

"How's that coming?" Larry asked as they approached a door that had Dr. Thompson's name stenciled on it.

"Classes are okay. A few hours of research on some of the topics I don't fully understand," Jim said as they stopped at the door.

"How about the thesis?" Larry asked as he opened the door to enter Dr. Thompson's office.

"Kind of nowhere," Jim admitted as they walked into a small area with file cabinets covering two of the walls.

"What's the problem?" Larry asked as he nodded at the secretary.

"My project seems to have disappeared," Jim admitted.

"Dr. Thompson in?" Larry asked the secretary.

"He's in one of the labs," she answered. "How can I help you?"

"Mr. Jackson's supposed to meet him here this morning," Larry explained.

"Have a seat, and I'll page him," the secretary said, picking up her phone.

Taking the two chairs under the single window that looked in, Larry asked, "So, what do you mean that it disappeared?"

"It was a patent that you folks developed," Jim explained. "I found it in a random search for complex GMOs and tried to find out if it ever made it into production."

"Did it?" Larry asked.

"I can't find any data that it ever went anywhere after the patent was granted," Jim answered.

"What do you plan to do about the thesis? I mean, I can't imagine a thesis that just proves a GMO can be patented," Larry told him.

"Not sure," Jim answered. "If I can't find any more information, I'll have to switch to another GMO."

"Maybe I can help you with that if you have to switch," Larry was saying as Dr. Thompson came in.

"Morning," Dr. Thompson said, stopping in front of their chairs.

"Good morning, sir," Larry said, rising to his feet.

Jim stood also and said, "Good morning."

"What do you need help with?" Dr. Thompson asked, shaking Jim's hand.

"I just told Jim that I might be able to help him if he needs to change the basis of his thesis," Larry answered for Jim.

"Having a problem?" Dr. Thompson asked.

"Sort of," Jim replied. "And, time's getting short to make a change to the GMO I've been researching. But I may have to."

"Well, if we can be of any assistance with research, let us know," Dr. Thompson said. "That's one of Larry's specialties. I'm sure he can get you all the data on any GMO we've developed."

"That'd be great," Jim said. "But I'd still like to pursue this one for a week or so."

"Is it our patent?" Dr. Thompson asked.

"Yes, sir," Jim answered.

"Do you have the patent number or product name?" Larry asked. "I can research it while you're with Dr. Thompson today."

"It was Barley MBM 106729," Jim told him.

"I see what I can do," Larry said as he prepared to leave.

"Well, let's get to work," Dr. Thompson said as he headed into his office. "I think you'll enjoy this more than looking through old computer records.

Chapter 38

After Dr. Thompson explained the new project they'd be working on, they left for the lab where the GMO was to begin. As they entered the cubicle that led into the actual lab, the blast of air hit them, ensuring all loose particles were removed.

"We'll suit up again when we get inside," Dr. Thompson said as the door to the lab buzzed open.

There was a solid glass wall that separated them from the various stations within the lab that Jim hadn't noticed when he had looked in the windows from the hall.

"Is this the same in every lab?" Jim asked as he followed Dr. Thompson toward a door at the end of the glassed-in hall.

"No," Dr. Thompson answered. "Just where we need absolute sterility for the actual gene extraction or insertion. The rest of them have the same procedures to enter but don't require the same precautions we require in this lab."

Once they'd entered the door, Jim saw containers for the overalls and things he'd been wearing. As Dr. Thompson began to remove his white overalls, Jim followed suit and tossed his into the marked containers.

A fresh set of whites were in stacks on an adjacent table and both of them redressed. The only difference was the cap was replaced with a hood that covered all of the face except the eyes and a pair of white cloth gloves.

Taking a clear face shield from a shelf, Dr. Thompson put his on and waited for Jim to do the same. Then back into another chamber that again blasted them with air.

Once the gust of air subsided, Dr. Thompson pressed the code to unlock the door. As it opened, Jim felt a slight breeze coming from within the lab, confirming that this had a positive pressure system to prevent anything left on them or from the chamber from entering the purified environment of the lab.

Dr. Thompson introduced Jim to several lab assistants who were preparing for the procedure. No one shook hands. Just nodded to acknowledge the introduction.

As they watched, Dr. Thompson explained exactly what was being done. Jim was allowed to look into the electron microscope as each step in the process was being performed. Following the procedure from station to station, Jim watched the entire protocol until the minuscule strand of DNA was ready to transfer to the next lab to see if it survived the process and would begin to grow.

It was almost five o'clock when they returned to the chamber to leave the lab. They kept the new whites on, except for the gloves and face shields, and left by a one-way door to exit back into the central hall.

"Well, what'd you think?" Dr. Thompson said as he headed toward his office.

"Amazing," Jim said, following him. "Most of the stuff I've only seen in videos or read about."

As they entered the office, the secretary smiled and said, "Mr. Jackson, Larry said he had some information for you and would like to give it to you when you leave the lab."

"Thanks," Jim said as he stood beside Dr. Thompson.

"Tomorrow, we'll follow the product to its next stage if you'd like," Dr. Thompson said. "If you have no further questions, why don't you meet with Larry and see what information he has for you."

"Lots of questions, sir," Jim answered, "but I don't know where to start."

Dr. Thompson laughed and said, "A lot to take in for the first time."

He turned to the secretary and said, "Page Larry and have him meet Jim here, please."

Turning back to Jim, he continued, "We'll start at eight o'clock tomorrow morning. If you're not here, I'll assume you had other priorities, like class, that prevented you from coming."

"No class in the morning," Jim said, shaking the outstretched hand. "I'll be here."

"Good, see you then," Dr. Thompson said as he turned to his office.

"You can have a seat, Mr. Jackson," the secretary said as she listened for someone to answer her page.

"He's on his way," she said a few seconds later as she hung up the phone. "Shouldn't be but a minute or so."

Jim sat back in the chair to wait as the secretary resumed her work at her desk. When her phone rang, Jim heard her say, "I'll get him on the line for you, sir."

"Dr. Thompson for Mr. Hawk, please," Jim then heard her say into the phone just as Larry walked into the room.

"How'd it go?" Larry asked as Jim stood up.

"Great," Jim said as he followed Larry out of the office. "Beats the hell out of anything the school's been trying to teach me. Sure, it makes a lot more sense now other than just seeing videos or reading about it."

"I know," Larry said as they headed down the hall to leave the facility. "That's why I think my time here will make it easier when I go back to school."

"It should," Jim agreed as they entered the room to remove their whites. "By the way, Dr. Thompson's secretary said you had some information for me."

"I do," Larry said as he opened the door to the reception area. "I left it with the guard just in case I didn't get to see you before I had to leave."

Jim followed Larry to the guard's desk and waited as he asked for the envelope he'd left. Taking it, Larry handed it to Jim, saying, "I'm afraid I can't find anything on that barley that shows what happened."

Jim opened the envelope and saw a duplicate of the data he had originally gotten and frowned. "This is the same as I got from Mr. Moss. I was hoping there would be something more showing what happened to the barley strain."

"I don't know," Larry said, walking toward the exit. "I searched every place I could think of. Maybe the people in Austin have something more, but I doubt it."

"Why's that?" Jim asked as they left the building.

"This strain of barley was developed here," Larry explained. "Austin would have gotten all of their information from us. If it was available, we'd still have it somewhere in our files."

"What's your guess about ever finding anything more?" Jim said, disappointed that it seemed he'd never get any more information on his thesis project.

"I don't think you ever will," Larry said, shaking his head. "But I'd be glad to look through our patents here and see if there's another one that meets your requirements."

"I'll let you know tomorrow," Jim said, shaking his hand. "Thanks for doing this for me anyway."

"No problem," Larry said as he headed for his car. "I'll see you tomorrow if you come in."

As Jim was walking to his car, Dr. Thompson was discussing Jim's visit to the lab that morning.

"Anything unusual?" Mike asked him.

"No, he just mainly observed all of the procedures," Dr. Thompson answered. "He seems to know what we're doing, just lacks practical experience."

"Good," Mike said. "Did he have any questions?"

Dr. Thompson laughed and answered, "No, I think he was overwhelmed. He said he had lots of questions but didn't know what to ask."

"I understand," Mike agreed. "Anything else?"

"I asked Larry to do some research for him," Dr. Thompson answered.

"On what?" Mike asked, suddenly alert.

"One of our patents," Dr. Thompson said. "Some strain of barley he's researching for his thesis."

"Do you know which one?" Mike asked, already knowing the answer.

"Not off the top of my head," Dr. Thompson answered. "But Larry did have some information for him. I'll have Larry call you if you'd like to know."

"That'd be fine," Mike said, not wanting to seem too interested. "Just have him call me tomorrow." "Sure," Dr. Thompson said. "I told Jim that Larry would be available to help with any research on any of our patents. I hope that's alright."

"Of course," Mike told him. "I even suggested that Larry do some preliminary research on one of our corn strains if Jim needs to switch projects."

"Good," Dr. Thompson said. "Jim seems like an intelligent man, and I'd like to help him with his thesis if he needs it. I still remember some of the problems I had with mine."

"Well, as I've always said, we'll support any of the A&M students in any way we can," Mike said. "Call me tomorrow after Jim leaves, please."

"Certainly," Dr. Thompson said before hanging up.

Chapter 39

Jim had left the lab and walked to his little VW. As soon as he got there, he checked the tape he'd placed on the trunk lid. Surprised that it was still there, exactly as he'd placed it, he opened the trunk and retrieved his briefcase.

Closing the lid, he climbed into the car, did a quick check of the briefcase, and saw nothing amiss. He tossed it onto the passenger seat and started the car, still amazed that it hadn't been searched.

'Maybe,' he thought as he drove away, *'I've been suspicious over nothing.'*

On the drive back to the campus, he mentally reviewed the previous times he thought someone had handled the briefcase. All of them were strange, but as Maria had said, there was no proof that anyone had done anything.

That, and the fact that Larry had found nothing, made him start to wonder if he was seeing a forest where there was only a single tree. Mountain out of a molehill, much ado about nothing, chicken little, and every other wise old saying came to mind as he drove.

A few minutes after five, Jim pulled up to the curb in front of the library and parked. Taking his briefcase, he walked slowly toward the entrance and tried to decide if he might as well change his thesis now instead of waiting another week. Or even another day.

As he walked into the computer section, ready to start a new search for a different GMO, he spotted Maria busy making notes as she ran her mouse back and forth across the pad. "Hey," he said as he put his briefcase on the unoccupied desk next to her.

"Hey," she replied without looking up. "How'd it go?"

"Great," Jim said, taking the empty seat next to her and booting up the computer. "I got to see a lot of the things we talked about in the classes."

"Good," she said, barely glancing at him. "That's what you've been wanting to do, isn't it?"

"Yeah," Jim said as he logged on. "And I think you're right about changing GMOs for my thesis."

Maria paused and turned to look at him, asking, "Why?"

"A guy I work with at the lab, Larry, tried to find more information on the barley," Jim explained as he found the original list of GMOs he had used before. "He spent most of the day going through Monogenic's files and couldn't find anything."

Maria smiled and said, "Well, at least you can say you tried. What's your plan now?"

"Start all over," Jim said as he scrolled down the list of potential candidates for his new project.

"Bummer," Maria said as she returned to her computer.

"Sure is," Jim said as he found a GMO that had been patented by Monogenic's. "Wish there was another way, but it looks like I'll be spending lots more time here than I thought."

"What about asking for that extension?" Maria asked as she made more notes.

"I'm going to wait until I'm sure I need it," Jim answered as he found more information on the GMO he had selected.

"Still think there's something up at Mono-you know?" she asked turning to look at him.

"I still don't know," Jim answered. "But I put the tape back on the trunk, and it was still there when I came out of the lab."

"Told you so," Maria said. "Now, can the people at the lab help you with your research, or do you still not trust them?"

"They, mainly Larry, said they could help if I needed it," Jim said as he read the information on the GMO he'd selected.

"I'd take it," Maria advised as she turned back to her computer.

"I may have to," Jim said, nodding his head. Returning to the original list of GMOs, he said, "Crap!"

"What?" Maria asked, glancing at him.

"That GMO didn't fit my parameters," Jim answered as he scrolled down the list again.

"Surprise!" Brett said as he walked up silently behind them.

Jim glanced up at him and said, "Nice ninja moves, grasshopper."

"Oh, I've got more than ninja moves, Sensei," Brett said, smiling at Jim.

"Hi, Brett," Maria said, glancing at him.

"Evening, Maria," Brett said as he pulled a chair up between them. "By the way, I come bearing gifts."

"Really? Did you bring beer?" Jim asked, still searching the list of prospective GMOs.

"Better than that," Brett answered as he tossed an envelope in front of Jim. "Much better."

Jim sat back and picked up the envelope, asking, "What's this?"

"What you asked for," Brett answered as Jim pulled the sheets of paper out of the envelope.

"That was fast," Jim said as he looked at the top sheet.

"My man has no life outside of his computer," Brett said, watching Jim's face.

"Holy shit!" Jim exclaimed as he saw the highlighted area on one of the sheets.

"What?" Maria asked.

"The connection with Monogenic's," Jim said, smiling at her.

"Not again," she said, exasperated at Jim's renewed interest. "I thought you just said you were going to change your subject."

"Still may," Jim mumbled as he continued to read more of the sheets. "But this may be something to look into anyway."

"What's this connection you're suddenly interested in?" Maria asked, sitting back in her chair.

"The President of Mombasa," Jim said. "He worked at Monogenic's right after they started the lab here at College Station."

"So?" Maria asked. "How does that tie them together? Lots of people start out at one company and then move on. That really proves nothing."

"No, not by itself," Jim argued. "But he was also the chief of the genetic programs at Agrigenic's."

"So, he got promoted," Maria said. "Again, left Monogenic's, went to Agrigenic, and got promoted to run Mombasa. I still don't see a conspiracy there."

"And you haven't proven that the two patents are the same anyway," she continued.

"I know," Jim said as he finished reading the papers Brett had brought. "

But I know the two patents are almost, if not perfectly, identical. I still think there's something going on."

Brett waited for a pause and then handed Jim another envelope, saying, "This may give you some more questions to ponder, my friend."

Jim took the envelope and pulled out a single sheet. As soon as he'd read it, he asked Brett, "What do you think?"

"Let's recap," Brett said, sitting back and crossing his arms. "A certain Doctor of Molecular Biology runs a genetic lab in Zwairiland. He was formerly at Mombasa and at Monogenic's before that."

Pausing to let Maria get on the same train of thought as he and Jim were, he continued, "This gentleman was at Monogenic's about the time their patent was applied for, as you can see from his resume. He then returns to Ethiopia, where he was born, goes to work with Mombasa, and they're granted a patent shortly after he gets there...maybe the same one."

"Coincidence? Maybe," Brett said. "But, another fly in the ointment. His older brother, who was the Prime Minister during the period while our good doctor was at Monogenic's, became the President of Ethiopia right after the doctor returned home."

"Now, bear in mind, this all happened over 20 years ago," Brett continued as he looked at Maria. "About the same time as the birthrate decline you discovered."

Maria looked from Brett to Jim and back before saying, "What you're inferring is called Genocide."

Chapter 40

For several moments, they just sat there wondering how this could have happened, if indeed it had. Finally, Jim said, "We don't know that for sure."

"Agreed," Brett said. "But there sure are a lot of coincidences going on."

"Even if a lot of things seem to point to that, how do we know that a plant's causing the drop in birthrates?" Maria asked. "I've been looking at it for several days, and I can't say what's causing it."

"How much information do you have on that corn you said was a contraceptive?" Jim asked Brett.

"Other than knowing it existed, none," Brett admitted.

"Can you get enough data that we could compare it with the barley?" Jim asked.

"Probably," Brett said. "How much information on the Mombasa patent do you have?"

"Everything that was in the patent," Jim answered.

"Do either of you know enough to prove that whatever caused the corn problem would be in the barley?" Maria asked.

Brett and Jim looked at each other for a second, and Jim said, "I don't."

"Me neither," Brett admitted.

"First, we don't even know if the barley is being grown or used in Zwairiland," Jim said.

"How would we find out?" Brett asked. "We can't just call some farmer down there and ask him what barley seed he's using."

"And, we can't go to any government official with what's just an unproven theory based on so far unrelated events," Jim said.

"What do you suggest?" Maria asked.

"First, we need to get the information on the corn, if it really did exist," Jim suggested. "Then we can compare the specific gene that was inserted into the corn's DNA with the gene that was inserted into the barley's."

"Even if we can show that the same gene was used, that doesn't mean that it's the cause of the birthrate decline," Brett offered.

"No," Jim said, shaking his head, "but it's at least a tie between the corn and barley."

"Back to the start," Brett said, "how do we determine if the Monogenic's patent and Mombasa's are the same and that barley is either being grown or distributed in Zwairiland?"

"I already have both of their patents, and they are virtually identical," Jim answered. "All we need is the patent on the corn to make the comparison. If it's the same, then we can logically argue that the barley carries the same contraceptive effect."

"Okay, what then?" Maria asked.

"Somehow, we have to determine that the *probable* contraceptive barley is being consumed in Zwairiland, "Brett repeated. "If it's not, we're wasting our time on the genetic makeup of any of these patents."

"Isn't there some international organization that monitors that sort of thing?" Maria asked.

"What about the US Department of Agriculture, the USDA?" Jim suggested. "They should be able to find some information on the corn thing. And they probably have some involvement with the World Health Organization (WHO) or some other international food or health group."

"That's as good a place to start as any," Brett agreed. "There's another source of information that's available, but I'm not sure we want to involve them at this stage."

"Who's that?" Maria asked.

"There're several organizations," Brett answered. "One of them is called the 'Say No to GMO'. I'm sure there's a list of them somewhere on the internet."

"I'd rather not get involved with them," Jim said, shaking his head. "You never know what sort of kooks you're dealing with or what their real objectives are. Plus, I'm in favor of GMOs. At least as long as they're used cautiously."

"Okay," Maria said. "Let's start with the USDA. Maybe we can get some information from the World Food Programme."

"Agreed," Jim said. "As long as we stay away from the anti-GMO organizations until we run out of options."

"At this point, I don't think even they'd find us credible," Brett said. "We have too little information and no proof or evidence that a GMO is the cause of our perceived problem."

"So," Jim surmised, "where do we start?"

"I'll keep digging into the birthrate thing in Zwairiland," Maria said. "I'll make sure there hasn't been anything else that could possibly account for the drastic drop in either population or birthrate."

"I'll get the data on the corn," Brett said. "Then we'll compare it with your data on the barley."

"If nothing else, we can probably get one of the genetics professors to double-check our analysis," Jim suggested. "Hell, this would make a great thesis for you, Brett!"

"You bet," Brett laughed. "I'll expose the worst side of pharming and GMOs for the world to see. That'll earn me a job with the companies I may put out of business. You bet!"

"Look at it this way," Jim argued. "If we prove it wasn't the barley, that's good. If we prove it was, then we've demonstrated how the GMO industry's responsible for eliminating any product that adversely affects our food supplies."

"Say, I have an idea!" Maria excitedly said.

"What?" Jim asked.

"What if Monogenic's isn't involved? What if Mombasa got the data and pirated it without Monogenic's knowledge?" she asked. "How about if we ask them if they know anything about it? Maybe they'd even be willing to help."

"Absolutely not!" Jim scolded. "I'm still not sure they're not involved, and if they are, we'd probably be putting ourselves in danger."

"I agree with Jim," Brett said. "Until we determine that there's no connection between the corn and Monogenic's, we keep our little investigation a secret."

"Speaking of involving Monogenic's, what're you going to do about working for them from now on?" Maria asked.

"I'll keep going there," Jim answered. "As Brett said, until we prove there's a connection between the corn, them, and Mombasa's barley, I'll remain an intern."

"Plus, you may be able to get more information from them," Brett said.

"I doubt it," Jim said. "I've tried twice and gotten nowhere. If I try again, they'll think I'm up to something. I'll just go along with their program and wait to see if anything develops."

"Okay," Jim said, standing up. "Why don't we plan on meeting here tomorrow evening and see what we've come up with? Then, we can plan our next steps."

"I'll be here," Brett said as he got out of his chair. "Hopefully, I'll have the corn data by then."

Maria got up and stood looking at them and said, "I'm in. Shouldn't we come up with a catchy name for our sleuth club?"

"Sure," Jim said as they started heading for the exit. "How about the 'The Three Miceketeers'?"

"Good enough for me," Maria said.

"If we're going with TV series, I like 'The Barley Bunch'," Brett said laughing.

"Too gay," Jim said. "I vote for the Miceketeers."

"Two for rodents, one for gay," Maria announced, smiling. "Rats we are, all for one, one for all!"

Chapter 41

The following morning, Jim woke early and gently shook Maria. "I've got to be at Monogenic's by eight," he said as she rolled over and threw an arm across his chest.

"I don't," she mumbled, snuggling up against him.

"No, you don't," Jim said as he ran his fingers down her bare back. "But, if you aren't up when I need to leave, you'll spend the rest of the day here. Or find your own way home."

"Can't you call in sick?" she asked, nuzzling his neck.

"Nope," Jim said, wishing he could. "Don't forget, we rodents have work to do. And you still have classes."

"What time are you coming back?" she asked as she rolled away from him.

"Around noon, maybe a little sooner," Jim answered as he sat up on the bed. "I have a class at one that lasts until three."

Pulling the sheet up over her breasts, Maria sat up and stretched, saying, "I have one from 10 to noon. Can we have lunch?"

"Sure," Jim said, swinging his legs off the bed. "Anything special that you want?"

"How about ice cream for lunch?" she asked, grinning at Jim.

Jim turned and saw the grin, saying, "And I suppose we're to just forget what we planned to do this afternoon."

"You know the old saying, 'the rats will play while the mouse is away,'" she said as she stretched her arms over her head, intentionally letting the sheet fall down.

"You mean the mice will play when the cat's away," Jim corrected, looking at her breasts. "And you're not going to get me to delay getting out to the lab, so either pull the sheet back up or get dressed."

"You're a R-A-T!" she said, jumping out of the bed.

"And you're trying to set the rat trap," Jim laughed as he walked over to where he'd tossed his underwear.

"Fine, Mr. Jackson," Maria pouted as she pulled on another of Jim's T-shirts. "Will you at least make some coffee for us before we have to go back to our normal, boring lives?"

"On my way, m'lady," Jim said, heading to the kitchen. "Would you like a shower before I take mine?"

Maria rushed up behind him and grabbed the waist of his underwear, saying, "I'll make the coffee while you shower. I'll take mine at the dorm."

Jim slapped her gently on the butt as she went by him and said, "Thanks, cutie butt. But don't try that *joining you in the shower* trick!"

"I don't shower with vermin," she quipped as she went into the kitchen. "You have absolutely no worries about your precious shower."

Jim laughed and reversed course to the bathroom. As soon as the water was sufficiently hot, he dropped his shorts and climbed in. With the shampoo over his head and his eyes closed, he never saw Maria quietly slip into the shower behind him.

When she reached around him and cupped her hand between his legs, she whispered, "Mmmm, mice like nuts!"

Jim's eyes flew open, and he almost banged his head on the shower as he jerked backward. "You sneaky rat!" he yelled as Maria pressed up against him.

"Never trust rodents," Maria said, noticing Jim's sudden interest.

Jim turned around and shook his head as Maria began stroking him. "I think I'm starting to like rats," he said, smiling at her.

A few minutes later, Maria kissed him on the cheek before climbing out of the shower laughing and said, "I believe the coffee's ready, but it looks like you've spilled the cream. Good thing we both take it black!"

After dropping Maria off at the dorm, Jim drove to the lab and headed for Dr. Thompson's office. When he arrived, Larry was standing by the desk and talking to the secretary.

"Good morning, Jim," Larry said, turning to greet him.

"Hi, Larry," Jim said, shaking his hand. "What're you doing this morning?"

"Not much," Larry replied. "I was going to help in one of the labs, but they ran into some problems with the genes they're working with, so I'm kind of here to see if you need anything."

"Not that I know of," Jim said, nodding to the secretary. "My thesis project is sort of dead in the water since I can't find any data that brings it to a successful conclusion."

"Maybe I can help," Larry offered. "What are your parameters?"

"Complex GMO, normal procedures for lab testing, successful field tests, and improved production levels when on the market," Jim told him. "Nothing too amazing, just proving that a GMO can improve the quality of life either through less costly food or increased production in areas of the world where famine is more the norm than readily available food."

"Nothing amazing you say," Larry laughed. "Isn't that the definition of amazing?"

"Isn't that the goal of GMOs?" Jim asked as Dr. Thompson joined them.

"What's the goal of GMOs? " the doctor asked.

"Improving the supply of quality food across the globe," Jim answered. "Otherwise, why are so many companies doing this?"

"You're correct to a point," Dr. Thompson said. "But, don't forget the profit motive. Without profit, these companies wouldn't be interested in investing billions of dollars for pure humanity's sake."

"I understand that, sir," Jim said, nodding his head. "But a successful product can do both. If it's good for the consumer, it's good for the producer. Our job is to develop the product that satisfies the need."

"True," Dr. Thompson said. "As long as everyone realizes that it's not altruistic. As much as I love the pure science, I certainly couldn't afford to do it without the backing of millions of investors that want a return on their investments."

"Now, speaking of the investors' money, we need to continue yesterday's beginnings," Dr. Thompson said as he turned toward the door.

Stopping in the door frame, he turned and asked, "What're you doing today, Larry?"

"Nothing's been assigned since my project is sort of on hold," Larry answered.

Turning to Jim, he asked, "How much help was his research yesterday?"

"Not much," Jim answered. "I already had most of the data."

"Are you still looking at that barley strain?" Dr. Thompson asked.

"I think I may have to find another GMO," Jim answered.

"Why don't you look through our patents and find something that may fit his requirements, Larry," Dr. Thompson asked. "Do you need for him to provide you with his parameters?"

"No, sir," Larry answered. "We were just discussing them when you joined us. I'm pretty sure I can narrow it down to several for him to choose from."

"Excellent," Dr. Thompson said, turning to Jim. "Would that help you?"

"Certainly," Jim said, nodding his head. "If Larry can find a program that proves conclusively that a properly researched and tested GMO can provide substantial benefits to humanity, I'll take it from there."

"Now you have something to fill your day, Larry," Dr. Thompson said, turning back to the door. "Unless there are more pressing needs for you, I'd appreciate it if you'd have something before Jim leaves for class today."

"Yes, sir," Larry nodded. "I'll get to work on it."

"Now, let's get to work," Dr. Thompson said as he headed toward the lab.

Chapter 42

For the rest of the morning, Jim followed Dr. Thompson around the lab as they observed the other scientists and technicians working with the single strand of DNA they'd created yesterday.

Jim was allowed to assist in several of the procedures as each step of the process was being done. The composition of the various mediums used to accelerate the growth of the DNA strand was a closely guarded secret, and some of the techniques were not revealed either.

As noon approached, Jim told Dr. Thompson that he needed to leave in order to get to his class. When the doctor asked if he needed someone to escort him out, Jim said, "No, sir. I remember the procedures from yesterday. I can make it on my own."

"Stop by the office on your way out," Dr. Thompson said. "My secretary will page Larry for you. Maybe he's got a list of potential candidates for your thesis ready."

"Yes, sir," Jim said, nodding his head.

"Will you be available again tomorrow?" Dr. Thompson asked as he glanced at his watch.

"Probably not," Jim answered. "If I get Larry's list, I'll need to spend some time to determine which GMO I want to investigate."

"If it'd help, you can use one of the computers here," the doctor suggested. "And, if Larry's not busy, he can help you narrow your search down even further."

"I appreciate the offer," Jim said. "But I don't want to take up any more of your staff's time on my personal project."

"Don't worry about that," Dr. Thompson said, shaking his head. "Mr. Hawk wants us to help you any way we can, as he always does for students from A&M. Part of his community service commitment."

"I'll certainly think about that," Jim said. "But I'll see what Larry's found and then see if I'll need his assistance."

"Good," Dr. Thompson said. "Just let my secretary know if you ever need our help. She'll give you my office phone number. I hope we've enlightened you at least a little these last couple of days."

"You sure have," Jim said before turning to leave. "I look forward to coming back and watching this project's progress."

"Then I'll see you later," Dr. Thompson said as he headed toward one of the technicians who was using an electron microscope to peer into a Petri dish.

Jim exited through the chamber and left his face shield and gloves before entering the hall. As he approached Dr. Thompson's office, he spotted Larry coming toward him.

Waiting for Larry to join him, Jim mentally reviewed what he needed to do this afternoon after class. Thinking about lunch, he smiled as he remembered this morning's shower.

"Well, you seem happy about something," Larry said, stopping beside Jim. "Or was there something funny in the lab?"

"No, just thinking about something," Jim answered.

"I've got a list of several patents that should meet your criteria," Larry said, handing Jim a single sheet of paper.

Jim looked at it and asked, "Is the complete protocol for each of these available, and are they all currently in production commercially?"

"Yes, and yes," Larry answered. "If you'd like, I can provide all of that information on any of them you select."

"Is there any way for me to access your computers from another location, such as at the school's computer section?" Jim asked.

"I'm afraid not," Larry answered. "The company won't allow anyone to remote with the main computers here or in Austin. Too much of a chance for someone to have unauthorized access to proprietary information."

"I understand," Jim said. "But how much information can I get from public records?"

"Not a lot," Larry answered, shaking his head. "The patents are recorded, but unless you know someone at the US Patent Office, I doubt if you can get more than basic information about who holds the patent and its brand name."

"Then I guess I'll need your help," Jim said, thinking about how he had gotten the information on the other two patents.

"That's not a problem," Larry said as they entered the office.

"Dr. Thompson asked me to get your phone number," Jim told the secretary as she looked up from her work.

"Certainly," she said, taking a business card from the small box on her desk. "You can reach me during normal business hours or leave a message otherwise. I'll be sure to pass it on to Dr. Thompson."

"Thanks," Jim said, putting the card in his shirt pocket.

"Where are you going now?" Larry asked, following Jim out of the office.

"I've got a class this afternoon," Jim answered as he walked to the room where he would leave his overalls and booties. "Then some time at the library working on a project."

"Okay," Larry said, taking his overalls off. "If you decide you need me to help you, just call Dr. Thompson's office, and they'll find me."

"What have they got you doing this afternoon?" Jim asked as they entered the reception area.

"After lunch, I'm transcribing notes from the lab people where you were yesterday and today," Larry said as Jim signed out. "It shouldn't take more than an hour or so to enter everything into the computer files. After that, I'll be available."

"Good," Jim said, putting the pen down. "If you get a chance, can you take one of the patents on the list and get me a printout of everything from conception to production? Maybe some data regarding field production as well?"

"Certainly," Larry eagerly answered. "Any specific one?"

"Just take the one at the top," Jim said. "Unless you know of one that really stands out as a success."

"I'll dig around and see if there's one that really stands out," Larry said as he followed Jim to the exit.

"That'd be great," Jim said, shaking Larry's hand. "I'll check back later this afternoon and see what you've found."

Jim walked across the asphalt parking lot and got in his car, wondering if it was ethical to let someone else pick his project and do the research. Rationalizing that if a professor could pick the subject for him, it was no different if another person selected it. And help with research wasn't uncommon. That's what student aides did for the professors all of the time.

The biggest issue with this was that the company could skew the project by selecting what they wanted him to use. But that was basically what Jim had told Larry to do: find a successful GMO.

The only thing that really did was prevent him from looking at other companies' patents. Even if he had, he might have randomly selected Monogenic's as he'd already done. Therefore, he selected the company and had control over which of their patents he used. No ethical violations as long as he picked the GMO, and he'd told Larry to just look at the one at the top of the list. The randomness of the list Larry had generated prevented Monogenic's from picking his GMO.

Chapter 43

Larry left the labs and drove to the office as soon as Jim left. Telling Barbara that he wanted to see Mr. Moss, he sat waiting in one of the chairs, holding a copy of the list he had given Jim.

A couple of minutes later, Barbara told him that Jerry could see him. Thanking her, Larry got up and walked to the door that led to the offices.

"Come on in," Jerry called out before Larry could knock. "Have a seat, please."

Larry took one of the chairs across from Jerry's desk and waited for him to start the conversation.

Laying his pen on the desk, Jerry asked, "What can I do for you, Larry?"

"You wanted me to *assist* Jim with his GMO research," Larry said.

"Yes, how's that going?" Jerry asked.

"He asked for a list of our patents that he could use to select a product," Larry answered as he handed the list to Jerry. "This is a copy of the list I gave him just a few minutes ago."

Jerry looked at it and asked, "Did he ask for anything else?"

"He asked me to gather as much data as I could on one of the patents," Larry answered, nodding his head.

"Did he tell you which one?" Jerry asked.

"Not exactly," Larry said, smiling.

"What does that mean?" Jerry asked, getting annoyed at the question-and-answer game Larry seemed to be playing.

"He just told me to use the one at the top of the list," Larry answered.

Jerry looked at the first one on the list and asked, "Is this the one I told you we needed him to use?"

"Yes, sir," Larry answered. "That's why I put it at the top of the list. I figured if he started at the top and found a successful GMO, he wouldn't bother going any further."

"Smart thinking," Jerry said as he laid the list down on his desk. "How much data have you gotten already."

"Everything from conception to several years of production," Larry answered.

"Good," Jerry said, nodding his head. "But be sure you don't appear to be forcing data on him that he doesn't request."

"Not a problem," Larry said. "He's already asked for everything I can find on the product, including any production statistics we have."

Jerry leaned back in his chair and asked, "Do you think he'll use this or keep looking at his barley project?"

"I think he'll take this corn GMO," Larry answered. "He'd asked me to try to get the data on the barley and then said that he already had the stuff I gave him. I think he's decided that he can't get enough information on that barley to continue looking."

"I really think he'll take the corn when I show him everything from the research I've already done," Larry continued. "The next time he comes to the lab, I'll have everything he's asked for ready."

"Good," Jerry said. "I also want you to do the same thing with three or four of the others. Pick ones that are close in complexity and production rates but that don't approach the success we've had with the corn."

"Yes, sir," Larry said, preparing to leave. "May I ask a question?"

"Sure," Jerry said, sitting up and picking up his pen. "What's that?"

"I was just wondering why we're trying to get him to write his thesis on the corn instead of one of the others," Larry said.

"Better publicity for us," Jerry lied. "If, by chance, his thesis is ever published, we stand to gain from showing how successful our products are. By picking one of our most successful recent GMOs, we're helping a student prove his thesis about the benefits of GMOs, and we may gain from favorable publicity."

"I understand," Larry said, getting out of his chair. "Is there anything else you need me to do?"

"No," Jerry said, scribbling some notes on the papers he was now reading. "Just stay with him and help him in any way you can."

Jerry looked up, smiling, and said, "Thanks, Larry. You've done a good job on this. I really appreciate it."

"Yes, sir," Larry said as he turned toward the door. "I'll let you know when he decides to use the corn for sure."

As Larry went down the hall to leave, Jerry picked the list up from his desk and walked to Mike's office. Tapping on the door frame, he asked, "Got a minute?"

"Sure," Mike said, putting his pen down and sitting back in his chair. "Come on in."

Jerry handed the list of patents to Mike and took one of the chairs in front of his desk, saying, "That's the list Larry gave Jim for potential thesis material."

Mike looked at the list quickly and asked, "What was Jim's reaction?"

"Apparently, he's going to select one from that list and drop the barley thing," Jerry answered.

"When will we know?" Mike asked as he placed the list on his desk.

"The next time Jim goes to the lab, Larry will give him all of the data on the corn GMO we talked about the other day," Jerry answered.

"Make sure he doesn't suspect we're pushing it," Mike warned.

"Not a problem," Jerry explained. "He asked Larry to gather the data for the first patent on the list. And he was smart enough to have put it there intentionally."

"Good," Mike said, relaxing slightly. "I hope he chooses it without looking at any of the others."

"That's being covered," Jerry told him. "I asked Larry to pick some others that were successful but not as dramatically as the corn."

Nodding his concurrence, Mike said, "Sounds good. We're not pushing him. We're just providing data and letting him pick the GMO that best suits his needs."

"Exactly," Jerry agreed.

"By the way," Mike said, leaning forward with his elbows on the desk, "Rocky came in this morning with his daily   report."
"Anything notable?" Jerry asked.

"Not really, unless you find the sexual escapades of college students notable," Mike answered.

"I'd find a *lack* of sexual escapades more notable," Jerry said, laughing.

"There were a couple of references to mice, rats, rodents, and vermin," Mike added. "But it was never used in context with barley, so I don't tie it to his project."

"Who knows what those kids are talking about," Jerry said. "Or what they're even thinking."

"You're right about that," Mike said, sitting back and picking up his pen. "Anyway, let me know when Jim's changed his project. I'll relax a lot when he gives up on that damned barley."

Chapter 44

Jim drove to the library, assuming that Maria would be waiting there so they could go to lunch. If she wasn't out of her class, he'd go talk to Kay to see if she would get her friend in the patent office to run his list.

As he pulled into the parking lot, he saw Brett coming up the sidewalk toward the library. Jim killed the engine, grabbed his briefcase, and waited for Brett to join him.

"Hey, Jim," Brett said when he got to where Jim was standing. "How's the day going?"

"Pretty good," Jim said, shaking Brett's hand. "I've been at the lab all morning, and I'm supposed to take Maria to lunch. She should be getting out of class about now."

"Learn anything at the lab?" Brett asked as they walked toward the library.

"Not about the barley," Jim said as they neared the entrance. "But it was interesting to see how they cultivate the DNA strand we developed yesterday."

Jim opened the door and held it for Brett to go in and said, "I did get a list of GMOs that Monogenic's patented."

"You could have gotten that from public records," Brett said as they walked toward the computer section.

"I know," Jim said. "This is a list of GMOs that were successfully developed and have a production history."

"How did you get it?" Brett asked as he pulled out a chair in front of one of the computers.

"One of the lab technicians got it for me," Jim answered as he sat at the terminal next to Brett.

"Aren't you still interested in the barley?" Brett asked as he logged into the system.

"Of course," Jim said as his screen filled. "I requested a list so that I'm not so far behind if I have to change GMOs."

"Don't you think they'd rig it?" Brett asked.

"No, I've thought about that, and I'd already selected Monogenic's as the company to use," Jim explained. "I've still got control over the specific GMO I pick, so all they're doing for me is basic research."

"Okay," Brett said, scrolling down the screen. "What're you looking for today?"

"I was going to ask Dr. Lindsay if she can help me get some information on the patents that are on the list," Jim answered.

"How's she supposed to do that?" Brett asked. "I doubt if she can get into the patent office's computers any better than you can."

Not wanting to tell Brett what she'd previously done for him, he answered, "I was hoping that she might have some influence with them, at least find out if it's possible to get the information."

"Why don't you let me give the list to my hacker?" Brett asked, turning to look at Jim. "If anyone can dig through their files, he can."

"That's a good idea," Jim said, handing Brett the list. "He doesn't need permission the way he does it. I just hope he doesn't leave a trail that could lead back to him or us."

"Not a single track," Brett said, smiling and looking at the list.

"Have you found out anything on the corn?" Jim asked, wandering aimlessly around the computer with his mouse.

"Not much," Brett said. "I did verify that it was an actual GMO and was patented. I gave that to my hacker, and he's supposed to let me know what he's found when I meet him for lunch. I'm hoping to have it when we meet this evening."

"When I see him, I'll give him this list," Brett continued. "Do you need it for now?"

"No," Jim said. "The lab tech was going to start with the top GMO on the list and gather all of the available data for me, and I can get another copy tomorrow when I go back out there."

Brett folded the list and stuck it in his shirt pocket as Maria waved to them from the door. "Looks like the club's all here," Brett said, waving back.

"Too bad you can't have lunch with us," Jim said, standing up to hug Maria as she walked up. "Then, I have a class this afternoon."

Brett logged off his computer and said, "Then I guess I'll see you two back here around five."

"I'll be here," Maria said as Jim logged off and slid his chair under the desk.

"Me, too," Jim said as the three of them headed for the door.

"Okay, I'll see you then," Brett said, turning toward the restrooms. "Maybe we'll have some new issues to talk about."

"Still want ice cream for lunch?" teased Jim as they headed for the exit.

"Maybe later," Maria said as Jim held the door open for her. "I've got a meeting in about 30 minutes with one of my professors who's helping me with the birthrate thing."

"How'd you manage that?" Jim asked as they jostled down the sidewalk between the other students.

"I just asked him if he knew of any studies that had been done in Zwairiland over the last decade or so on their population decline," Maria said as they got to the car.

"What'd he say?" Jim asked, opening the passenger door for her.

"He said he didn't know, and then when I showed him my numbers on the birthrates, he said he'd look into it," Maria answered as Jim shut her door.

"Well, with not much time, where'd you like to go?" Jim asked, getting into the car.

"Isn't there a little Italian sandwich shop just down University?" she asked as Jim started the car.

"Yeah, I think it's called Tomato Joe's," Jim answered as he pulled out of the parking lot.

"Let's go there," Maria said, putting her hand on the back of Jim's neck. "I'm not real hungry anyway, maybe a salad or something."

"What about tonight?" Jim asked as he approached University. "I thought the three of us could go for Bar-B-Q and have a couple of beers after the meeting."

"Sounds good to me," Maria said. "Why don't we just meet there instead of the library?"

"Fine with me," Jim said as he maneuvered through the noon hour traffic on University. "We'll have to meet at the library to start since I don't know where Brett will be this afternoon."

"Did he get any information on the corn?" Maria asked as they spotted Tomato Joe's just ahead.

"Some," Jim said, pulling into the parking lot. "He hopes he'll get more when he meets his hacker today for lunch.

Jim killed the car and turned to Maria, saying, "I hope we can find the relationship between all of these things. Otherwise, we've wasted a lot of time."

"I know," Maria said, looking at Jim. "But I'm starting to believe you were right the first time. There's got to be a connection."

Chapter 45

As Jim and Maria were having lunch, Rocky was gathering the transcript from their conversation in the car. Not knowing if what they'd heard, or thought they'd heard, was important, Rocky wanted to get this to Mike as soon as possible.

Rocky called as soon as the recordings had been transcribed and got an appointment to see Mike as quickly as he could get there. Maybe nothing, but after the chastisement he'd gotten over the botched briefcase issue, Rocky wanted to provide anything that might put him back in good graces with Mr. Hawk.

"Come in, Rocky," Mike said as he heard the gentle tapping on his open door. "What've you got that's so important that it couldn't wait until tomorrow morning?"

"Well, sir, you wanted any information about Mr. Jackson's interest in any GMO project," Rocky answered.

"Yes," Mike said, sitting back in his chair. "Has he said or done something that's different than what you've found thus far?"

Rocky handed the transcribed sheets to Mike and said, "I don't absolutely know if he's changing his interest, but he had a conversation with Ms. Pompillio about corn. I know his previous searches were involving barley, so I thought this might prove he's shifted his focus."

Mike sat for a couple of minutes reading the transcript and then asked, "What's this birthrate comment she made?"

"I'm not sure," Rocky admitted. "It seemed sort of out of context to me, but we included it as part of the entire conversation as they were driving to a place called Tomato Joe's."

"And this hacker comment, what's that in reference to?" Mike asked as he started adding the tidbits of conversation together.

"Again, I don't know," Rocky answered. "It seemed to be more about the man we've heard about before, Brett, than either Jim or Maria."

"And you still have no information on him?" Mike asked, looking up.

"No, sir," Rocky answered. "We still only have his first name, and there are several enrolled at A&M."

"It appears that the three of them are having a meeting this afternoon," Mike said rereading the last of the transcript. "Perhaps you can find out something at this Bar-B-Q place where they plan to meet."

"Do you know where that is?" Mike asked, looking up again.

"It's most likely the same one where we tracked them to last time," Rocky surmised. "That's the first time Jackson ever mentioned Brett after they had dinner there a couple of days ago."

"I agree," Mike said, setting the transcript on his desk. Leaning forward and placing his elbows on the table, he continued, "I think you need to have someone there when they arrive. If nothing else, get a couple of pictures of this 'Brett' and see if you can identify him."

"Yes, sir," Rocky agreed. "We can use the school's yearbooks and see if we can find him there."

"Now, I need you to bring me the tapes that you used to make this transcript," Mike directed. "And you need to figure out a way to tape their meeting this afternoon. I want the transcript of that meeting as soon as you can get it to me, regardless of the time."

"I understand, sir," Rocky said, knowing he was being dismissed. "I'll get those tapes here within the hour."

"Have them here in 15 minutes," Mike ordered as he picked up his phone.

"Get in here," Mike said into the phone as Rocky hurried down the hall.

"Something happen?" Jerry said, coming through the door.

"Shut the door and have a seat," Mike said, getting up and rounding the desk.

Handing Jerry the transcript, Mike followed him and took a seat across the table from him.

"What do you think?" Mike asked as Jerry finished reading.

"This corn thing could be because of the list Larry gave him," Jerry said, hoping it was true.

"Then what's the hacker about? If it's the corn Larry gave him, he knows he can get the information from us," Mike argued.

Jerry looked at the transcript again and answered, "It may be something Brett's working on. Nothing to do with Jim's project."

"Just a coincidence?" Mike asked incredulously. "And, that final comment? Maria thinks there's a connection, just as Jim's been thinking. And when you add that comment about birthrates, it's just too damn coincidental!"

"What do you plan to do?" Jerry asked, laying the transcript on the table between them.

"I told Rocky to bring the actual recordings," Mike said, sitting back in his chair. "I want to hear them for myself. Maybe there's something he missed or didn't connect because he doesn't understand what connections Jim's been trying to make."

"When will he be back?" Jerry asked.

"I told him 15 minutes," Mike answered. "And I told him to tape the meeting this afternoon. We need to figure out who this Brett is and what's his interest in Jim's project."

They were still discussing the transcript when the phone rang. Mike rose from his seat and walked to the desk as he said, "Things are getting out of hand here, and if we can't stop it, others will."

After listening to the phone, Mike said, "Send him in."

Mike walked to the door and stood holding it open, saying, "Rocky's back with the tape. I want you to stay and listen to it with me."

As soon as he took the tape from Rocky, Mike said, "Let me know immediately if you get anything else from Jim's car."

"Yes, sir," Rocky said as the door closed in front of him.

Mike placed the recorder on the table and hit the play button. They listened to the entire tape before saying a word.

"Play that again from the beginning," Jerry said, leaning forward. "There's something that Maria said just as they were getting to the car that I want to hear again." Mike rewound the tape and started it again. "Again," Jerry said. "There's something I can't quite make out just before she gets into the car."

Mike repeated the rewind and start sequence, listening closely to see if he could hear what Jerry was talking about.

"It's something about the last decade of population decline," Jerry said, listening intently. "I can't make out the few words before she says that, but I swear I hear 'something-land' just before the part we can start hearing clearly."

"I don't know," Mike said, sitting back and staring at the recorder on the table. "Maybe Rocky can take the tape and see if he can have it enhanced."

"This is starting to really worry me, too," Jerry said, sitting back in his chair. "As you said, there are getting to be way too many coincidences. With a hacker in the mix, who knows what information they may be able to get."

"You assured me that the computers were clean," Mike said, looking at Jerry. "That there wasn't anything incriminating in them."

"It's not our computers," Jerry said. "If they learn about Microbiotics and trace the original corn patent to them, they can trace it to us."

"How's that possible?" Mike asked. "They no longer exist. Their computers would have been shut down for years. He can't possibly get into systems that aren't there."

"No, but the company's public records are. That includes the patent," Jerry told him. "If they find that Microbiotics developed the corn patent that we used on the barley, it would tie it to us."

"But we weren't involved with the particular project that produced the original patent," Mike argued.

"No," Jerry said, shaking his head. "We weren't, but if they find that patent and can prove it's identical to ours, which is identical to Mombasa's, we have a problem."

"Oh shit," Mike said, falling back in his chair. "I thought when they went out of business, all of their records would be removed from the system."

"They were," Jerry said. "We made sure of that when we acquired what was left of the company after bankruptcy. But their corn patent is still in the system, and it can be the one thing that can blow this whole thing apart."

"Alright," Mike said, sitting up. "Let's not get too worked up yet. There's still a lot of unknowns about this hacker, Brett, and Maria's birthrate thing. We'll just have to wait to see what Rocky learns this evening."

"I agree," Jerry said, standing up. "Besides, if Jim takes our corn GMO, maybe this whole thing will evaporate before any of them find the string that will unravel our little ball."

"I'll call you when I hear from Rocky," Mike said, getting up and returning to his desk. "It may be late, so make sure I can contact you."

CHAPTER 46

After lunch, Jim dropped Maria off at the dorm while he went to his only class for the afternoon. Promising to be at the library later, Jim waved and drove off. A few blocks later, he parked in the library lot, grabbed his briefcase, and walked to his class.

Three hours later, Jim was walking down the sidewalk when Brett pulled up alongside. "Need a ride?" Brett asked as he came to a stop.

"Sure," Jim said, tossing his briefcase into the backseat. "Library, please."

"No problem, heading there myself," Brett said, pulling out into the traffic. "How'd the class go?"

"Pretty good," Jim said. "There are several things I watched at Monogenic's that were relevant, especially when we got to the lab portion."

"Excellent," Brett said. "Are you ready for some more good news?"

"I can hardly wait," Jim said, grinning.

"You know my hacker, let's call him Deep Throat, that I asked to run the corn GMO patent?" Brett said as he pulled into the library parking lot and parked a couple of spaces from Jim's VW.

"Sure, you were meeting him for lunch today," Jim answered, wondering what Brett had found out.

"I think we may have hit the jackpot," Brett said as he shut off the motor.

"How?" Jim asked.

"Take a look at this," Brett said as he handed Jim a thick envelope.

Jim pulled a stack of sheets out of the envelope and started rapidly skimming them. Several times while he was reading, he would stop and look at Brett as if to say, *'You gotta be shitting me.'*

When he had finished the last sheet, he asked, "Where did he get all of this? It can't be a matter of public record."

"Surprisingly, most of it is," Brett said leaning back and half turned in his seat.

"For example," Brett continued, "the data on Microbiotic's is available since it went through bankruptcy court and was a publicly registered corporation before that."

"The patent, our infamous corn GMO, was registered with the US Patent Office, also public information," Brett further explained. "The exact patent wasn't, but that's the only thing that wasn't in the labyrinth of information available to the astute researcher. He *may* have violated a minor law or two delving beyond the shallow end of the pool to garner that tidbit."

"Who's this company, New Tech Biogenics?" Jim asked, looking at one of the sheets he held in his hands.

"That's the company that bought all of Microbiotic's assets in the bankruptcy proceedings," Brett answered.

"What does that have to do with us?" Jim asked, looking at Brett. "They aren't in any part of the patents we've been looking at."

"Wrong, my unwise fellow," Brett said, smiling as he explained. "One of the 'assets' New Tech bought was a certain patent."

"Why aren't they listed on the patent as the holder?" Jim asked.

"The patent only shows who it was granted to," Brett said. "Further, since it was never used, as in corn, it never showed up again after the initial registration. And since New Tech never put it on their corporate list of assets, it virtually died with the death of New Tech."

"Alright, I follow that," Jim said, still trying to figure out where Brett was heading. "But I still don't see any tie between this New Tech and Monogenic's."

"Ahhh, that's because you don't know what information I have in this envelope," Brett said holding out another envelope.

Jim took the envelope and removed the single sheet. Almost immediately he looked at Brett and said, "The sole stockholders and board members of New Tech are one Mr. Mike Hawk and one Mr. Jerry Moss."

"You wanted a connection," Brett said, smiling like a Cheshire cat. "Now you have it, in spades."

"Now, we need to get these patents over to one of the genetic professors to see if the corn GMO matches the two barley GMOs," Jim said as Maria was sneaking up behind them.

"Talking about anything interesting boys?" she joked as she walked to the passenger side and kissed Jim's cheek.

"Just about the loves of our lives," Brett smiled and told her.

"Probably a very short discussion," Maria quipped as she stood beside the door. "Are you guys heading to the library or what?"

"No reason to go there," Jim answered. "That was just the meeting place, and that's no longer needed since we're all here."

"So, what's the plan?" Maria asked, tossing her bag into the backseat on top of Jim's briefcase."

"I guess we can go for Bar-B-Q early," Jim said, getting out of his seat to let Maria climb into the back.

"Can we change?" Maria asked, settling into her seat.

"Sure, what'd you have in mind?" Brett asked as Jim got back in.

"Pizza," Maria answered. "And beer."

"Not a problem," Brett told her as he started the Jeep. "I happen to know of a little pizza and pasta place that makes Pizza Hut pizza taste worse than the boxes they use. And, they have beer!"

"Sounds good to me," Jim said, smiling as Maria reached around the seat and squeezed his arm.

CHAPTER 47

When they arrived at the restaurant, the hostess led them to a table in the empty back section away from the bar, where they were virtually assured of privacy.

The waitress arrived almost immediately with menus and water. Asking what they would like to drink, she announced that none of the draft beers were available due to a malfunction in the cooler that held the kegs.

"That's fine," Brett said. "I'd like a Shiner, and I believe these two would be happy with bottles of Budweiser."

"Sounds good to me," Jim said as he studied the menu.

"Me too," Maria said, smiling at the waitress.

"Be right back," the waitress said after scribbling their drinks on the order ticket.

"Want to fill her in?" Jim asked Brett while waiting for their beers.

"Why don't we wait until we place our orders," Brett answered. "That way, we won't be disturbed for 20 minutes or so."

"Fill me in on what?" Maria asked, looking from Brett to Jim.

"What we were discussing when you found us in the Jeep," Jim answered. "Did you get anything from your professor on the birthrate thing?"

"A little," Maria told them. "He's ruled out diseases because the WHO didn't have any data that would support any illness in that region that would affect normal conception."

"Are there diseases that'll do that?" Jim asked.

"There are several, such as autoimmune disease," Maria explained. "There, the body's immune system attacks the very organs it was meant to protect."

"What causes it to do that?" Jim asked.

"Usually hormones," Brett answered.

"Could it be possible for a high level of hormones derived from the barley to do that?" Maria asked.

"Possible," Brett said. "There have been studies that show high testosterone levels from implants in cattle have worked their way into humans. I suppose the same thing could happen with a plant."

"I doubt that," Jim countered. "We don't deal in hormones with plants."

"What about things that resist fungi?" Maria asked. "Maybe that's a plant hormone."

"Don't think so," Jim repeated, shaking his head.

"But couldn't some hybrid plant cause hormone changes in a human?" Brett asked. "We use bacteria to engineer medicines; how can you be sure?"

"I'm not absolutely sure," Jim admitted. "But I think the problem lies elsewhere."

"What other causes do you have?" Brett asked as their drinks arrived.

"I'll tell you in a minute," Maria said as she returned to looking at the menu.

"Why don't we just get a large pizza?" Jim asked, sliding his menu to the waitress.

"How about 'The Works'?" Brett asked, sliding his menu over.

Maria closed her menu and placed it on the others and said, "Fine with me."

"One large 'Works,'" the waitress said, writing it on her order ticket.

"Anything else?" she asked before turning away.

"Give us a few minutes, and then check on the beer problem we may have," Jim said, smiling at her.

As the waitress walked away, Maria said, "Endometriosis is also a problem, but it only affects less than 50 percent of infertile women."

"Since it only affects infertile women, it doesn't cause infertility on a scale as we're discussing," Brett offered.

"Unless something in the barley is causing widespread endometriosis," Jim countered.

"Even if it did, studies show that more than 50 percent wouldn't be affected," Maria argued.

"Okay, what else?" Brett asked to stop the argument.

"Polycystic Ovary Syndrome, or PCOS, is probably the most frequent cause of infertility," Maria answered. "I tend to see this as the most logical due to the percentage of women that it affects."

"How does it cause infertility?" Jim asked.

"It causes the adrenal glands to secrete more androgen, a hormone that interferes with the development of the ovarian follicles and egg release during ovulation," Brett explained. "There's been quite a bit of research on it in the Pharming industry."

"So, there are at least two hormone-related causes," Jim said. "Maybe there's something in the barley that causes a spike in hormones."

"What about causing a decrease in sperm?" Maria asked. "Maybe the problem is with the man, not the woman."

"That's entirely possible," Brett said, nodding his head. "The corn we were discussing apparently caused a protein to attach to the sperm and caused it to become too heavy to successfully reach the egg."

"Lots of ways to cause the infertility problem, if it is infertility," Jim said. "And the only one we have any data on is the corn that affected the male. Maybe that's where we need to look."

"We still haven't proven that Zwairiland is using the barley GMO," Brett argued. "That still must be proven."

"True," Maria said. "But you were going to tell me about what you were discussing earlier."

"Oh yes," Brett said. "Basically, we can connect Mr. Hawk and Mr. Moss with the corn GMO that appears to be identical to the barley GMO. That's the tie Jim was looking for to tie Monogenic's to Mombasa."

"Just Hawk and Moss?" Maria asked.

"Yes, they're the only ones listed in New Tech Biogenics corporate information," Brett answered.

"Who's New Tech Biogenics?" Maria asked. "I thought we were just looking at Monogenic's and Mombasa."

"They're the company that actually owns the patent on the corn," Brett explained. "And, since they run Monogenic's, they could've given it to Mombasa."

"They run Monogenic's?" Maria asked. "I thought they were just the President and Vice President of the part here in College Station."

"They are," Jim said, nodding his head.

"Well then," Maria continued, "what if they, Hawk and Moss, are doing this without their boss's knowledge? What if it's not Monogenic's but a couple of rogue officers?"

"I suppose that's possible," Jim said as he thought about it.

"Makes more sense to me," Brett said, getting enthused about the direction they were heading. "It's easier for a couple of people to conspire together than an entire corporation. If you get too many people involved, the probability of a leak increases."

"Do you think we should see if we can get someone above these guys to listen to us?" Maria asked hopefully.

"Not yet" Jim cautioned. "We don't know for sure how high this goes and letting them know we've discovered their secret wouldn't be wise right now."

"Not to mention that we only have suppositions right now," Brett said as the waitress rounded the corner with their pizza. "We still have to show that it's the same barley, the same as the corn, it's being grown or distributed in Zwairiland, and it's the cause."

CHAPTER 48

As they were eating their pizza, Rocky called Mike at his office. "Bad news," he said as Mike answered the phone.

"What's gone wrong now?" Mike asked getting more upset with his Chief of Security as things appeared to continually spiral downhill, or at least out of Rocky's control.

"I guess nothing's really wrong," Rocky clarified. "Just not what we wanted."

"Again, what's gone wrong?" Mike repeated.

"Mr. Jackson and Ms. Pompillio never went to the Bar-B-Q place," Rocky answered.

"Where did they go?" Mike asked.

"We don't know," Rocky admitted. "I had two people at separate tables waiting for them to arrive, and they're still there, but it's long past when they were supposed to be there with this Brett fellow."

"Maybe they're on their way," suggested Mike.

"Don't think so," Rocky said. "Jackson's car is still in the library parking lot, and one of my men walked through the computer section, and they weren't there."

"So, what's your plan now?" Mike asked.

"I'll leave the men at the restaurant for another hour or until we see where Jackson's car goes," Rocky answered.

"I suppose there's no other choice," Mike said, disappointed that he had such little control over the situation.

"Mind if I ask what's so important about this Brett guy?" Rocky asked. "I didn't know we were investigating him."

"We don't know what role he's playing," Mike lied. "It's possible that he's Jim's contact with a competing company. Or, it's also possible that he's one of those GMO opponents that's looking for any adverse effects of any of our products."

"I see," Rocky said, nodding his head. "I'll get someone to park at the school and see if we can catch them coming back for Jackson's car. If this Brett is with them, as they planned, we'll at least get the license tag and be able to identify him from that."

"That's a good idea," Mike said. "Just make damn sure whoever's there isn't spotted."

"I'll do it myself," Rocky said. "I'll use an old Falcon that one of my men drives. That piece of crap won't be noticed among all of the other junky student cars."

"Fine," Mike said. "Give me a call when you have something."

"Yes, sir," Rocky said as the connection was broken.

Mike called Jerry's office and said, "We lost them. Maybe you better come in for a minute."

"Yes?" Jerry said as he arrived at Mike's office door.

"Have a seat," Mike said, getting out of his chair. "Have you had any contact with Jim lately?"

"No, sir," Jerry answered, taking his usual chair.

"What about Larry?" Mike asked, sitting down across the table from Jerry.

"The last I got was that Jim was supposed to check back with him this afternoon about his research on an alternate GMO," Jerry answered.

"Has he heard from Jim?" Mike asked.

"Not sure," Jerry admitted. "Jim was supposed to get the data Larry had gathered the next time he came to the lab, and that's tomorrow at the earliest."

"Give Larry a quick call and see if he's had any contact since he briefed you on the list he gave Jim," Mike directed.

"Sure," Jerry said, getting out of his chair and going to Mike's desk. Dialing the number Larry had listed as his home phone, Jerry waited until it had rang several times before saying, "He's not at home."

"Try the lab," Mike said. "Maybe he's there working on that list."

Jerry dialed Dr. Thompson's number from memory and waited while it rang. "No answer there," he said as he dialed the security desk at the entrance. "I'll see if the guard can page him."

A few seconds later, Jerry held his hand over the phone and said, "The guard says that Larry just signed out a minute ago. He's going to see if he can catch him before he leaves."

Minutes later, Jerry removed his hand from the phone and said, "Larry? Jerry Moss here."

After waiting for Larry's response, Jerry asked, "Have you heard from Jim this afternoon?"

Hearing that he hadn't, Jerry asked, "If you aren't busy, can you swing by Mr. Hawk's office before you go home?"

"That'd be fine," Jerry said before hanging up.

Jerry walked back to his seat and said, "He'll be here in about 10 or 15 minutes. He said he's bringing the data he's collected on the corn GMO and a couple of others with him.

"Rocky's been questioning our investigation," Mike said as Jerry took his seat.

"What do you mean?" Jerry asked.

"Initially, he wondered why we were digging this far into Jim's activities," Mike answered. "Then this afternoon, when he called to tell me that he couldn't identify Brett because they didn't go to the restaurant where he expected them to be, he asked why we were interested in Brett."

"What did you tell him?" Jerry asked.

"Just that we're concerned that he may be a contact between Jim and some other organization," Mike answered. "I'm not sure how much longer we can use him before he starts asking the wrong questions."

"Do you have any other options?" Jerry asked.

"We can hire that little company we used when we were trying to force Microbiotics into bankruptcy," Mike answered. "At least they don't ask questions; you just tell them the objective and let them earn their rather exorbitant fees."

"Do you think that's wise?" Jerry asked. "They may tie that operation to this one and start adding the parts together as Jim's been inadvertently doing."

"I doubt it," Mike said. "They've got no expertise in GMOs or reason to try to find out what happened to Microbiotics after they went bankrupt."

"You're probably right," Jerry said nodding his head. "When will you contact them?"

"Let's give Rocky another day or two," Mike said. "Or, if he keeps asking questions, we'll tell him we have all the information we need and give him something else to do."

"Sounds reasonable," Jerry said as Larry knocked on the open door.

"Come in, Larry," Mike said. "Take a seat."

"Thanks," Larry said as he walked to the open chair beside Jerry.

"Thanks for coming so quickly," Mike told him as he took his seat.

"Is that the GMO data?" Jerry asked as Larry started to put a folder on the table.

"Yes, sir," Larry said, handing the folder to Jerry. "There's a complete workup on the corn GMO and three others that I used."

Jerry glanced through the information Larry had compiled and handed each to Mike as he finished. "Looks good," Jerry said as he handed the last sheet to Mike.

"This should certainly satisfy Jim," Mike agreed as he finished reading the material.

"Did Jim say anything about when he's coming back to the lab?" Jerry asked.

"No, sir," Larry answered. "He said he'd call me this afternoon, but I never heard from him. Since he didn't say anything about classes, I expect to see him sometime tomorrow."

"He didn't say anything about it?" Mike asked.

"No, sir," Larry repeated. "But I think he's running out of time on his thesis and wants to see the data I've gotten for him as soon as he can."

"Good," Mike said, handing the folder back to Larry. "Just give us a call when you hear from him or when he shows up."

"Yes, sir," Larry said, taking the folder from Mike's hand as he stood up. "I'll let you know if I hear anything."

"Thanks for coming," Jerry said, standing to escort Larry to the door.

As he turned back toward his chair, the phone rang. Answering, he said, "Mr. Hawk's office."

"He's right here, Rocky," Jerry said, handing Mike the phone.

"Yes, Rocky," Mike said as he took the phone.

Listening for a few seconds, he then said, "Great. Let me know what you've found tomorrow morning."

Hanging up the phone, Mike said, "He's got the license plate number from a Jeep that Jim and Maria were in. He'll know who it belongs to tomorrow morning when he can get his contact at the Sheriff's office to run them.

"Think that's Brett?" Jerry asked, still standing.

"Probably," Mike answered. "He was supposed to be with them this afternoon. Looks like they took his car instead of Jim's."

"Too bad we don't have a bug in his," Jerry said as Mike started preparing to leave.

"We'll see," Mike said as he headed for the door. "I'll talk to Rocky in the morning and let you know if we need to do anything else."

CHAPTER 49

The following morning, Jim headed to the lab, hoping to be there by eight o'clock. He hadn't made any arrangements with Dr. Thompson, but he felt sure that the doctor would include him in any of the procedures they were doing today.

He was also anxious to see what Larry had found on the GMOs on the list. The more he thought about it, the more he wanted to get one of them for his thesis. Not only would it allow him to complete it on time, but it would hopefully show Mike and Jerry that he had lost interest in the barley.

If he stayed focused on something else for a couple of more days while Maria and Brett did their digging, maybe he would be enough of a diversion to keep them from discovering that the three of them were slowly uncovering their secret, whatever that was.

As he pulled into the parking lot, he spotted Larry heading for the entrance. Killing the engine and getting out, he yelled, "Hey Larry!"

Larry turned and saw Jim coming toward him. Waiting until he was just a few feet away, he said, "I didn't know you were coming in this morning."

"Guess I forgot to mention it," Jim said, shaking Larry's hand. "I was hoping that Dr. Thompson had something interesting for me to do today."

"He's always got something interesting going on," Larry said as he held the door open.

"I imagine so," Jim agreed as he approached the guard's desk and started signing in.

Waiting for Larry to sign in, Jim watched the guard inspect the envelope Larry had handed him. When the guard handed the envelope back, and they were entering the dressing chamber, he asked, "Do they always inspect packages coming in?"

"And out," Larry answered as he pulled on his white overalls. "Not that a guard would know what the papers really mean, but I think it's more to make sure that we know they'll look at everything."

"Sort of a deterrence," Jim said, pulling on his booties.

"I suppose so," Larry said, standing by the door that led to the hall. "I guess if someone was to deliver a strange package, or someone that hadn't been here as long as I have, was to try to bring something in or take something out, they might call for one of the techs to look at it."

"Sounds reasonable," Jim said as Larry handed him the envelope.

"Here's your GMOs," Larry said as they approached Dr. Thompson's door. "I did a complete search on the first one on the list, some corn products, and some others. You can take your pick, and I'll help you if you pick one I haven't researched."

"Thanks," Jim said as they entered the office.

"Good morning, Mr. Mallory, Mr. Jackson," the secretary said as she looked up from her desk. "How can I help you today?"

"Good morning," Jim replied. "I was hoping that Dr. Thompson had something available for me to do this morning."

"I'm afraid he's not coming in until around noon today," she told him. "Is there anything I can do for you?"

"I guess not," Jim said, disappointed and mildly chastising himself for not letting the doctor know he would be available this morning.

"I have a suggestion," Larry said.

"What?" Jim asked.

"I'm not scheduled for anything too important this morning," Larry answered. "Why don't we find a room and go over these GMOs and see if there's something you're interested in."

"Might as well," Jim said, looking at the envelope. "At least I won't be wasting my morning."

"Why don't you use the conference room next door?" the secretary suggested. "There're a couple of computers in there that aren't being used this morning."

"Thanks," Larry said. "That sounds perfect. The computers aren't password protected, are they?"

"Of course they are," the secretary said, smiling and getting up. "I'll take you in and get them online."

After unlocking the door, she walked to the row of computers and asked, "Do you want one or two?"

"Better make it two," Larry said as he followed her. "That way, I can use one to find whatever Jim may need, and I can use the other one to dig into the files whenever he needs my help."

"Okay, there you are," she said as she logged onto the two computers that were side by side. "Just call if you run into any problems."

As she turned to leave, she asked, "Mr. Jackson, is there any message you want to leave for Dr. Thompson?"

"No, Ma'am," Jim answered. "I'll stop by when we're done if I think of anything. Oh, I do need to leave him a copy of my class schedule."

"Fine," she said, heading for the door. "Just leave it with me when you get a chance."

"Where do you want to start?" Larry asked, taking his seat.

"Might as well start at the top," Jim said, sitting down and pulling the sheets from the envelope.

"Is this one from the top of the list?" Jim asked, studying the information.

Larry leaned over and looked at it before saying, "Yes, that was the first one on the list."

Jim sat it on the table and asked, "What are these?"

Larry took the papers and said, "This one's another corn GMO we did several years ago. There's also one in here for soybeans and another for rice."

Handing them back, he continued, "I just picked these randomly from the rest of the list for you to look at."

"Did you notice anything different about any of them?" Jim asked, picking up the sheets on the first corn GMO.

"Of course," Larry answered. "I didn't notice it until I'd looked at the others, but that one has more of the criteria you asked for, and more importantly, it's proven to be very successful in production."

"Alright," Jim said. "Let's start with it. Could you give me a quick brief on everything here and we'll see if I have any questions."

"Sure," Larry said, typing the GMO's ID number into the search bar. "I'll have it on the screen in a second."

Jim took a new yellow legal pad and pencil from the stack that was on his desk, asking, "Is it alright if I use these?"

"Use anything in here that you need," Larry answered as he found the GMO he was looking for.

Copying the basic information on the top of the first sheet, Jim asked, "When was the project started?"

Larry scrolled up and down the screen as he walked Jim through all of the information on the product. Reciting his prepared litany of answers to the questions he'd anticipated, he elaborated on all of the things he thought would lead Jim to this GMO.

After about an hour, Jim said, "Okay, that's enough on that one. Let's look at the rice."

For the next 20 minutes or so, Larry walked Jim through the entire procedure to the production statistics before Jim called a halt to the rice.

"Do you have the list with you?" Jim asked, sitting back in his chair.

Larry typed a few words into the computer and answered, "It's right here. What are you interested in?"

Jim leaned over and looked at the screen. Seeing the four GMOs Larry had researched, Jim pointed to a tomato GMO and said, "Let's look at that one."

"No problem," Larry said, typing the GMO's ID number into the search bar. "Any particular reason?"

"I just want to know what's in my catsup," Jim joked.

Jim waited until Larry had retrieved all of the data and then said, "It looks like that one didn't last too long in the field."

"Nope," Larry agreed. Typing a new subject into the search bar, he said, "Looks like it was replaced by another GMO that came out a year or so later."

"Okay," Jim said, looking at his notes. "I think I'll take this corn GMO. As you said, it satisfies all of my criteria and has proven its value in the actual production area."

"Good," Larry said, returning his screen to the original corn data. "Is there anything else you'd like to see?"

"Do you have the results of all of the tests on this one?" Jim asked, scribbling more notes on his pad.

"Such as?" Larry asked, searching his screen for lab test results.

"Oh, I don't know," Jim answered. "Any problems with animal reaction to prolonged use, information on next-generation abnormalities, percent of allergic reactions. Any adverse conditions resulting from ingesting the corn."

Larry searched the files for several minutes with Jim watching and finally said, "It looks like there was a .0017 percent of abdominal stress in the test mice."

"How's that compare with other tests?" Jim asked, scribbling notes of what he was seeing on the screen.

"That would be way below the acceptable tolerance," Larry said. "There are acceptable thresholds on every product. Just as a certain percentage of people are allergic to peanuts, there's a percentage that is going to exhibit an intolerance to any product. Most importantly, a mild upset stomach in a few of the test subjects is a very minor consideration to the improved product."

"I agree," Jim said, putting his notes away. "Even mother nature can't please everyone. I think I'll call it a day, go to the library, and try to put all of this information into a reasonable format for my thesis."

"Glad I could help," Larry said, getting out of his chair. "When are you coming back?"

"Probably tomorrow afternoon," Jim said as he tore his notes from the yellow pad. "I'll let Dr. Thompson's secretary know if I'm coming in."

"Well, if you need any more help, let her know, and she'll call me," Larry said as he watched Jim put all of the material back in the envelope along with his notes.

CHAPTER 50

Jim left the lab and headed back to the campus to see if he could locate either Maria or Brett. Glancing at his briefcase and wondering if he was making the right decision on using the corn GMO, he didn't see the cooler that must have fallen from someone's car and was in the middle of his lane until it was almost too late.

Slamming on his brakes and swerving at the last second, he hit the curb and came to a stop with his right front wheel on the grass just short of the sidewalk. Thankful that there wasn't anyone on the sidewalk, he sat back and took a deep breath. Looking at the passenger seat, he saw that his briefcase had fallen onto the floorboard.

Leaning over to retrieve it, he turned his head slightly and was staring at the underside of the dash on the passenger side. Just as his hand grabbed the briefcase, something shiny caught his eye. Letting go of the briefcase, he bent further into the area in front of the passenger seat.

Reaching under the dash, he pulled a small piece of electronic equipment loose from the metal backside of the dash. Holding it, he noticed that it'd been held in place by a magnet on the back. Although he wasn't the greatest at keeping the car spotless, he knew that this was something he'd never seen when he'd cleaned the interior.

Holding it in his hand, he sat up and turned it over and over. The most notable thing was the wire that extended a couple of inches from the circular object. Although he'd never seen a micro transmitter, he suspected that was exactly what he was holding in his hand.

'Son of a Bitch!' he thought, *'The bastards have bugged my car.'*

Now, it became clear that he hadn't been wrong when he suspected that someone had been in his briefcase. Wondering what else they'd done, he stuck the transmitter back under the dash and drove home to check if they'd done anything there.

Parking in an open slot close to his apartment, he took his briefcase and headed for his door. Shaking his head at the incredibility of them eavesdropping on him in his car, he just couldn't believe they'd bug his home.

Inside, he tossed his briefcase on the kitchen table and looked around. Remembering the white dust he'd seen the other day, he went to the same area and started looking around. Looking beneath the cupboard, he noticed a small scratch in the sheetrock. As he rubbed it with his fingers, he felt a wire and a piece of tape directly above the scratch. Running his hand along the wire, he touched something on the bottom of the cupboard. Almost lying on the countertop and looking up, he saw a black rectangular object taped to the wood just above his face.

Now furious, he pulled his head back and looked around to see if there was anything else that seemed out of place or unusual. Seeing nothing, he went into the living room and swept the area with his eyes. Spotting the telephone, he picked it up and unscrewed the mouthpiece.

Not seeing anything there, he replaced it, turned the base over, and saw another small circular device identical to the one he'd discovered in his car. Setting the phone down on the table, he silently cussed Monogenic's or whoever had done this to him.

Standing there thinking about everything he and Maria had said or done that they'd probably monitored, he was tempted to rip the house apart to see just how many of these little bugs they'd installed.

Realizing that if they knew he'd found them, they'd just deny any knowledge about it, and he couldn't prove anything. But, now knowing they were there, he'd make sure nothing was ever said that hinted at what he was still, now more than ever, looking into.

Going back into the kitchen, he grabbed his briefcase from the table and headed for the door. Halfway to his car, he stopped and thought about someone listening to him and Maria when they'd been in bed. Or the shower. *'Alright,'* he said to himself as he continued to the car, *'you bastards want to listen to everything I do or say. I'll see if I can accommodate you.'*

Driving to the campus, he wondered just how Maria would take knowing that someone had been listening to their most intimate moments. He debated only half a second about not telling her, but she needed to know regardless of how she felt about it or how angry she got.

Now, near lunchtime, he parked on the curb in front of the library and hurried up the steps. Not seeing her inside, he went back to his car and was just starting the engine when Brett pulled up beside him with Maria in his passenger seat.

"Going somewhere?" Maria asked, smiling at Jim.

"No," Jim answered, killing the engine. Almost saying that he needed to show her something, he just said, "Hey Brett, how about we take your Jeep and go grab a burger?"

"Sure," Brett said. "Jump in and we'll go."

"Let me park over in the lot instead of here at the curb," Jim said, starting the car.

"We'll be right behind you," Brett said as Jim put the VW in gear.

After parking, Jim got his briefcase from the passenger seat and walked to where Brett sat idling. Maria had climbed into the rear seat, and Jim handed her his briefcase as he got into his seat.

"What-a-Burger?" Brett asked, putting the Jeep in gear.

"Fine," Jim said, waiting for them to get away from his car before saying anything.

Suddenly thinking about his briefcase, he turned to Maria and asked, "Could you hand me my briefcase, please?"

As she handed it to him, she asked, "What'd you do today?"

Putting his index finger to his lips, he motioned for her to be quiet for a moment. Opening the briefcase, he started pulling all of his notes and other papers from inside. Handing them to Maria, he emptied everything else out and ran his hand around the inside before being sure there wasn't another listening device.

"Thanks," Jim said as he took everything from Maria and put it back in the briefcase.

"What was that all about?" Brett asked, having watched Jim motion for quiet and inspecting the briefcase.

"We've got a problem," Jim said, handing the briefcase back to Maria.

"What?" Maria asked.

"They, or somebody, have been listening to everything we've said for the last few days," Jim answered.

"How do you know that?" Brett asked as they pulled onto University Drive.

"First, I found something in my car," Jim explained. "It must have gotten dislodged when I jumped the curb trying not to hit a cooler that was in the road."

"What'd you find?" Maria asked, leaning forward and placing her arms on the back of Jim's seat.

"I'm not positive, but I think it's a transmitter of some kind," Jim answered. "And that's not all."

"What else?" Maria asked.

Jim turned to look at her and said, "My apartment was bugged."

Maria sat back with a look of astonishment on her face and asked, "Are you sure?"

"Positive," Jim said, waiting for her to fully comprehend what it meant.

"You mean someone listened to everything we said or did at your place?" she asked as she realized the same thing that Jim had just minutes ago.

"I'm afraid so," Jim said, shaking his head.

"Those son-of-a-bitching BASTARDS!" Maria shouted, pounding the back of Jim's seat. "I'll kill the bastards! Spying on us in bed, perverted pieces of shit. I'll kill every one of them."

Brett pulled over to the curb and killed the engine, waiting for Maria to settle down. "Are you sure about all of this, Jim? Could there be some other explanation?"

"I've never really seen transmitters like these, but that's all they could be," Jim said.

"How long do you think they've been there," Maria asked still shocked at the invasion to her, their, privacy.

"I'm not sure," Jim answered. "But I noticed something a couple of days ago that looked like powdered sugar, or that powdered cream stuff, on the counter. I didn't think anything about it until I found the thing in my car."

"Then I went home and found the ones there," he concluded. "So, it must have been right after my first visit to the lab. The day I first told you, I thought someone had been in my briefcase."

"So, they know everything you've talked about," Brett said. "That could be bad."

"I don't think so," Jim said, shaking his head. "I don't think we ever discussed much of it either at home or in my car. It was mostly in the library or when we were with you, like the restaurant."

"I don't give a rat's ass about that," Maria angrily said. "I'm pissed about them listening to us at your house."

"I understand," Jim said, turning to her. "That's something that upsets me, too. I never thought anyone would be spying on us for any reason."

"You'll rip every one of those damn things out of your house right now!" Maria demanded, crossing her arms. "Or, you'll never get me in that bed again."

"I wish I could," Jim said, shaking his head. "But what if I miss one? How would I ever know for sure?"

"Fine," she said, turning her head from Jim. "You can forget ever having me in your apartment again."

"I know," Jim agreed. "I agree that we can't meet there. I'll have to think of somewhere else or move."

"Why don't you think about this for a few minutes," Brett advised. "If anything changes in your normal routines, they'll know something's up. Why don't you just keep doing everything you've been doing until we get this sorted out?"

"I will *not* be in that apartment!" Maria stated firmly. "Never again!"

"I understand," Jim repeated. "I don't want to either. But this may be an opportunity for us to use their little spy bugs for our benefit."

"What do you mean?" Maria asked. "You want to put on a show for them? Give them some X-rated stuff? Count me out!"

"Of course not," Jim answered. "I mean about what we're doing on the GMO thing. I don't expect you to ever come to my place again. I'll change apartments as soon as we figure out what's going on with the birthrate thing and the barley in Zwairiland."

"Since we know where they can hear us, we pretend we've moved on and forgotten about anything we've talked about," Jim continued. "If they think we've given up on the barley thing, maybe they won't watch us so much."

"I agree," Brett said. "Since most of the work's already in progress, we're just really waiting for the professors or my hacker to get more information. We can always meet at some restaurant or bar to discuss it."

"Alright," Maria said, somewhat mollified. "But I plan to stick it to those bastards as soon as I can. Now that I'm sure they're hiding something, I'll spend as much time as it takes to get them.

CHAPTER 51

While Jim was revealing what *'they'* had done to him, Rocky was briefing Mike and Jerry on what he'd discovered about Brett. "His name's Brett Weston, and he's originally from some little town up around Seattle. Nothing at all on his record, not even a speeding ticket that we could find."

"He's been here for almost seven years, now working on his Ph.D. in Pharmaceuticals," Rocky told them as he looked at his notes. "He has an apartment off campus, apparently lives by himself, and has no current girlfriend that we've been able to identify."

"What's his tie with Jim?" Mike asked as Rocky closed his notepad.

"Other than seeing them together for the last couple of days, I don't know," Rocky answered.

"I'd guess that they probably shared some classes over the years," Jerry offered. "Since both of them have been here about the same amount of time and both are studying genetic subjects, I'd just guess they're sort of like classmates."

"That's a reasonable assumption," Mike agreed. "Do you have anything else, Rocky?"

"No, sir," Rocky answered, preparing to leave. "Would you like for me to look into him any further?"

"No, that won't be necessary," Mike answered. "It looks like he's just some friend of Jim's and of no concern to us. Just keep your eyes open on Jim and let us know if you hear anything."

"Yes, sir," Rocky said as he turned to leave.

"What do you really think?" Jerry asked as soon as Rocky was out of earshot.

"Not sure," Mike answered as the phone rang. "He could be helping Jim, and we'll find that out soon enough."

"Put him on," Mike said into the phone after answering it.

"Good morning, Larry," Mike said, looking at Jerry. "What have you got for us?"

Listening for a minute, Mike then said, "Thanks. I hope we've been able to help Jim with his project. You keep up the good work and let us know if he needs anything else."

Hanging up, Mike said, "Jim's decided to take the corn GMO as his thesis project."

"Are we sure?" Jerry asked hopefully.

"Pretty positive," Mike said, relieved that their scare may be over. "Larry spent the morning with him, and Jim told him he'd take the data to the library and try to organize it for his thesis."

"That sounds pretty positive," Jerry said. "What do we do about him now? Drop the surveillance?"

"Not yet," Mike said. "I want to hold off for a few more days. Even if he's changed his thesis, I still think he may want to find out about the barley."

"Alright," Jerry said. "I'll see if Dr. Thompson can get him a little more involved in something at the lab. If he's spending all of his time on his new thesis, classes, and the lab, he won't have much time to dig around on the barley."

"Even if he does," Mike said, leaning back in his chair, "we'll certainly hear about it from the bugs."

"What about this hacker thing?" Jerry asked.

"I wish I knew," Mike answered. "But, unless we start monitoring Brett, which would really make Rocky suspicious, we just have to get our information through Jim's conversations."

As Mike and Jerry were beginning to relax a little, Brett was driving toward What-a-Burger and talking about what his hacker had found.

"Deep Throat came up with some interesting information," Brett said as he pulled into the drive thru.

"What's that?" Jim asked as they inched toward the ordering station.

"He decided to take a deeper look at New Tech Biogenics," Brett answered.

"I thought he had all of the information on them already," Maria asked.

"He did, on the corporation and its operations here," Brett said, pulling forward as another car gave its order and left.

"He decided to look into the financials," Brett said, looking at both of them. "He found something very interesting."

Pulling up to the order station, Brett said, "I'll take a number one combo with cheese, jalapenos, and a Dr Pepper.

"Make it two," Jim said, leaning over Brett.

"Same," Maria said from the back.

Listening to the static and trying to interpret the broken English, Brett finally said, "Three number-one combos with cheese, jalapenos, and three Dr Peppers."

Hearing something that sounded like his order and directions to pull to the window, Brett shook his head and pulled up to the window the car in front had just left.

"I got it," Brett said as he pulled out his wallet. "You can get tonight."

After paying and getting their food, Brett said, "Why don't we just pull over here and eat? That way, nobody will bother us, and we don't have to worry about being overheard."

"Sure," Jim said as he handed Maria one of the sacks.

"Okay," Maria said as they parked, and Brett killed the engine. "What about the financials?"

"Just a second," Brett said as he pulled the thin film from the top of the catsup container. "I'd like to at least have a bite before I have to start answering questions."

"Take your time," Jim said smiling that Maria seemed to have dropped her outrage over the bugging of his apartment.

"Okay," Brett finally said after taking a bite of his burger, "Deep Throat couldn't find any financial institution here in the States that had more than a couple thousand dollars belonging to New Tech."

"Not much for a genetic company," Jim said. "That wouldn't last an hour at Monogenic's."

"Well, they're not much of a genetic company," Brett said as he munched on a fry.

"What are they?" Maria asked, wiping her mouth with a napkin.

"More of a holding company," Brett said. "Since they took over all of Microbiotic's assets, meaning the patent, they've had no activity."

"That's sort of strange, isn't it?" Jim asked. "I mean, why start a company that owns a patent you don't intend to use?"

"I'm not done," Brett said, taking a drink of his Dr Pepper.

"I said there weren't any substantial assets here in the States," Brett told them as they waited for him to say what'd been found.

"Okay, I'll bite," Maria asked. "Where did he find assets?"

"The Grand Caymans," Brett answered.

"How much?" Jim asked, surprised that even Deep Throat could discover offshore banking information.

"Just over 100 million dollars," Brett announced.

"Holy shit," Jim said, amazed at the amount. "How did they get that much money without the US finding out?"

"It appears that it was electronically transferred from another account at the same bank over a period of almost 20 years," Brett answered as he finished his meal.

"That's five million every year," Maria said. "What could they have that would be worth that much? Like you said, they only have the patent."

"My guess?" Brett said, looking at both of them. "The patent."

"No way a patent that can't be used due to the fertility issue would be worth that much," Jim said.

"Unless it's as you've both been thinking," Brett countered. "The ties with Mombasa and Monogenic's? The birthrate in Zwairiland? Maybe that barley patent you stumbled upon is worth more than a few million dollars to a country if they needed to eliminate a neighboring country's population."

"Who do you mean?" Maria asked as she thought about the enormity of what they'd discovered.

"The relationship between the President of Ethiopia and the head of Mombasa," Jim said, nodding his head. "Somehow, he found out about the problems the patent caused while he was working at Monogenic's and told his brother."

"Probably," Brett agreed. "And I'd bet that they're trying to reduce the population of Zwairiland for some reason."

"I think I know the reason," Maria said, sitting up in her seat.

"You mean that stuff you were telling me about what happened during the famine and rebellion?" Jim asked.

"That's exactly what I mean," Maria said.

"What are you talking about?" Brett asked as Jim and Maria smiled knowingly at each other.

"The motive," Jim answered. "Why would someone want to annihilate an entire population? And, there's all of that untapped oil reserves. Ethiopia certainly has a motive."

"That'd take generations this way," Brett said, shaking his head. "Why not another way? And what about the high possibility that some of their own population could be affected?"

"If you go undiscovered, as they have so far," Maria answered, "no one can charge you with genocide."

"And I really doubt if a little *collateral damage* would concern a man that's willing to try to annihilate an entire population," Jim added.

"That's the second time we've come to this conclusion," Brett said, looking at Jim.

CHAPTER 52

After lunch, Jim went to his afternoon class while Brett and Maria went their separate ways. Maria stopped by to see the professor who was looking into the population decline in Zwairiland.

Using his contacts at WHO, he found that there had been no disease outbreaks in the area, no skirmishes that'd reduced the male population, and certainly no famine.

"As a matter of fact," the professor told her, "there's been an abundant source of nutrition. According to the WHO and the World Food Programme, the WFP, there's been a dramatic increase of supplies in Zwairiland."

"Then what could be causing the population decline and the birthrate decrease?" Maria asked.

"That's being looked into," the professor said. "Once I brought this to their attention, the WHO and WFB have agreed to send agents over there to see if they can find out what's going on."

"When will we know what they've found?" Maria asked.

"Could be months, could be years," the professor told her. "Once they do their investigations, they'll collaborate and come up with a joint conclusion. That may be the hardest because of somewhat conflicting interests."

"How can they not have the same interests?" Maria asked, dumbfounded.

"The WHO is more into disease issues while the WFP is basically concerned with nutritional issues and poverty," the professor explained. "While they're both part of the United Nations (UN), they jealously guard their turf and want to use anything like this to increase their program's funding."

"So, the people at the UN are going to let this go unsolved because of politics?" Maria asked.

"That's the way it works," the professor agreed. "It's about funding and power, not to mention each country wants to use the organizations to get more international assistance."

"Okay," Maria said as she prepared to leave. "I'll see if I can't find another way to bring this to someone's attention that can make a faster decision."

"I wish you luck," the professor said as he escorted her to the door. "Let me know what you're doing, and if I can help, I'll be glad to."

"Thanks," Maria said as she left the office. "I appreciate what you've done so far."

While Maria was getting disappointing news about how long governmental involvement was going to take, Brett was talking to the Head of the Pharmaceutical Department, Dr. Holder.

Presenting him with copies of all the information they'd gathered on Microbiotics corn GMO patent, Monogenic's' barley GMO patent, and Mombasa's barley GMO patent, Brett asked, "Is it possible to determine the similarities between these patents?"

"Let me see," Dr. Holder said. "I'll take a quick look and run them through the computer to see if it can match the exact genes that were inserted."

"How long do you think that will take?" Brett asked as the doctor read through the data.

"Could take a day or so," Dr. Holder replied, engrossed in the complexity of the patents. "How soon do you need this?"

"As soon as possible," Brett answered.

"May I ask why?" Dr. Holder asked, looking up from the papers.

"I'd rather not say," Brett answered. "At this point, all I can tell you is that it appears that the Mombasa patent is being used unethically if it's a version of the Microbiotics corn patent."

"How did you come to this conclusion?" the doctor asked, wondering if this was just some case of crying wolf by a student.

"I can't give you all of the information," Brett said, "but there are other issues that led me, and a couple of others, to this theory. It's not a conclusion yet."

"What other issues are you talking about?" Dr. Holder asked as he got more interested in what Brett was saying.

Brett thought about it for a minute and then said, "A fellow Ph.D. student stumbled upon the Monogenic's patent while working on his thesis; that sort of started it."

"What do you mean 'stumbled'?" Dr. Holder asked.

"Just a random search for potential GMOs dealing with crop production," Brett answered.

"So, he's not in my department," the doctor surmised.

"No, sir," Brett said, shaking his head. "His degree is in Molecular Biology."

"Alright, that's a logical area to be working on this," the doctor said, nodding his head. "Anything else?"

"Yes, sir," Brett said. "Another student in the Master's program for Archaeogenetics found a problem with declining birthrates."

"So, how does all this tie together?" Dr. Holder asked.

"That Microbiotics patent, the corn, was pulled from production after it demonstrated a contraceptive effect," Brett answered.

"So, you're saying that a corn GMO that had a contraceptive effect may have been introduced into a population that has shown a decline in birthrates," Dr. Holder said.

"Yes, sir," Brett answered, nodding his head. "That's why I need to know if the three GMOs are essentially the same."

"You believe it's the barley, not the corn," Dr. Holder said, now understanding what Brett was trying not to tell him.

"All I can really say is that I, or we, think something has caused the decline in birthrates," Brett answered. "Since the corn GMO isn't being used but appears to be similar to the barley GMOs, there's potentially a tie."

"Alright," Dr. Holder said, standing up. "I'll run these through our program to see if they're the same or share a common gene insertion. Stop by around noon tomorrow, and I'll see if I can give you the answer."

"Thanks," Brett said, shaking the doctor's hand. "I appreciate it. And, please, I'd rather keep this just between us for now."

"Not a problem," Dr. Holder said, laughing. "I'd never discuss something as farfetched as this and risk the credibility of this University without absolute proof."

When Jim finished his class, he walked to the library and looked for either Maria or Brett inside. Seeing neither, he left and was walking toward his car when Brett pulled up.

"Done with class?" Brett asked, stopping beside him.

"Finally," Jim answered. "There was some jerk that kept asking questions after the class was supposed to be over. That'd normally be fine, and I certainly understand the need to ask questions when you don't understand something, but why didn't he ask when the topic was being discussed instead of 30 minutes later."

"I know what you mean," Brett said, nodding his head. "Where are you going now?"

"I was hoping to find you and Maria and see what you've found out today," Jim said, leaning on the door of the Jeep.

"I dropped her off at one of the Sociology buildings," Brett said. "She was going to find out if her professor had learned anything."

"What about you?" Jim asked.

"I got Dr. Holder, the head of our department, to run the patents to determine if they're the same or at least share a common gene that was inserted," Brett answered.

"When will we know?" Jim asked.

"He hopes by noon tomorrow," Brett said. "Why don't you jump in and we'll head over there to see if Maria's still around?"

"Sounds good," Jim said, tossing his briefcase in the rear seat and opening the door. "Maybe she's got some good information."

"I hope so," Brett said as he headed out of the parking lot. "I'd like to nail down the links between these things if there is a link."

"There's got to be," Jim said as they drove. "Too many things that point to it. Especially now that we know Hawk and Moss are getting five million dollars a year for something."

"Speaking of that," Brett said, turning to look at Jim. "Deep Throat found out who owns the account in the Caymans that's putting money in New Tech's account."

"Let me guess," Jim said, smiling. "The country of Ethiopia."

"Nope," Brett told him. "But you're heading in the right direction."

"Mombasa?" Jim guessed.

"You've gone too far, turn around," Brett said.

"Agrigenic?" Jim guessed.

"Bingo!" Brett said, raising his hands from the wheel.

"Now, it really looks like the problem isn't with Monogenic's, just our little genocidal folks right here in College Station," Jim said.

"Looks that way," Brett said as he stopped by the building where he'd left Maria. "The question now is, what do we do?"

CHAPTER 53

When Maria came out of the building, she saw Jim and Brett sitting at the curb waiting for her. "Hey, Jim. How was class?" she asked as she got to Brett's Jeep.

"Another class, come and gone," he said as he got out and let her climb in the backseat.

"How'd it go with the professor?" Brett asked as Jim got back in the Jeep.

"Not good," Maria answered.

"No answers?" Jim asked, shutting his door.

"Oh, he had answers," Maria said as Brett started the engine.

"Well, what'd he tell you?" Jim asked.

"He did say that he had contacted WHO and WFP, the world food people, and they were interested in what caused the decline in birthrates," she answered.

"So, they're going to look into it," Brett said as he pulled away from the curb.

"Short answer, yes," Maria said. "Long answer. It can take months or years for them to get an answer."

"Well, if they're at least looking into it, we've gotten someone with some authority to resolve the problem," Brett said, knowing that neither Jim nor Maria would let it go that long.

"Not a chance," Maria said. "There's got to be a faster way."

"I agree," Jim said. "I think that we're getting enough facts to take it to someone who can demand answers and find a quick solution."

"How about you, Brett?" Maria asked. "How'd it go on the gene thing?"

"Pretty good," Brett said as he headed for the library parking lot. "I'll know tomorrow, I hope, if the genetic issue with the corn is identical to the barley."

"Okay," Jim said. "We're still getting pieces. We've confirmed that the birthrate decline isn't something that can be attributed to any elements known to the WHO or WFP. We're getting the data on the three GMOs tomorrow around noon. So, that, combined with our knowledge and proof that Hawk and Moss are involved with Agrigenics, we're almost there."

"I agree," Brett said as he pulled into the parking lot.

"Don't park close to my car," Jim advised. "I don't know what range that little insect has that they snuck into my car."

"I know," Brett said, parking several cars away.

"What about tomorrow?" Maria asked Jim. "Are you still going to their lab after lunch?"

"Of course," Jim said. "It'd look strange if I didn't. Plus, I'm going to spend the rest of the afternoon formatting my thesis so they can see it."

"How do you know Hawk or Moss will know that you've changed GMOs?" Brett asked. "Have you told them?"

"No," Jim said. "But, if they're bugging me, I'd bet they have someone in the lab that's informing them of everything I do."

"You think so?" Maria asked rhetorically.

"I do," Jim said. "And I'd bet it's the guy, Larry, that's been assigned to *help* me."

"Do you think he's in on the barley thing in Zwairiland?" Brett asked.

"No, I doubt it," Jim answered. "He's just a tech that quit school after he got his Master's. I don't think they'd trust someone that far down the food chain, so to speak."

"What about that doctor, Thompson, you've been working with?" Maria asked.

"I doubt that also," Jim said. "I don't think he'd be part of this."

"Besides," Brett interrupted, "there's just the two names on the New Tech company roster and on the banking account."

"Why don't you have Deep Throat dig around and see if there's maybe an employee list for New Tech?" Maria asked. "Maybe there are others that'll get a share of the money in the Caymans."

"He didn't find any employees when he did the search," Brett said. "He's convinced that it's just a front or holding company."

"Do you think you'll have enough time this afternoon to throw together a reasonable thesis?" Maria asked Jim, changing the subject.

"Probably not one that I can submit," Jim acknowledged. "But, for right now, all I really have to show Larry is a basic outline with most of the data. I doubt if he's ever seen a Doctoral thesis."

"What if we helped you?" Brett asked. "I can write the portion that deals with the protocol on the corn while you concentrate on the production end."

"I can do the computer inputs from your notes," Maria suggested.

"I don't know, guys," Jim told them. "I sort of feel as if I'll be getting credit for someone else's work."

"Not at all," Brett said. "You get the information and dictate the stuff to Maria. All I'm doing is assembling your data into a reasonable format. All she's doing is computer assistance."

"What about your thesis?" Jim asked Brett.

"And yours?" he asked as he turned to look at Maria.

"You're helping me with mine right now," Brett said.

"And mine," Maria agreed.

"How do you figure that?" Jim asked as he realized that they were going to help him regardless of what he wanted.

"As you said awhile back, this whole ethical issue will be the basis for mine," Brett said.

"And I'm going to use the birthrate thing in mine," Maria said, nodding her head.

"How does birthrate apply to Archaeogenetics?" Jim asked, trying to find a reason to deny them their desire to assist him.

"I'll use it as a sociology topic that has implications for Archaeogenetics," Maria said.

"I doubt if your professor will allow that," Jim argued.

"I bet that when everything is done, I can convince them that I discovered this while researching the DNA of Ethiopia and its ties to the inhabitants of Zwairiland," Maria said.

"Probably for a Master's thesis," Brett agreed. "Especially if you were looking for genetic reasons for one population to differ from another."

"Easy," Maria said, getting excited. "I'll just say that while I was comparing the two and could find no genetic reason for them to have such differences yet be experiencing such differing birthrates."

"Then, you can say that you learned about the GMO thing from Jim, being as you two are an item," Brett joked.

"And you'll use the data how?" Jim asked Brett, ignoring the 'item' remark.

"You're looking at it from a Molecular Biology standpoint," Brett explained. "You're all about improved plants. I'll approach it from a Pharming angle, how some GMOs can impact pharmaceutical issues."

"Hell, I may even try to buy the corn patent and sell it as a contraceptive in the vegetable or produce section of every grocery store in the United States!" Brett proclaimed as he puffed out his chest.

"Or the world! We may be billionaires!" Maria exclaimed.

"Whoa there, missy," Brett said. "What's this *we'* stuff?

"Alright, guys, I guess I'll let you help, but the 'we' stuff will be in the acknowledgment section of the thesis," Jim finally said as he opened his door.

"And I'll be sure to reference your work in mine, old buddy," Brett announced as he got out of the Jeep.

"I may do the same," Maria said, climbing out of the back seat. "Just remember that all credit is listed in alphabetical order. 'P' then 'J' then 'W.'"

"J comes before P," Jim said.

"Not if he wants to keep seeing P," Maria said, laughing as they headed to the library.

CHAPTER 54

After they'd been in the library for a little over two hours, they decided to wrap it up and go out for dinner. Maria sent the rough draft thesis to the printer while Brett and Jim gathered up all of their notes and the information Larry had provided.

"What do you think?" Brett asked as they walked toward the parking lot.

"Pretty good," Jim answered. "I'll take it with me to the lab and let Larry see it, maybe even ask him what he thinks about it."

"How much more will you have to do on it before it's ready to submit?" Maria asked.

"Actually, not much," Jim answered. "With the information I got from Larry and you guys working with me, I'd say a couple of hours just refining some of the wording, double checking the spelling, and one last fact check, and it'll be ready."

"I have an idea," Brett announced.

"What?" Maria asked.

"Why don't we use the bug they put in Jim's car to make sure they know he's shifted his focus," Brett answered.

"Not a bad idea," Jim said, nodding his head.

"How do you plan to do that?" Maria asked.

"You and Jim take his car, and I'll follow you," Brett explained. "We'll go to the Bar-B-Q place, and while you're driving, you discuss how happy you are with the new GMO and how much time you've saved instead of continuing with the barley."

"I'm not sure I even want to be in the car knowing they're listening to me," Maria said.

"Think of it as an acting audition," Brett said. "Pretend you've no idea they're listening, but play the part of girlfriend for the audience."

"That way, even if Larry isn't reporting back to them, they'll think I'm no longer interested in the barley," Jim agreed. "You can just tell me how glad you are that I've changed and how much more time we'll have together, talk about going to the Gulf for a weekend, anything that we'd normally be saying."

"Alright, I'll try," Maria finally said. "But I can't stand for those sick bastards to listen to us, even if it's just school talk or something. What we say to each other is private, and they've got no right to hear it."

"I know," Jim said. "I don't like it either, but if they're convinced I've given up on the barley, maybe we can get our lives back a little sooner."

"Good, it's settled," Brett said as they walked across the parking lot. "You two play your part, and we'll make sure they pay for everything they've done to you."

Jim stopped suddenly and said, "You better check your Jeep. They may have bugged it, too."

"I doubt it," Brett said. "How would they know about me or my Jeep?"

"I don't know," Jim answered. "But they might. If they've heard about you from our conversations or anything, they'd probably think you're involved somehow."

"Okay, I'll look tomorrow at home," Brett said. "Until I'm sure, we just don't talk about any of this in either of our cars anymore. We'd better be very cautious anywhere we could be overheard also."

"I agree," Jim said. "And, it goes without saying, but other than the few people we've asked to help, nobody even gets a hint of what we've discovered."

"Understood," Maria said, nodding her head. "I know my professor has no clue about the barley thing."

"Dr. Holder knows that I suspect something unethical is being done with the barley," Brett said. "But I think he believes that it's too fanciful to be real."

"You told him about Zwairiland?" Maria asked incredulously.

"No, I just said that I think the barley is tied to a decline in birthrates," Brett said, shaking his head. "I didn't mention the country or continent. I didn't even specifically say people, but I assume he inferred that during our conversation."

"Alright," Jim told them. "From now on, we don't discuss this with anyone else unless absolutely necessary. Then we never talk about the two things together. It's either about the genetic makeup of the corn or barley, or it's about birthrates with no mention of what we suspect is causing it."

"Agreed," Brett said as they continued walking to his Jeep.

"Okay," Jim said as they got to the Jeep. "I'll see you at the restaurant."

"Right behind you," Brett said as he climbed in his seat.

Jim and Maria were silent during the short walk to the VW. As Jim opened the door for Maria, he said, "What would you like for dinner tonight?"

"How about Bar-B-Q?" she asked as she got in.

"Sounds good to me," Jim said as he shut her door.

"Brett did say he was following us, didn't he?" Maria asked as Jim got in the car.

"Yeah," Jim said as he started the engine.

"Shouldn't we ask him if that's okay?" Maria said as she looked where Jim was pointing on the dash.

"He doesn't care," Jim said as Maria nodded her understanding of where the bug was hidden.

"I think all he cares about is if the beer's cold," Maria laughed as they pulled out of the lot.

"That's important to him, alright," Jim said, looking in his rearview mirror to make sure Brett was behind them.

As they were driving to the restaurant, Rocky got a call from the men monitoring Jim's car. Learning where they were going, he called two other men and told them to go back to the restaurant where they'd previously waited for Jim, Maria, and Brett.

Next, he called Mike and told him of the news and that he'd sent his men to try to find out what role Brett played in Jim's investigation. After hearing that Mike was glad to know he was staying on top of things, he called the restaurant and asked for one of the waitresses who worked there.

Asking her if she still had the tiny transmitter she'd been given, he told her to wait until Jim arrived and to somehow attach it to the bottom of their table. Then, if possible, have his two men seated as close as possible. Satisfied that everything would be taken care of, he decided to go to his office and monitor what any of the bugs provided.

When Jim and Maria parked at the restaurant, they waited on the sidewalk for Brett to join them before going in. Once inside, the hostess took them to an open table near the rear and told them a waitress would be over shortly.

When the waitress arrived with the menus, Maria smiled at her and said, "I don't think we need the menus, but we really need beers."

"You're not eating?" the waitress asked, picking the menus up.

"Yes, Ma'am," Jim quickly said. "But we already know what we want to eat, so we don't need to look."

"Okay," the waitress said, smiling. "What would you like?"

"Three rib plates, two Budweiser's, and a Shiner," Brett said as Jim and Maria nodded their concurrence.

"Sounds like you've been here before," the waitress said as she scribbled their order on her pad. "I'll be right back with the beer."

While they were waiting for their beer, another waitress escorted two men to one of the tables about three feet from theirs. Jim nodded at one of the men who was facing him and received an answering nod in return. Watching him for a second, Jim then turned his attention to Brett and Maria.

A minute or so later, the waitress that had seated the two men arrived with a tray carrying their beer. Setting it on the table, she asked, "Who had the Shiner?"

"I did," Brett said, holding out his hand.

"I guess that means you two had the Buds," she said as she put them in front of Jim and Maria.

"What happened to our other waitress?" Maria asked as the waitress slid the tray half off the table.

"She just asked me to bring the beer while she's turning in your order," the waitress said as one of her hands slid beneath the tray.

"Okay," Maria said as the waitress leaned slightly forward as if to stretch her back. "Thanks."

"No problem," the waitress said as she picked up the tray. "Enjoy your dinner."

As soon as the waitress left, Brett leaned over to Jim and whispered, "Did you see that?"

"What?" Jim whispered as he picked up his beer.

"She reached under the table right after she gave you your beer," Brett said, holding his bottle in front of his mouth.

"What do you think she was doing?" Jim asked as he was pretending to sip his beer.

"I don't know," Brett said as he knocked his silverware off the table with his elbow. "But I'm taking a look."

Brett scooted his chair back and bent over to get his silverware off the floor. Letting the spoon fall from the napkin they were rolled in, he stuck his head under the table and looked up before picking it up.

Straightening up, he put the silverware and napkin on the table and took his seat. Picking up his beer, he tilted the bottle up and nodded his head slightly at Jim.

"Here's to a successful day on the road to graduation," Jim said, lifting his beer. "And to good friends that help a man when he's in need."

All three clinked their beers over the center of the table and took a drink. Holding his beer in his right hand, Jim leaned over to kiss Maria on the cheek.

With his lips close to her ear, he whispered, "We're bugged."

Sitting back, Jim said, "I appreciate all of your help with that corn GMO for my thesis. You've saved me hours of work."

"Not a problem, good buddy," Brett said. "I expect the same when I get back to work on mine."

"I assume you'll both help me," Maria said silently, fuming at this new invasion of her time with Jim.

"You bet," Brett said, smiling. "Of course, you'll be responsible for buying the beer afterward, just as Jim is tonight."

"Not fair," Maria said, laughing. "You guys drink twice as much as me. I should only have to buy half of it."

"Hey, an all-you-can-eat is the same price no matter how much you eat, isn't it?" Jim asked, looking at her and winking. "You don't like the price, don't go there."

CHAPTER 55

Sitting in his office listening to the conversation of Jim and Maria that'd been taped, Rocky nodded his head as he heard nothing unusual. As soon as Jim was at the restaurant, he got a call that his men were sitting near their table and that the bug had successfully been placed beneath their table.

Listening to the mundane college kid talk about numerous subjects, he only made a note of the fact that Jim had used the corn GMO for his thesis. Knowing that was what Mike wanted to hear, he made a copy of the table conversation and waited for his men to report back.

Now, unless something different was heard when Jim drove home or after he went into his apartment, his night was almost over. Knowing that the waitress would remove the bug when Jim left, that left only his men leaving. If they hadn't seen anything suspicious, then he'd wait until morning to brief Mike.

Rocky hoped that this would end his surveillance of Jim. He wasn't very comfortable about the entire situation and would rather have just stuck to the normal background stuff. But orders were orders, and Mike must have had his reasons to go this far.

As Jim drove Maria to her dorm, she talked about how she needed to spend the night there so she could catch up on some studying. Plans were made to meet for lunch the next day, and Jim reminded her that he was going to the lab in the afternoon.

After they reached the dorm, Jim walked her toward the entrance and stopped on the steps that led to the door. "Thanks," he said as he held Maria's hands.

"I can't believe the bastards had the nerve to put that thing under our table," she said looking at Jim.

"I'm not sure, but I think there were two men at the next table who were there to watch us also," Jim said.

"When this is over, what do you plan to do about all of this crap?" Maria asked.

"I'm not sure how to handle it yet," Jim admitted.

"Can't you call the police and have them arrest somebody?" Maria asked.

"Arrest who?" Jim asked. "You know everyone would deny any knowledge of any of it."

"Can't they trace the bugs?" Maria asked. "See who bought them?"

"I doubt it," Jim said, shaking his head. "That kind of stuff only happens on Law and Order or some super-cop show. Real life, even if they could be traced, it would probably be some fictitious name from another town or something."

"Besides," Jim continued, "I want the bugs still there after we expose Hawk and Moss. That'd be just one more little piece of evidence that they were trying to hide something and trying to find out if I knew anything."

"Have you figured out how to expose them?" Maria asked.

"Not yet," Jim answered. "But, if it's all true, and it looks that way, I think the best course of action would be to get one of the people from the District Attorney's office and show them what we've found."

"What can they do?" Maria asked. "There's been no crime here in College Station except for the bug thing. And as you said, you can't prove anything there."

"I don't know," Jim answered. "But at least they'd know who could do it. Maybe the state or some federal office. But we still need the link between the corn and the barley strains."

"Are you still against going to Hawk's boss?" Maria asked.

"No, not if we can prove what's happened," Jim answered. "Maybe that's something we could do with the DA. Especially if it's a state DA."

"I don't care who kicks his ass," Maria said. "I just want to be there when it happens."

"Me too, baby," Jim said, putting his arms around her. "But I better get home and let you go study."

"Okay," Maria said, kissing him. "I'll see you tomorrow."

Jim winked at her and said, "Maybe we'll get a motel room tomorrow night, and I'll bring the Pistachio almond ice cream."

Maria stood watching Jim as he walked back to his car, wishing she didn't have to wait until tomorrow.

Waving as he drove off, Jim left the campus and drove to his apartment. Once inside, he turned on the TV and listened to the show while he sat at the kitchen table, making notes on his thesis.

Even if they proved that barley was the culprit in the birthrate decline, that wasn't what he wanted to present as what he truly believed were the benefits of GMOs used responsibly.

The next morning Jim was driving to his only class for the day when Rocky was briefing Mike and Jerry on the conversations from yesterday. "What's your impression of Brett?" Mike asked.

"I still think he's just another student that Jim's known for a while," Rocky answered. "I haven't heard a word about him being interested in anything Jim's involved in besides helping him with some paper he's doing for his degree."

"I agree," Jerry said. "From everything we've heard or seen, he and Maria are just two more students that know Jim. I see no connection, other than the romance thing with Maria, between them."

"Okay," Mike said, sitting back in his chair. "I guess that's all for now."

"What about the bugs we've planted?" Rocky asked, standing up.

"Give it another day or two, and then pull them," Mike said. "Just don't get caught taking them out."

"No, sir," Rocky said, shaking his head. "We'll do it while he's at the lab so I can get his car, and we know he's not going to be in the apartment."

"Good," Mike said. "I'll see you in the morning."

"What do you think?" Mike asked Jerry as Rocky walked away.

"He's said he's using our corn GMO for his thesis," Jerry answered. "If he shows it to Larry or talks about it, I think we can assume that he's dropped the barley GMO."

"I'll agree with that," Mike said. "How do we know he isn't still looking into the barley anyway?"

"I don't think he's got time," Jerry said. "If he's like most students, he's probably tired of research and wasting his time. I honestly think it was just a fluke that he came across that particular strain, and since there's no data past the development stage, he's got no reason to pursue it."

"Okay," Mike said, getting up. "Talk to Larry this afternoon after Jim leaves the lab."

"I'm going out there while Jim's there," Jerry said, standing up. "I want to talk to Jim myself. I'll have a better feeling about it when I see his thesis."

"What if he doesn't have it with him?" Mike asked as he sat down at his desk.

"I'll suggest that he bring it out and let Dr. Thompson give it a look," Jerry said. "Just as a courtesy to us. Let us see how much help we've been. That sort of thing."

"Sounds good to me," Mike said, picking up the phone. "I'll tell Thompson you're coming out and that we'd appreciate it if he'd show some interest in Jim's paper."

"I'll let you know how it went this afternoon when I get back," Jerry said as he turned and headed for the door.

CHAPTER 56

That afternoon, when Jim got to the lab, he saw the company Suburban sitting in the reserved parking spot where Jerry always parked. Wondering if Jerry was here to see him or other company business, Jim knew he had to play his part when they met.

When Jim entered the building, he saw Jerry signing in and talking to the guard at the desk. "Good afternoon, Mr. Moss," Jim said as he walked up.

"Good afternoon, Jim," Jerry said as he turned his head.

"How're things at the front office?" Jim asked as he picked up the pen to sign in.

"Fine," Jerry answered. "How about you? School wearing you down?"

"It's alright," Jim said, handing the folder he'd brought in to the guard. "As a matter of fact, Larry's really helped me with my thesis, and that's saved me a lot of time."

"Great," Jerry said as the guard opened the folder and looked at the papers inside. "How's that going?"

"Pretty good," Jim answered taking the folder back from the guard. "As a matter of fact, I'm hoping he can do some fact-checking for me today."

"I'm sure he can," Jerry said. "If you need someone with a little more expertise, I'll see if Dr. Thompson has a little spare time."

"That'd be great," Jim said as he followed Jerry to the dressing chamber. "But I'm sure he has more important business than to critique a student's work."

"We'll see," Jerry said as he finished dressing in his whites.

"Either way, I really appreciate the opportunity you guys have given me here," Jim said as he pulled his booties on.

"Our pleasure," Jerry said as he opened the door to the hall. "You never know where you may find the talent you may need in the future. Have you given any consideration as to where you'll try to go to work?"

"Not yet," Jim answered as they walked down the hall. "First things first, you know. I've got to get that all-important piece of paper that says I get to start all over and really learn what they've tried to teach me."

"That's certainly true," Jerry said as they approached Dr. Thompson's office. "Even in my field of management, most of the things I learned didn't translate to being able to do my job. It took several years of actually doing it until I felt comfortable. Lots to learn when you start applying the basic knowledge."

"Yes, sir," Jim said, nodding his head as they entered the office.

"Good afternoon, Mr. Moss, Mr. Jackson," the secretary said as they walked up to her desk. "How can I help you today?"

"I was hoping Dr. Thompson could see me this afternoon," Jerry said.

"I'll let him know you're here," she said, picking up her phone.

A second after hearing her tell the doctor that both Jerry and Jim were at her desk, she hung up the phone and said, "Please, go right in."

"Thanks," Jerry said as he headed to the closed door behind her desk.

Just as he was about to knock, the door opened, and Dr. Thompson said, "Good afternoon, Mr. Moss, Jim."

"Good afternoon, Dr. Thompson," Jerry said. "I was wondering if you could spare us a little of your time this afternoon."

"Not a problem," Dr. Thompson said, gesturing for them to come in. "As a matter of fact, I just got a call that postponed a meeting I was supposed to be in."

"Problems?" Jerry asked as he followed the doctor to his desk.

"Not really," Dr. Thompson said. "Please, have a seat and tell me what you need."

"If you have the time and interest, I was wondering if you'd take a quick look at Jim's thesis," Jerry asked as they took their seats.

"Sure," Dr. Thompson said. "As I said, I've got a little time on my hands right now, and maybe I'll learn something from Jim."

"I doubt that," Jim said as he handed the doctor the folder he'd brought in.

"I'm sure you've seen all of this before, and reading it'll be about as boring as watching grass grow."

"Isn't that our job?" Dr. Thompson asked as he took the folder. "Making plants grow? Maybe we'll find a grass that grows so fast it's fun to watch."

"As long as I don't have to mow it!" Jerry said, laughing. "Mine grows fast enough as it is."

"Well, maybe not yard grass," Dr. Thompson said. "But can you imagine a pasture grass that could grow fast enough that you could graze 100 head of cattle per acre year-round? There are some areas in West Texas, New Mexico, and Arizona that take 100 acres for just one cow."

"Let's see what we've got," he continued as he opened the folder.

After skimming through the thesis for a couple of minutes, Dr. Thompson put the papers on his desk and asked, "Have you verified all of the data here?"

"Sort of," Jim said. "Larry gave me most of the numbers and protocol information. I just tried to translate the scientific jargon into understandable language."

"I see," Dr. Thompson said. "Would you like my impression?"

"Certainly, sir," Jim answered. "Any advice would be greatly appreciated."

"First off," the doctor said, "I'd go a little easier on the details involved. Too boring, even to college professors. You've got a good paper here, but I'd emphasize the results of the product more."

"The actual protocol for developing this GMO isn't near as important as the result," he continued. "Genetic manipulation is so commonplace now that it isn't as unique as it was 20 years ago. Spending so much time on which gene went where isn't as important as placing more emphasis on the real benefits."

"I agree, sir," Jim said, nodding his head. "But I was really trying to place the emphasis on how complex some of the GMOs have become more than just production rates. Although they're important, as I demonstrated at the end of the paper."

"Of course," Dr. Thompson said. "Maybe I'm just so used to doing this all day and tend to forget that the purpose of the school is to teach you how to manipulate the genetic makeup of various combinations. Perhaps your approach is more important in an academic environment."

"What do you think overall?" Jerry asked. "Do you think he selected a good subject for his paper?"

"Certainly," Dr. Thompson said, handing the folder back to Jim. "When viewed as Jim just said, it's outstanding work. He's taken a simple kernel of corn, built an improved version, and demonstrated an increase in production. I'd say that would meet anyone's standards for a Doctoral thesis."

"Thank you, sir," Jim said as he took the folder.

"By the way," Jerry asked, turning to Jim. "Whatever happened to your first subject, GMO, the one that led you to us to start with?"

"Not enough data to complete the thesis as I wanted," Jim answered. "I could show how it was made, but as Dr. Thompson said about the value of production rates, I had no information to demonstrate the value of GMOs."

"Well, I'm glad we could help you with this one," Jerry said, satisfied that Jim was no longer digging into the barley. "When you finalize it, if possible, I'd like a copy. We can always use some good publicity. It's very competitive out there, and since you've done so much work to verify our product, I'd like to use some of the data in our advertising."

"Of course," Jim said. "After all, it was mostly your people that gave it to me. I just tried to tie everything together."

"Sometimes seeing the forest is more important than seeing just the trees," Dr. Thompson said. "We tend to focus on making the trees and lose sight of what we're really trying to accomplish. Science, for science's sake, isn't what we're here for, is it?"

"No, it isn't," Jerry said as he rose from his chair. "We're here to benefit humanity, and products like this corn GMO do just that."

"And make a little profit, too?" Dr. Thompson quipped as he rose from behind the desk.

"We need just a little money to support your research, don't we?" Jerry answered. "But a superior product produces the funding, doesn't it?"

"Indeed it does," Dr. Thompson said as he came around his desk.

Jim rose and said," Thank you, Dr. Thompson. I truly appreciate you taking the time to give me your opinion."

Shaking Jim's hand, he said, "Not at all, Jim. I'm looking forward to working with you between now and graduation."

"Maybe we can convince him to join us after he graduates," Jerry said, shaking the doctor's hand. "That is if you think he's sharp enough to be on your staff."

"I'd bet he is," Dr. Thompson said, ushering them to the door. "I wouldn't be surprised at what he can accomplish when he puts his mind to it.

CHAPTER 57

Jim was ready to go home after over four hours at the lab while Larry did a fact-check of the thesis. Having spent most of that time sitting in meetings with Dr. Thompson and several of the senior scientists, Jim had all he needed for one day.

One thing he did learn. Meetings tended to be like classroom time, with lots of information given, some of it useful, but most of the time, it was listening to countering viewpoints on several issues that had no bearing on the actual production of GMOs.

Once he got back to the library, he quickly parked and headed for the computer section to see if either Maria or Brett were there. Not seeing them, he headed back through the library, intending to go to Maria's dorm. Almost at the exit, he heard Kay calling his name.

"Yes, Ma'am," Jim said as he walked over to her.

"Your friend Maria asked me to give you this if you came in," she said handing Jim an envelope she picked up off of her secretary's desk.

"Thanks," Jim said, opening the envelope.

"How's the thesis coming?" Kay asked, watching Jim read the note Maria had left for him.

"Pretty good," Jim answered as he stuck the note in his shirt pocket. "I've got it in the rough draft right now. I'll have it finished in a week or so."

"Glad to hear it," Kay said. "Did the information on the patents help you at all?"

"Not really," Jim explained. "I still couldn't find any production on either of the barley GMOs, so I switched to one with proven production."

"Too bad," Kay said. "I know that you spent a lot of time on it. A shame that all of that work was for nothing."

"I guess that's the way it is," Jim said, nodding his head. "I'm sure that won't be the last time I work on a project that never comes to fruition."

"Well, I'm just glad that you found a subject that you could use to finish your thesis," Kay said. "Stop by every now and then and let me know how things are going."

"I'll do that," Jim said. "Thanks again for all of your help."

As Kay headed back to her office, Jim pulled the note from his pocket and reread Maria's note, telling him to meet her and Brett at the little pizza restaurant at five o'clock.

Looking at the clock on the wall, he knew that he needed to leave right now to make it there by then. Hurrying down the sidewalk and dodging the students with their armloads of books, he checked the traffic on the road before crossing to where his car was parked.

At least he didn't think anyone would know where he was going this time and didn't expect to be under surveillance as they were last time. But he'd make sure to check under the table and be aware of anyone that came in after he got there.

As he pulled into the small parking lot, he saw Brett's Jeep and pulled up beside it. No longer worried about his briefcase being inspected, he left it in the front passenger seat and walked the short distance to the entrance.

Seeing Brett, Maria, and another young man sitting near the rear drinking beer, Jim walked over and said, "Looks like you started without me."

"Hey, Jim," Brett said as Maria got up and kissed Jim. "Pull up a chair and join us."

Jim pulled out the chair beside Maria and was bending over to look under the table when Brett laughed and said, "I've already done that!"

Smiling, Jim sat down and scooted up the chair as the waitress came over and asked if he'd like a beer. "Budweiser," he said as Maria scooted her chair a little closer to his.

"Jim, I'd like for you to meet my friend that you've come to know as Deep Throat," Brett said. "His real name is Jack Sinclair."

"Glad to meet you, Jack," Jim said, extending his hand across the table. "I certainly do appreciate you using your unusual talents to help us."

"My pleasure," Jack said, shaking Jim's hand. "It's good to meet you also. Brett's said good things about you."

"Let me start by telling you a little about Jack," Brett said after the waitress delivered Jim's beer.

"You remember that I told you he came from a rather affluent family," Brett began. "I just didn't tell you how affluent."

"His family just happens to own several thousand acres around the Midland Odessa area," he continued. "And most of it covered with those little pumps that bring many, many barrels of oil to the surface every day of every week, etc., etc., etc.

Now, as an affluent man in that part of the country, you can already guess that his dad's not without influence in other parts of the state as well. As a matter of fact, his dad, Jack Sr., was a major contributor to a former Governor of our great state.

Although Jack Jr. is somewhat the black sheep of the family, he's still the only male child and the ultimate heir to a rather large inheritance. So, when I explained our situation about getting some governmental assistance with our problem, he volunteered to intercede with his father and get us in to see the former Governor."

"Now, Jack doesn't know the whole picture, and I certainly wouldn't tell him any more about it without your concurrence," Brett concluded. "But I think we're going to need some major league help here if we're going to expose their operation."

"Exactly how much do you know?" Jim asked Jack.

"I know some people have a patent that you're interested in," Jack began. "I know that it's somehow tied to a company called New Tech, and the officers of that company are tied to Monogenic's. I also know about the funds in the Caymans. You already knew that since I'm the one that gave you most of the information."

"What I don't know, and I'm a very curious fellow, is what sort of business these boys are in that garners that much money for a company that has no actual product," Jack finished.

"Now, before you make any decision about Jack," Brett interrupted, "I'll tell you that he wants no part of this other than to help arrange the introductions we're going to need and to vouch for us to his father."

"Why don't you want to be involved?" Jim asked, looking at Jack.

Jack grinned and said, "I'm supposed to tell my dad and a former Governor, and who knows who else, that I've been hacking into computers all over the world? Not a chance in hell! My only stipulation is that you swear that you got your information from anybody but me."

Jim sat back, sipping his beer as the three of them watched him. Sitting his beer on the table, he turned to Maria and asked, "What do you think?"

"I'm with Brett on this," she answered. "We've got the information, but we can't get it to the right people without some help. Jack's got no dog in this fight but wants to help us, and his dad can certainly get us an audience with those people."

"Alright," Jim finally said after a lengthy pause while he looked at Jack. "How much do you want to know?"

CHAPTER 58

Over the next two hours, Brett and Jim revealed how much they'd found out about the apparent activities culminating in the population reduction that was happening in Zwairiland.

Maria told him that although the WHO and WPF were involved in solving the mystery, it would take them entirely too long to reach a conclusion that may or may not result in charges being brought against the individuals responsible.

Not only may it not result in any criminal charges, but when those organizations descended on Zwairiland, it would signal those involved that they were under scrutiny, and they'd probably disappear.

Jim told Jack about the bugs he'd discovered and that he was certain that all of his movements had been tracked, as well as everything that had been said in his apartment.

Brett said that he'd gotten the results of the three GMOs and that although they had an almost identical genetic makeup in certain areas, absolute proof could only come from obtaining samples to test. Possibly even duplicating the GMOs in the lab since there were no samples of the original corn GMO or Monogenic's version of the barley.

When all of the elements of the puzzle were revealed, Jim concluded by saying, "While we have all of these suspicions, the only actual proof of anything is the bugs I've discovered and the bank accounts in the Caymans."

"And those accounts can't be used as evidence," Jack reminded them. "Even if it was known how you got that information, there's not a court in the world that would allow it since it was obtained by illegal methods."

"Alright," Brett said after another round of beers had been delivered, "we've got to develop a comprehensive plan to present to Jack Sr."

"Who do you think we need to include in the investigation?" Maria asked.

"Let's start with the local police," Jim suggested. "They'll be the ones that are concerned with the illegal monitoring of my home and car."

"I'm not sure who'd be the logical people to investigate the financial aspect," Jack said. "But I'd bet Dad, or the Governor would have some ideas."

"There's the International War Crimes Tribunal that investigates crimes against humanity," Maria said. "They'd certainly need to be involved."

"Do you think we have enough information to convince your dad to get involved?" Jim asked Jack.

"I'm sure we do," Jack answered. "We have the statistics from Maria's research on the birthrate decline, we have proof of the contraceptive effects of the corn GMO, we have almost conclusive evidence of the genetic similarity of the three GMOs, and we can tie the association of Hawk, Moss, and the head of Mombasa."

"Don't forget that we have New Tech," Brett suggested. "I know we can't use what we found, but I'd bet there's a branch of the banking system that can do their own investigation based on a credible informant. Maybe tie it back to the bankruptcy thing. Then they'd find the money trail."

"That's a real sticky point," Jack said, shaking his head. "Dad knows about my little issue with the school and he'll suspect that I was involved when you present your proof about how you tied New Tech, the money, and the guys at Monogenic's together."

"You may have to confide in him that you're involved," Jim said. "Without that financial information, we don't have any motive for Hawk or Moss to be behind the whole thing."

"Can't we use the Mombasa connection?" Jack asked.

"Then Hawk and Moss would get off scot-free," Brett said.

"With millions," Maria added. "Not to mention their invasion of my privacy. I want them included in every bit of this."

"There's no other way, is there?" Jack asked, knowing that he'd have to reveal what he'd done.

"If there is, I don't know what it would be," Jim said. "I wish there was."

"How'll your dad take this?" Maria asked.

"He's not going to be happy," Jack answered.

"But, if he's convinced that it was the only way to get proof of the ties between all of the people involved, maybe he'd understand why you did it," Maria explained.

Jack sat quietly for a few minutes while trying to figure out what his father's reaction would probably be. "I don't see any way around it. Even if you guys never mention my name, he'll suspect it. And Dad's always taught me that it's better to take responsibility for any mistake than try to hide it."

"Okay, what's the plan?" Brett asked. "When do we get this ball rolling?"

"I'll call Dad tonight," Jack said. "I'll ask him to meet us in Austin with the Governor as soon as possible."

"Call me when you find out," Brett said. "I'll let Jim and Maria know."

"In the meantime, we need to get copies of everything we've found so we can present them at the meeting," Jim said. "We want this to be done as professionally as possible."

"Who's going to be the one to actually present the information?" Jack asked.

"It's got to be Jim," Brett said. "He's the one that discovered the genetic connection."

"But Maria found the birthrate issue," Jim argued.

"Nope," Maria said, shaking her head. "It would come better from you. You're the only one that's actually worked with Hawk or Moss and can tell why you became suspicious to start with."

"She's right," Brett said. "The rest of us were just assisting you. You started this. Now you've got to finish it."

"Fine," Jim said. "If Jack has to take responsibility for his mistakes, I guess I do, too."

"Never think this was a mistake," Maria said, putting her hand on his arm. "This just may be the biggest accomplishment in your life."

As the four of them were making plans for meeting the next day, Jerry was briefing Mike about his afternoon at the lab.

"You're convinced he's forgotten the barley?" Mike asked as they sat around the table.

"Absolutely," Jerry answered, handing a folder to Mike. "I saw the thesis and had Larry make a copy for me while he was checking it when Jim was with Dr. Thompson."

"But does that mean he's still not suspicious?" Mike asked, taking the folder and glancing at the papers inside.

"It's impossible to know that for sure," Jerry answered, sitting back in his chair. "But there's been no real evidence that he ever knew about what really happened to the barley."

"And we still have the bugs," he continued. "If we hear anything in the next couple of days, we'll deal with it then."

Mike tossed the folder on the table and sat back, saying, "It looks like we've dodged the bullet so far. If we hear nothing from Rocky or Larry over the next few days, I'll feel a whole lot better."

"We've managed to keep this secret for almost 20 years so far," Jerry said. "I think the odds of a mere college student putting all of the pieces together are extremely remote. Even if he did, who could he go to and manage to convince them that he'd discovered what's going on in some tiny unheard-of country in Africa?"

"You're probably right," Mike said, getting out of his chair. "I'll just be glad when he graduates and disappears from our lives."

CHAPTER 59

The next morning, Jim was making a few corrections to his thesis while he waited for the coffee to finish brewing when the phone rang. Knowing that whatever he said would be heard, he cautiously answered, "Hello?"

"Good morning, handsome," he heard Maria say.

"Good morning, Maria," he said, knowing that she wouldn't say anything he didn't want overheard. "What's up?"

"I finished all of my homework last night and was hoping that you'd want to take me to breakfast," she answered.

"Sure," Jim said. "It'll take me about 15 minutes to get there. Is that alright?"

"That's good for me," she answered. "I'll meet you out front."

"See you there," Jim said as he hung up.

After turning off the coffee pot that'd just finished brewing, Jim got a clean shirt out of the bedroom and left. As he drove to Maria's dorm, he wondered if she'd heard from Brett.

As he was pulling up to the curb, Maria came down the sidewalk waving at him. When she reached the car, she pulled the door open, slipped into the passenger seat, and kissed him.

"I've missed you," she said. "I hope they don't keep giving me so much homework that I have to be away from you for much longer."

"Well," Jim said as he pulled away from the curb, "we're here to learn, not to play."

"Your attitude's a lot different when we're at your place," she joked as he drove down University Drive. "Don't even pretend that you'd rather study."

"You wouldn't believe me if I tried," Jim said, grinning at her. "Where to for breakfast?"

"IHOP, okay?" she answered.

"Fine with me," Jim said as he merged with the morning traffic.

"Get much more done on your thesis?" Maria asked to keep the conversation moving.

"Pretty much," Jim said as he saw IHOP come into view. "Just a few minor corrections, and I'll get it on the computer. Then, one last review before I print it and get ready to submit it."

"Good," Maria said. "I'm glad that's over. Now you have no excuses to avoid seeing me."

"What about my homework?" Jim asked as he pulled into the parking lot.

"I'll give you plenty of work to do at home," Maria joked as he parked.

"Guess I should've bought those oysters after all," Jim said as he killed the engine and opened his door.

"You're going to need them," Maria said as she got out.

Once they were several feet from the car, Maria said, "Brett and Jack are meeting us here. Brett wanted me to call since it might seem strange for him to be heard talking to you."

"I'd rather talk to you anyway," Jim said, smiling and holding her hand as they reached the door.

As they stepped inside, the hostess asked, "How many, sir?"

"Four, please," Jim said, not seeing either Brett or Jack at any of the booths or tables.

The hostess took them to their seats, and the waitress was just arriving when Brett and Jack came walking up.

"Hey guys," Jim said. "Grab a seat."

"Good morning," Brett said, taking the seat across from Maria. "How's your day so far?"

"Pretty good," she answered. "But the day could go south at any minute."

"Well, I'll bet that it'll go west more than south," Jack said, taking his seat. "If you can make it, Dad's agreed to meet us at the Governor's house at noon today."

"Wow! That was fast," Jim said.

"It wasn't too hard after I explained what we'd discovered," Jack said. "It took him about an hour to get the Governor on the phone, but we're lucky that he wasn't busy for lunch today."

"What'd your dad say about the computer stuff?" Maria asked.

"He's not too happy," Jack answered. "As a matter of fact, I'm meeting him about an hour before we go to see the Governor."

"Would you like for us to go with you?" Jim asked.

"I don't know if that'd help," Jack answered. "He's pretty steamed about what I did, but for now, he's going to overlook it if we can convince him and the Governor that the Zwairiland thing is real."

"I don't see how they can ignore it," Brett said. "All of the pieces are there."

"Except you can't prove that the barley is being grown or consumed in Zwairiland," Jack said. "That's actually the only thing Dad was skeptical about."

"I don't know how we can ever get that proof," Jim said. "Unless someone goes over there and finds it. I'm sure anyone over there who's involved, and it may just be one or two people, would just hand us the barley."

"That's why we need the Governor," Jack said. "He can pull strings at the federal level, and I'm sure the State Department can make things happen."

"Too bad your dad doesn't know the President," Maria said.

"That'd be nice," Jack said, "but let's not forget that a former Governor of Texas would probably have access to either the current President or a former one."

"To think that a couple of college students can get the attention of the President of the United States," Brett said, sitting back. "Pretty amazing."

"We don't have anybody's attention yet," Jim reminded him. "We've got to convince Jack Sr. and the Governor first. And then they have to convince somebody up the food chain that this is real."

"Back to the question of your dad," Maria interrupted, "do you want us to go with you?"

"It might help," Jack answered. "But the bigger question is if Dad wants to see you when he's chewing my ass out."

"How much time do we have before we need to leave," Jim asked.

"Couple of hours," Brett said. "It's about a two-hour drive, so we need to leave no later than 10."

"I don't think we have time for breakfast," Maria said. "I need to get back to the dorm and start getting dressed."

"It takes more than an hour?" Brett asked.

"If I'm meeting Jack's dad and a former Governor, at least an hour," Maria answered. "And you guys need to find a suit and tie."

"Do we have copies of everything to give them?" Jim asked.

"I got them last night," Brett said. "I thought we'd have more time to do a run-through just to make sure we cover everything."

"We've got the two-hour drive," Jim told them. "But that'd mean taking one car. And we sure as hell can't take mine."

"Mine neither," Brett said. "I'm not sure where the top for it is right now, and I don't think Maria would sit for two hours with the wind blowing her hair."

"Not a chance," Maria agreed.

"No problem," Jack said. "Dad gave me his old Mercedes last year. We can take it."

"Alright, breakfast is out," Jim said. "Where do we want to meet?"

"How about the library?" Brett said. "Since we're there almost every day, there wouldn't be anything strange about our cars being there all day."

"Sounds good to me," Jack said.

"Me, too," Jim said. "I'll drop Maria off at the dorm and then go home to clean up. I should be at the library in about an hour."

"Maybe we should leave your car here for now," Maria suggested. "They heard us say we're coming here for breakfast, and it'd be strange if we left so quickly."

"She's right," Brett said. "Why don't I take her to the dorm and then drop you off at your place? Then, when I'm dressed, I'll come get you, and we'll come back for your car."

"Won't work," Jim said. "If I'm in my house, they'll know it. I've got to stay out of there until my car gets back there."

"Okay, here's an idea," Jack said to Brett and Jim. "I'll go home and get ready. You and Brett take Maria to her dorm and drop her off, and then go to the library to double-check the copies or whatever. Spend 30 minutes or so and then come back here to get Jim's car. That gives both of you half an hour to get ready and be back at the library."

"The only problem with that is that they won't hear Maria in my car," Jim argued.

"Good point," Brett said.

Jim turned to Maria and asked, "Can you get ready in less than an hour?"

"Not really," Maria said. "It'll take me an hour to do my makeup and hair."

Jim sat thinking for a moment and then asked, "How about if Brett and I come to get you after your shower? We'll stay at the library until then. We come to get my car, and I'll take you back to the dorm to do your hair and makeup."

"Then, I go home and get ready," he continued. "When I'm dressed, I'll come back to the dorm for you, and we can meet Brett and Jack at the library as planned."

"Sounds good," Brett said, getting out of his chair. "I'll take you guys, and Jack can head home to get ready. Then, if he's ready before the two hours are up, he can do whatever he needs to do before we meet at the library."

"Sorry, we forgot we needed to be somewhere," Jim said to the waitress as she arrived. "We'll come back another time."

CHAPTER 60

Slightly less than two hours later, Jim arrived at the library with Maria. Parking his VW a few spots from Brett's Jeep, he took his briefcase from the rear seat and got out.

As Maria was getting out, a late-model black Mercedes pulled up in front of them. "Wow!" Jack said as he looked at Jim and Maria standing beside his car, "I've never seen such a darling couple! And so finely dressed! You must be going somewhere important."

"Up yours, Jack," Jim said as he opened the rear door of the Mercedes. "Seen Brett?"

"I just got here, so no," Jack said, killing the engine as Maria slid into the rear seat and Jim shut her door. "But he's here somewhere since his Jeep's here."

"Here he comes," Jim said, spotting Brett coming down the sidewalk from the library.

Jim walked around the front of the car and got in the backseat with Maria, placing his briefcase with all of the materials he thought he'd need to brief Jack Sr. and the Governor between them.

Maria picked up the briefcase, slid over to Jim's side, and set the briefcase on the seat beside her, saying, "I'll pretend I'm your secretary, and if you need something, you just smile sweetly and ask."

"May I have my briefcase?" Jim asked, smiling as Brett climbed into the front seat.

"I'm sorry, sir," Maria teased. "I'm on break right now. Please call back in 15 minutes."

"What's going on back there?" Brett asked as he shut his door.

"They're playing office," Jack said, smiling as he started the car.

"Who's the boss?" Brett asked, looking at Jim.

"I'd like to say that I am," Jim said as Maria took his hand. "But, as we all know, when there's a female involved, she's always in charge."

"But we let you pretend you are," Maria said, kissing Jim on the cheek.

"Too bad I don't have one of those dark partitions like the limos have," Jack said as he pulled out of the parking lot. "We wouldn't have to watch them play their little game."

"We're not here to play games," Jim said, shaking his head as they left the campus. "Let's get started with what we're going to say when we get there."

"How do you plan to handle it?" Jack asked as he drove toward Highway 21.

"I figured that I'd sort of do it chronologically," Jim answered. "Start with the search parameters for a GMO that fit my requirements, and then talk about how random it was that I found the Monogenic's barley."

"Then I'd talk about how I kept running into a brick wall getting past the patent," Jim told them. "Next, I'll tell them about my first exposure to Monogenic's and their lack of information on one of their own patents."

"What about the ties to Zwairiland?" Maria asked.

"That would come next," Jim answered. "I plan to let you talk about how you discovered the declining birthrate if they want to know more about that."

"I'd rather you do it all," Maria said.

"I don't remember all of the details," Jim protested. "I think it'd come better from you since you did the research. After that, I'll explain how I found out about the patent Mombasa had that appeared to be a duplicate of Monogenic's."

"You're not going to tell them how you got the information, are you?" Maria asked.

"Not exactly," Jim answered. "I promised I wouldn't let anyone know who gave it to me, but I've got to point them to the patent office somehow."

"Kind of like how you got the financial information?" Jack asked, looking in the rearview mirror.

"Exactly," Jim answered. "Anyway, the next issue is the corn. I'll bring it up and then let Brett talk about it since he knows more about that than I do."

"I brought all of my notes on that," Brett said. "I've also got the printouts on the genetic similarities that the professor gave me for reference if they need them."

"Good," Jim said. "I guess the only thing left is how we tied all of the companies, the people, and the money together. That's where you take over, Jack."

"I know," Jack said. "I've got all of the material that I gathered researching the companies, their officers, their employees, and their financial data. I don't think Dad will bring up the methods that I used, but we'll see."

"I wonder how they'll determine if the barley is actually being used in Zwairiland?" Maria asked.

"Like most of this, we just present the information and let them figure out how to prove or disprove it," Jim answered. "I'm sure they've had situations before that required assistance from federal or international organizations. And, likely as not, some of their actions weren't exactly kosher."

Slightly less than two hours from when they'd left, Jack pulled into a gated mansion covering almost an entire block in Austin. As they stopped at the massive gates, a uniformed guard came out, checked their IDs, and verified that they'd been invited.

Once cleared, the gates swung open, and Jack drove down a long paved driveway to the sprawling mansion. Seeing his dad's Mercedes parked close to the house on the circular drive, Jack pulled in behind it and parked.

"Ready for the show to start?" Jack asked as he killed the engine.

"What do you want us to do while you're with your dad?" Maria asked.

"I'm sure one of the Governor's staff will take care of that," Jack said, getting out of the car. "We'll have to wait and see if when Dad wants to meet you."

As they gathered on the wide porch that fronted the double oak doors, a man wearing a dark suit opened the door and invited them in.

"Which one of you is Jack Jr.?" he asked as they entered a large reception area."

"I am," Jack said.

"If you'd follow me, please," he said as he looked at Jim, Brett, and Maria. "And if you three would kindly wait here, I'll escort you to the library."

"Yes, sir," Jim said as the man turned to take Jack to see his father.

A couple of minutes later, he returned and directed, "Follow me, please."

They followed him a short distance down a wide hall covered with a runner decorated with various scenes of Texas landmarks. Finally, at a tall oak door that stood open, he said, "If you'll please wait in here, I'll send someone by shortly to take care of you."

"Thanks," Jim said as he led them into a room that was twice as large as his apartment.

Looking around, Maria said, "Wow, I've never seen a place like this. It must've cost a fortune."

Walking to a wall covered with leather bound books, Brett added, "And it still costs a lot. I doubt if I'd ever be able to just pay the taxes, let alone the staff it must take to run someplace like this."

Seeing an ornate table with four chairs around it, Jim walked over and took one of the leather armchairs. "I wonder what Jack's house looks like," he said as the others joined him.

"I've never been there," Brett said, running his hand across the polished tabletop, "but from what Jack's told me, it's still a fairly small house. His dad never went in for extravagance. I assume it's nice, but nothing like this."

"He probably doesn't have to entertain the type of people that the Governor has to," Maria said, still in awe of their surroundings.

"Kind of intimidating," Jim said. "Really makes me wonder if we're ready for this level of discussion."

A few minutes later, a middle-aged lady came in and asked if they'd like anything to drink or eat. Just as Jim started to answer, Jack came in the door and told her, "They'll be in the front sitting room with Dad and me. There's already coffee and tea available. Thank you, though."

Jack looked at them and smiled. "Not as bad as I thought," he told them. "Now, he wants to talk to you guys."

CHAPTER 61

After following Jack into the room, they were met by Jack Sr., who rose from an overstuffed leather chair to meet them. "Dad, this is Jim Jackson," Jack Jr. said as Jim approached.

"Good to meet you, Jim," Jack Sr. said, extending his hand. "I guess you're the start of this little escapade."

"Very nice to meet you, sir," Jim said, shaking his hand. "And yes, sir, I guess you could say that this is all my fault."

"And this is Brett Weston," Jack Jr. said as he introduced him.

"Good to meet you," Jack Sr. said, shaking Brett's hand.

"You too, sir," Brett said.

"And this is Maria Pompillio," Jack Jr. said.

"Good to meet you, Maria," Jack Sr. said, taking her hand. "Please, all of you have a seat."

"Alright," Jack Sr. said as they sat down. "Let me see if I've got this right. You, Jim, found a barley GMO that you wanted to use for your thesis. Correct?"

"Yes, sir," Jim answered, nodding his head.

"And then you discovered a similar barley used somewhere in Africa," Jack continued. "How did you discover the barley in Africa?"

"A friend made some calls, sir," Jim answered. "Then another friend did some research and matched the two."

"And these *'friends'* wish to remain anonymous," Jack said.

"Yes, sir," Jim answered.

"I assume that their methods of gathering this information are somewhat like what my son did," Jack said turning to frown at Jack, Jr. "By that I mean that it wasn't quite legal."

"That I don't know," Jim answered, shaking his head. "As far as I know, they were entitled to the information because of their jobs. I'm not sure they were supposed to give me the information, but I don't think there was anything illegal about them getting it."

"Okay, let's assume the only questionable thing is divulging information to an unauthorized person," Jack said, nodding his head. "When did you tie these two barley strains to a corn GMO that causes infertility?"

"That came from Brett," Jim answered. "Maria and I were having dinner one evening when I ran into him. During our discussion about failed patents, he told me he had heard about a contraceptive corn."

Jack Sr. turned to Brett and asked, "Okay, how did you find out about this corn?"

"I don't really remember when I first heard about it, sir," Brett said. "It was probably during one of my classes. Not sure, maybe a professor or another student."

"How did you get the information that tied the corn to the barley?" Jack asked.

"Jack found the information for me, sir," Brett answered.

Jack Sr. glanced at his son for a moment and turned back to Brett, asking, "And you can prove that the three GMOs, two barleys and a corn, are identical?"

"Yes, sir," Brett answered. "I have the results of the tests that were run by the university."

"Okay, now, about the financial data," Jack Sr. said. "I know how that was obtained, and we obviously can't give the Governor that data. But I think I know how it can be discovered by more traditional methods."

"Now, let's talk about the birthrate issue," he continued.

"That's Maria's area," Jim said. "She's the one that discovered that."

"Tell me about that," Jack Sr. said to Maria.

"Well, sir," Maria started. "I was just talking to Jim about how Ethiopia was where all of our ancestors began according to DNA."

"What does Ethiopia have to do with the birthrate in Zwairiland?" he interrupted.

"Really nothing," Maria admitted. "But, when Jim told me about the barley in Zwairiland, I sort of looked at it and saw how close to Ethiopia it was. Then I noticed that the birthrate had declined dramatically over the last 20 years or so."

"So, you more or less stumbled across that," Jack said, nodding his head.

"Yes, sir," she answered.

"Now, the final thing," Jack said, looking at the four of them. "You have no proof that the barley is the cause, is that correct?"

"No, we don't, sir," Jim answered. "We have no way of proving that. Someone would have to go over there and get samples of the barley if it's being used, and then we could have it analyzed to prove it's the same as the one they patented."

"Alright, you guys stay here for a minute while I go talk to the Governor," Jack Sr. said, standing up. "I'll see if he can meet with us right now or if we need to schedule another meeting."

"Yes, sir," Jim said as the four of them stood.

About ten minutes later, Jack Sr. came back in and said, "The Governor wants to know if you guys can stick around for a couple of hours and brief him and a couple of members of his staff."

"Not a problem," Jim said. "All of us sort of planned to take the whole day off for this."

"Good," Jack said nodding his head. "I've got a few things to take care of while you go to lunch. We'll present all of the information, along with any material you've brought, to him when you get back. All of it but the financial data that is."

Jack led them out of the house after his dad left them. "Not too bad," he said as they walked to his car. "I think it went about as well as we could expect."

"How do you think he'll manage the financial part?" Brett asked as they drove toward the entrance gates.

"Not sure," Jack answered. "But I know that he has something in mind."

About an hour later, they pulled back up to the gates and waited for the guard to recognize them and let them in. Going up the driveway, they saw four cars parked in front of the house.

As they parked behind the rear car, the door to the house opened, and the man who had originally met them came out and waited for them to get out of the car. "The Governor will meet you in the library," he said as he escorted them down the hall. "Mr. Sinclair is waiting for you there."

"Enjoy your lunch?" Jack Sr. said, rising to greet them.

"Yes, sir," Jack Jr. said as they walked to the chairs that were arranged around an oak table. "Not like Mom's cooking, but pretty good."

"Good," Jack Sr. said. "Y'all have a seat. The Governor should be in shortly.

"Do the cars out front have anything to do with this?" Jack Jr. asked as they all sat down.

"Most assuredly," Jack Sr. answered. "He made a few calls after I explained everything we discussed. The people he called will be in the meeting, and they'll take over the investigation."

Just as Jim started to say something, the Governor entered the room, followed by four men wearing suits and carrying briefcases. "Good afternoon, folks," the Governor said as he walked over to them.

"Governor, I'd like to introduce these people," Jack Sr. said as all of them stood.

"You remember my son, Jack Jr.," he said.

"Of course," the Governor said, shaking Jack's hand. "How are you, son?"

"Fine, sir," Jack said.

"And this is one of his friends from college, Brett Weston," Jack said.

"Nice to meet you, Brett," the Governor said, shaking Brett's hand.

"Glad to meet you too, sir," Brett said.

"And this is another friend, Maria Pompillio," Jack said.

"Pleased to meet you, Ms. Pompillio," the Governor said as he took her hand.

"Thank you, sir. It's very nice to meet you," Maria said as she shook his hand.

"And, finally, the guy who got this all started, Jim Jackson," Jack said.

"I'm glad to meet you, Jim," the Governor said, stepping in front of Jim. "I guess we have you to thank for uncovering what may well be a disaster in the making."

"Thank you, sir," Jim said, shaking the Governor's hand. "And thank you for meeting with us on such short notice."

"My pleasure," he said. "Now, let's all take a seat and see if we can't find a solution to a few little issues."

As soon as they were all seated, the Governor asked Jim, "What do you see as the most critical issue right now?"

"Finding out if the barley is being used in Zwairiland," Jim answered. "Then, getting a sample, if it is, and proving that it's identical to the barley and corn GMOs we've tested."

The Governor nodded his head and said, "That seems to be the right place to start. If the people over there aren't consuming this flawed barley, we really don't have a case, do we?"

"No, sir," Jim agreed.

The Governor turned to one of the four men who had accompanied him into the room and said, "Give this to one of your contacts and get me the information and a sample, if necessary, as soon as you can."

"Yes, sir," the man said, nodding his head. "I can have someone get that within a couple of days."

"Now, I've heard a rumor from a reliable source that there may be some shenanigans going on with some people sheltering money in the Caymans," the Governor said, looking at Jack Jr.

"I think it came from a confidential informant that suggested someone look into it," the Governor continued, nodding his head at Jack Jr. "Since I'm acting solely on a tip from a reliable source, we'll investigate it and see if the information can be substantiated. Doesn't that sound reasonable?"

"Yes, sir," Jack Jr. said as he realized how his father had interceded on his behalf by being the reliable source.

For the next hour, they discussed all of the data Jim and the others had brought to the meeting. When the Governor had finally assigned his men their tasks, he said, "Well, that about wraps it up. Does anyone have anything to add?"

Jack Sr. looked around at everyone and answered, "No, sir. If something comes up, my boy can get in touch with me."

"Fine," the Governor said, rising from his chair.

As the rest of them stood, he continued, "Now, y'all head on back to school, and let us handle this. I'll get word to you when everything's ready. We'll have all of the appropriate authorities coordinate their actions so that it happens all at once to prevent any leak or notification of what we're about to do."

"Thanks, Governor," Jack Sr. said as they prepared to leave the room. "I'm sure we'll be talking within the next few days."

"That we will," the Governor said as he led his men from the room. "That we will."

CHAPTER 62

The next morning, when Jim left his apartment to head to the campus, he was met on the sidewalk by a man who was obviously waiting for him. "Can I help you?" Jim asked as he approached him.

"I think I may be the one to help you," the man said, holding out an envelope.

Jim tore open the envelope and pulled a single sheet of paper from inside. Noting that the letterhead was from the Governor's office, he quickly read it and stuck it in his briefcase.

"What do you need for me to do?" Jim asked.

"We need to go back into the house," the man answered. "I want you to show me where you found the bugs. I'll sweep the rest of the apartment for any more of them and get pictures. In order for me to do that, you need to make some minor noise. Nothing too dramatic, just a faucet running in the kitchen, pick up the phone and make a normal call, flush the toilet. Small normal things you'd do every day."

"Why do you need pictures?" Jim asked as he turned back toward his apartment.

"I don't know, sir," the man said, following Jim up the sidewalk. "I was just told to get some high-resolution photos of what you found in your apartment and car."

"Have you gotten them of the car?" Jim asked as he started to open the door.

"No, we'll do that next," the man answered. "And make sure you don't talk to me once we're in the apartment or at the car."

Nodding his head to show he understood, Jim opened the apartment door and walked into the kitchen. Tossing his briefcase on the table, he turned on a faucet and started rinsing out the cup he'd used for coffee.

As he swished the water around in the cup, he pointed to the spot under the cupboard where the bug was located. After the man had taken several shots and nodded, Jim turned off the faucet, got his briefcase from the table, and went into the living room. Sitting the briefcase on the couch, he picked up the phone and dialed the number for Maria's dorm. As he waited for it to be answered, he turned the phone over to reveal the bug that was attached to the bottom.

Again, waiting for the man to signal that he was done, Jim listened to the ringing of the phone in the dorm a couple more times and then hung up without speaking to anyone.

Then Jim went into the bathroom while the man checked the bedroom for bugs. Finding one, he took pictures as Jim flushed the toilet.

When the man nodded his head toward the door, they returned to the living room. Jim picked up his briefcase and led them out of the apartment. "Where in the car is the bug?" the man asked as Jim locked the apartment door.

"On the passenger side," Jim answered. "Sort of behind the dash."

"I'll need for you to open the passenger door, maybe put your briefcase in the seat," the man said. "Then, I don't know, open the glove box, move some papers, anything to give me a little noise cover."

"Not a problem," Jim said as they approached the car. "There's an old burger wrapper and a cup on the floor that I'll pick up. Then I can leave the door open as I take it to the trash can."

"That'll work," the man said. "I'll only need a couple of shots there. I'll do a quick check of the rest of the car to make sure there's nothing else."

Once all of the pictures had been taken, Jim followed the man a short distance from the VW and asked, "Did you find anything else?"

"Yeah," the man said. "There was a transmitter of some sort on the back of the car, probably a locator beacon. You know, not to listen, just to let them know where you are."

"What now?" Jim asked.

"I don't know," the man said. "I've done what I was sent to do. I don't have any idea about why they needed the pictures or anything else."

"If you have any questions," the man said as he prepared to leave, "I suggest you call the number on the letter.

As the man walked away, Jim shut the passenger door, went around the front, and opened his door. Climbing in and starting the engine, he wondered if everything was coming to an end today. That didn't seem likely since the Governor's staff or whoever he'd sent couldn't possibly have gotten back with the barley seed and information this fast.

Pulling up in front of Maria's dorm, Jim left the car at the curb and walked to the reception area. Asking for her to be paged, Jim looked around the empty lobby while the young girl behind the desk tried to locate Maria's room and let them know she had a visitor.

After waiting several minutes, he left a note saying that he'd be at the library for the next hour or so. Driving over, he spotted Brett's Jeep parked in front of the Genetic Research building and what appeared to be Jack's Mercedes parked behind it.

Jim pulled to the curb and parked behind the Mercedes, wondering if Jack had gotten some news and they'd been afraid to call his apartment. Remembering the building from his Master's program, Jim went through the front doors and down the hall to where he knew the department head's office would be.

As he approached the open doors, Jack and Brett came out, followed by someone in a lab coat. "I'll have the analysis done before noon," the man in the lab coat said.

"Thanks," Jack said. "I know Dad will be grateful that you've been able to rush this through."

"Hey, Jim," Brett said as they met. "We were hoping we'd find you this morning. Anything new with you?" Jim told them about the man who took pictures of the bugs and then asked, "Is that what I think it is?"

"You mean the analysis that'll be done by noon?" Jack asked. "Probably so. It was flown in this morning."

"What about it being used?" Jim asked.

"On almost the entire population," Jack answered. "The only thing left to cover is that it's the same as the corn and the other barley."

"What's going to happen then?" Jim asked.

"The Governor has a task force ready to hit Monogenic's in Austin, here in College Station, Mombasa, and Agrigenics at the same time," Jack answered.

"The guy at your place was probably trying to get evidence that supports your story," Brett said. "If they removed them, you couldn't prove they were spying on you."

"Probably," Jim agreed. "I wonder how soon this is going to happen."

"Soon," Jack said. "Dad called and said that it would be either this afternoon or tomorrow morning. The only thing they couldn't guarantee was getting someone in Ethiopia's government arrested."

"That's their problem," Brett said. "We can give them the information, and they can do what they wish."

"I'd be willing to bet that they isolate themselves from Mombasa and the President's brother so fast that it never makes the news over there," Jim said. "But that's alright with me. I just want things taken care of here."

"Maria's still pissed about what they did to you and her. More her I'd guess," Brett said. "If she had her way, she'd be there when the team walks into Monogenic's. I bet she'd flip off both of them as they're led away in cuffs."

"I'm sure she would," Jim agreed. "Have you seen her this morning?"

"No," Brett said.

"What about the financial issue?" Jim asked. "What's happening there?"

"I don't know," Jack said. "But, if I know Dad and the Governor, they've got years of experience with dealing with fund movements and the law. I'd bet that just Dad's lawyers alone could come up with a dozen ways to freeze the assets for years."

"Why would your dad's people know how to freeze assets?" Jim asked. "I thought they'd be more interested in knowing how to unfreeze them."

"They're the same," Jack explained. "If they know what the government can do, they can figure out a way to keep them from doing it. Sort of a know your enemy and his capabilities thing."

"What are you guys doing the rest of the day?" Jim asked.

"Thought we'd go over to the student union building," Jack answered. "I told Dad that I'd check back around noon to see what the plan is."

"Why don't we go to the library instead?" Jim asked. "I left a message for Maria that I'd be there."

"I'm not really welcome at the library," Jack said. "Not since I misused the school's computers. Now, any place that has computers is sort of off-limits for me."

"Not a problem," Jim said. "I'll get Maria at the library when she gets there, and we'll meet you over there."

CHAPTER 63

As Jim was heading toward the library, Rocky Ford was sitting alone at a table in What-a-Burger, having a cup of coffee. Watching the street and parking lot, he immediately noticed the black Chevy Suburban pull into an empty slot beside the door.

Both front doors of the Chevy opened, and two men in dark suits emerged and looked around before they entered. Spotting Rocky, the man who had been driving walked over to his table and asked, "Mr. Rocky Ford?"

"Yes," Rocky answered, sitting his cup down. "How can I help you?"

"Mind if I have a seat?" the man asked as he took the seat across from Rocky.

"Apparently not," Rocky said, getting nervous.

"Are you still working at Mongenic's?" the man asked, referring to a small notebook he had pulled from his inside coat pocket. "Corporate Security, I believe?"

"That depends on who you are and what you want," Rocky told him.

The man merely smiled and said, "I figured you'd want to know that."

Pulling a thin wallet from his coat, he opened it to reveal a photo ID and a badge that had "FBI" across the center. "Just call me Dale," he said as he showed Rocky the ID.

"Ok," Rocky said, shaking his head. "Just exactly what do you want with me?"

"I'm here to do you a favor," Dale said as he put his ID back inside his jacket.

"And how's that?" Rocky asked, leaning back in his seat.

"I'm going to give you a chance to stay out of prison," Dale whispered, leaning over on the table that separated them.

"Really," Rocky said, wondering just what sort of trouble he was in and how much this man knew.

"Really," Dale repeated, sitting back and waiting to see Rocky's response.

Rocky glanced to where the other man was standing and asked, "Just what makes you think I'm in any trouble or have done anything that would cause me any problems?"

Dale glanced at his partner and nodded slightly as he said, "I think you'll understand when my partner shows you what he's found in an apartment here in town."

As his partner approached, Dale held out his hand for the envelope and continued, "I'm pretty sure what he has in that envelope will be enough to convince you that my offer has some merit."

Taking the envelope, Dale pulled several enlarged photos from within and slid them across the table.

Rocky leaned forward and glanced at the first photo and knew immediately what he was seeing. Sitting back, he asked, "What do these have to do with me?"

Dale smiled as he leaned back and answered, "Lots, my friend. Lots."

"What exactly do you mean by lots?" Rocky asked, picking up the photos. "I'm not exactly sure what you're getting at, and I'm absolutely sure these have nothing to do with me."

"I'd reconsider that statement if I were you," Dale said, looking directly into Rocky's eyes. "We're not going from place to place showing these to just anybody. There's a reason I'm here with you, and you should know that I wouldn't be here unless I had pretty positive proof that I could tie you to the articles in the photos."

"Just why do you think I have anything to do with these," Rocky told him, tossing the photos back onto the table.

"Pretty simple," Dale said, leaving the pictures scattered across the tabletop. "We've identified each of these little listening devices, or bugs, as I'm sure you're used to calling them."

"Identified them as to what?" Rocky asked, knowing what was coming next.

"As to manufacturer, model, serial number, seller, and, in most cases, the buyer," Dale told him as he continued to stare at him.

Dale leaned forward and continued, "So, you see, I can track almost every one of these from where it was made to where it was found. And the one I can't positively track; I can definitely prove that you were one of the few people who handled it."

"So, you can prove I once, maybe, had or handled some of these," Rocky argued. "How does that relate to me going to jail or anything else? It's not against any law that I'm aware of that prohibits owning or handling a lawful device."

Leaning back and cocking his head slightly to the side, Dale asked, "Do you really want to play word games with me or dance around the facts that I know and can prove?"

Realizing that he really had no way out, Rocky asked, "Do you think I need a lawyer to continue this conversation?"

"That's up to you," Dale said. "But the offer I'm about to give you will only be made here and now. If you insist on a lawyer, which is your right, or decline to accept my offer, this conversation is over, and the gentleman standing patiently over there will hand you a piece of paper that will definitely ruin the next several days of your life. And most likely the next several years."

Nodding to his partner again, Dale watched as he pulled an arrest warrant from his jacket.

"Now he hasn't served it yet," Dale said as he saw the recognition in Rocky's eyes. "But once he does, I'm gone, and you can deal with that gentleman."

Dropping his head, Rocky asked, "What do you want, and what kind of deal are we talking about?"

Nodding his head, Dale answered, "We want to know who ordered you to place these devices, for what purpose, how long they were in use, and basically everything that has anything to do with the operation."

Watching Rocky nod his acceptance, Dale continued, "And as for what deal we are offering you; we'll offer complete immunity if the information is verified, and your cooperation is 100 percent. Any recanting or refusal to cooperate will nullify the agreement, and my friend there will start his process to ensure you get to spend the next few years at the government's expense."

"Alright," Rocky said, resigned to the fact that his options were limited, and he knew that Monogenic's wouldn't stand behind him. "How do we progress from here?"

Dale nodded at his partner again and slid over for him to sit beside him. "Mr. Ford, this is FBI agent Sproc. He'll tell you what he wants and how we'll proceed."

"Mr. Ford," the agent said as he slid a single piece of paper and a pen across the table, "this is a simple agreement that you will act as an informant for the FBI and will perform to the best of your ability any legal tasks the agency requests."

Rocky picked up the paper and quickly scanned it, noting that his name was already typed across the bottom, along with both agents' names.

Signing the paper, Rocky asked, "Where do we start?'

CHAPTER 64

When Jim was almost at the library, he saw Maria heading down the sidewalk. "Hey, Miss," he said as he pulled alongside her and stopped, "need a ride?"

"I'm pretty picky about who I ride with," she said, smiling at him as she stepped into the car. "What makes you think I'd like to ride with you?"

"Because I'm charming," Jim joked. "Charming, witty, sort of cute, and charming."

"You've said charming three times," Maria said, laughing.

"My best feature," Jim said, leaning over to open the door. "If you'll just get in, I'll demonstrate how charming I can be."

"Try for witty," Maria said as she got in.

"I'll try for cute," Jim said as she pulled her door shut.

"You'll never pull it off," Maria joked as Jim drove away. "Stick with charming."

Once Jim had parked in the student union building parking lot, they met Jack and Brett, who had also just pulled in. "Morning, folks," Brett said as he and Jack waited for Jim and Maria to join them.

"Good morning," Maria said as she put her arm around Jim's waist. "What's the word on the street?"

"Waiting to hear," Jack said as they headed toward the entrance. "I'll call Dad when we get inside and let him know where we are."

"We'll get some chairs and a table," Brett said as Jack went looking for a phone.

"How about over here?" Maria asked as she spotted a table with six chairs around it, none of them occupied.

"Fine," Brett said as he and Jim followed her. "Too bad this isn't Starbucks. We could get coffee and rolls or something."

"Not to mention that the chairs are more comfortable there," Jim said as he pulled out a hard wooden chair for Maria.

"I'll agree with that," Maria said as Jim sat down beside her. "But we poor students have to accept what we can get."

"Are you going to tell her about your morning adventure?" Brett asked as he took a seat.

"What this time?" Maria asked, turning in her chair to face Jim.

"Nothing, really," Jim said as he leaned back. "Just a guy wanting to take pictures of all of the bugs we found in the apartment and the car."

"Did they find any more?" Maria asked.

"Yup, one in the bedroom," Jim answered. "And what's probably a locator beacon on the car."

"Please tell me none of these things had video capability," Maria asked as she thought about what they would reveal.

"Not that I know of," Jim told her. "And the guy that took the pictures didn't say anything about videos."

"Good, I'd hate to think that there are videos of us out there somewhere," Maria said.

"I know," Jim said. "I still plan on changing apartments when this is over."

"Maybe you can sue Monogenic's," Brett said.

"If they're guilty of what's happening in Zwairiland, I doubt if there's enough money left after those folks get sued to buy me a decent dinner," Jim said.

"Ready for some good news?" Jack asked as he walked up.

"Sure," Jim said.

"The Governor decided to start without the barley confirmation," Jack said. "Due to the time difference between here and Zwairiland, they wanted to hit them as early as possible."

"When are they going after Monogenic's here?" Maria asked.

"Probably right now," Jack answered. "Dad just said that everything had been moved up for some reason."

"When will we know what's happening?" Jim asked.

"Dad's on his way here right now," Jack said. "He'll be in contact with the Governor and have the latest information."

"Where does he want to meet?" Brett asked.

"He's arranged for us to meet at the Mayor's office," Jack said. "If I know the Governor, he's already set up a press conference. And since the only two people we can tie to the Zwairiland issue are here in College Station, this may be the only place where actual arrests will be made today."

"When does he want us there?" Jim asked.

"His plane will land in less than 30 minutes, and the Mayor has sent a car for him," Jack answered. "So, we have about 30 minutes to get to the Mayor's office."

"I wish I had time to go back to the dorm and change clothes," Maria said as she thought about possibly being in the news.

"Not time," Jim said. "We need to get going if we're going to get there before the Mayor's office is overrun with reporters."

"I agree," Brett said. "Why don't we all go in Jack's car? No sense in taking three cars."

"Good idea," Jim said, standing up. "But I wish I could be at Hawk's office when the police arrive. I'd love to watch him, and Moss, get cuffed and hauled away."

"Me, too," Maria said as she pushed her chair back under the table. "I'd like to tell them how I feel about their listening to our private conversations. Assholes!"

"I doubt if you'll ever get that chance," Jack said as he led the way out of the building. "I imagine that once the FBI or whoever's in charge gets to them, the only people they'll talk to will be their lawyers."

About an hour later, the Mayor was just finishing delivering his speech about what had just become an international news event. He had praised the Governor for his speedy response to what was a humanitarian crisis of epic proportions.

As hundreds of cameras were rolling and microphones shoved toward the hastily erected stage, the Mayor described how international forces had cooperated and seized material from labs in Zwairiland and Ethiopia. It was expected to be matched with the patented corn and barley from Monogenic's.

Although no arrests had been made locally regarding the Zwairiland genocide, warrants had been issued for Hawk and Moss for tax evasion. It was certain that additional charges would be made for the rumored invasion of privacy, and additional people were being held pending further investigation.

For the next hour, the Mayor answered questions and promised that he would leave no stone unturned to make sure that anyone involved would be discovered and held accountable for their actions.

EPILOGUE

Two days after the graduation ceremony, where Jim, Maria, and Brett received their degrees, they were sitting around a table at the pizza restaurant drinking beer. "What now?" Jim asked, looking at Maria.

"I may stay for my Ph.D.," she answered. "What about you, Brett?"

"I'm sending out resumes," Brett answered. "Not sure where I'll end up."

As they continued discussing what their futures might hold in store, Jack walked in, followed by his father. "Good afternoon," Jack Jr. said as he got to their table. "Care for some company?"

"Please," Jim said, standing. "Pull up a couple of chairs and join us."

"Thanks," Jack Sr. said, taking the chair his son had brought over to the table for him. "I thought I'd try to catch you guys before you all left the area."

"I'll be right back," Jack Jr. said as he walked to get a couple of beers for him and his father.

"What can we do for you, sir?" Maria asked.

"It's what I can do for you," Jack Sr. answered. "Along with the Governor, I want to thank you for what you did. I know it won't ever be attributed to you, but we know."

"So, as a way of thanking you," he continued, "we've set up a fund for Ms. Pompillio to continue her education. Interviews with several pharmaceutical companies have been arranged for Mr. Weston. And Jack Jr. will be allowed to reenter A&M, with certain restrictions, of course."

Turning to Jim, he finished by saying, "It's up to you, but the President of Monogenic's has offered you a job. He's grateful to you for uncovering what trusted members of his company were doing. If you're interested, he'll make time to interview you personally at your convenience."

As they realized what opportunities had just been presented, Maria spoke saying, " Not bad for the Three Miceketeers."

"Not bad at all," Jim agreed. "But it looks like we need to add a fourth."

"No thanks, guys," Jack Jr. smiled and said. "I have no reason to be associated with any mouse other than the one on my computer. But I've enjoyed our little adventure."

"Likewise," Brett said, standing and raising his beer. "Here's to good friends and bright futures."

"Amen," Jim said as they all stood and clinked their bottles. "To the future!"

"To *our* bright future," Maria said, smiling and looking at Jim.

ABOUT THE AUTHOR

Jim West was born and raised in Texas. Following an unscheduled interruption in his college education, Jim served a tour in the U.S. Navy in photo intelligence. After that and college completion, Jim joined the U.S. Air Force as a pilot, retiring in 1989.

Next, American Airlines obviously lowered their standards and allowed Jim to be one of their family of pilots. Retiring after 16 years, Jim began writing, and this is his fourth published novel.

Finally, with ample time on his hands, writing became the primary focus of the spare time left over from running his ranch and competitive team roping. Telling a good story has long been a Texas tradition, even if it involves some fabrication of the facts.